Queen

a novel

by Suzanne Crain Miller

To Chad, who saw in me what I couldn't and has loved me like that's who I've always been. I can only hope for my love to be half as pure and true.

Other books by the author:

The Selections

Wage

My legacy is that I stayed on course...from beginning to the end because I believed in something inside of me.

Tina Turner

The Cop

He'd never hurt a baby. The list of people he'd battered and worked over was long, but it had never included someone so young or so helpless. He thought it could be similar to manhandling the old codger who'd caught him stealing from a drawer during an investigation. Not much different than pummeling the junkie housewife who'd pulled a knife on him when he'd responded to a domestic disturbance, though probably far more exciting.

In some ways, bruising a baby would prove far easier than either of these things. Though it wouldn't matter if it was or not. It would have to be done. There was no room for reneging. He reminded himself of this fact as he sat there in the dark.

If someone were to have driven by at that precise moment, seeing him idly sitting in his patrol car, they'd have dismissed him as just another cop clocking speeders or sitting comatose wasting taxpayer's money. The latter would be the closest thing to the truth. The only thing he was accomplishing was staring at Lara's house.

The same house where, as a teenager, he'd gone to more keggers than he could count. The same house where he'd tried to kiss her. Where she'd hastily turned her cheek, informing him she was in love with his friend, Tom. Where he'd gone to her mother's wake. The house she now lived in with only the baby- the sole monument to her troubled childhood.

The house where he and Tom had celebrated their being hired on as official *law enforcement officers*. Where they shot their guns out back as onlookers marveled at their marksmanship and skill. The same house where he'd spent the last few Christmases with them after they married.

Tom and Lara Forever engraved on the cake knife next to their wedding cake. The very knife he'd made a point to slip into his tuxedo pocket at the reception. The one that once she became aware was missing, he'd listened to her go on about.

"Who'd want it what with our names on it an all?" she'd asked him as he sat slouched on their couch. The same couch where he took up space once, if not twice weekly, watching football. He'd responded with only a shrug.

As he sat there Monday night after Monday night, he wondered what it was like to live with her. To watch her do the simple, day-to-day things like get dressed in the mornings, and feed the baby. He'd closed his eyes many a time and envisioned himself lying next to her in bed.

He'd watched closely as she'd presented Tom with a jersey from his favorite football team on his birthday. They'd often kiss more heavily than most would in public, allowing him opportunity to speculate about how it would feel to have her tongue in his own mouth. He'd never know. Of this he was certain.

Lara was one in a long line of unrequited loves. In fact, if he took the time to trace his losing streak back to its origins, the beginnings of his love of girls who did not love him in return, he'd have gone all the way back to grade school. All the way back to little Lisa Lawson to whom he'd confessed his undying love for by the slide at recess.

Even as grown man, when a woman rejected him, he replayed the answer she'd given him over and over. As if by uttering it all those years ago, she'd put a hex on him. As if the declarations of young girls hold any weight in the dealings of adults.

"You're strange." she'd stated very matter-of-factly as though it was something everyone knew like 2+2=4 or the alphabet.

"What do you mean?" he'd demanded with his hangdog look that, even then, he couldn't seem to shake.

" I don't know...you're just strange. You're always following me around like you don't have anywhere else to go. Every time I turn around you're just there, like a puppy or something." she'd gone on to explain.

Sitting there in his cruiser, all those years later, so properly dressed in his uniform, this still lingered. There he was, nearly two decades since the slide incident transpired, still wallowing. He wasn't a self-actualized person by any means, but he was intuitive enough to feel ashamed that such playground ruses continued to define him.

He wasn't entirely sure what had become of Lisa Lawson. Why, the last he'd heard around the restaurant her father owned, she'd moved to

Florida after high school. She'd quit college then soon after started waitressing at a restaurant with some guy she'd taken up with. Some guy who was a fraction of the man he was to be sure.

Sitting there listening as the calls came over his radio, he took them in, though they were indistinguishable to him. The only discernible words, were hers, *you're strange*...and in his mind, he checked this off as one of the reasons Lara too was not his. As possibly the singular reason he remained a bachelor.

There was no reason he would miss any sleep over having to hurt the baby, bruise his arm a bit. That's what he and Tom had agreed on, only bruising an arm. No, he'd never hurt a baby. The opportunity or need had never presented itself before, but he'd hurt a lot of people. Why should age or size make any difference?

Pain is pain. No matter who's on the receiving end. He theorized as he placed his hand on the door handle. The whole matter seemed so trivial to him, yet he reminded himself it was for his friend, a show of loyalty...and Tom had lied for him. Yes, in the fall of last year, Tom had done his part when that whole underage girl catastrophe had threatened to sear their world in two.

This reasoning didn't make his footsteps any less heavy as he trudged up to her door. He didn't like this. He didn't like anything that resembled reluctance, yet he knew it wasn't that he wasn't ready. He was always ready – a gun always loaded waiting for the safety to be clicked off.

No, he was irritated, frustrated rather, at having to take the time out of his day to do such a thing when he, more than anyone, knew he was capable of so much worse. Lifting his feet a bit higher, he decided to bite the bullet. He all but stomped up the last of her front steps.

The curtain on the window to his left parted slightly. The door remained closed. She knew why he'd come. After she and Tom separated, he'd taken Tom's side. She knew he wasn't there to watch a game or shoot the breeze.

Knocking again, far more loudly for effect, produced an irritated Lara frowning at him through a thin slit, chain still fastened at the top of the door.

"Ain't you got anythang better to do, Carter?" she accused, a feeble attempt at masking her fear.

"I'm coming in. Only thing up to you is how long that takes." he decreed.

She looked behind her, assessing the situation. There wasn't as much risk for her as there was for the baby. He hated that she did this. It reminded him of what a good mother she was. A much better mother than his own had been. With a deep sigh, she unfastened the chain, opening the door to him.

In a quick, swooping motion she crouched, scooping the baby out of his playpen and into her arms. Balancing him on one hip, holding him firmly to her, they stared at him together.

"I know he sent you. Motherfucker thinks he can send you to do his dirty work. Same ol' same ol'. Shit! He tell you he's tryin to get custody? You know he's wrong on that one. A baby belongs with his momma." she prattled on.

He stared back at them, picturing how it was to go. Picturing how to grab the baby without causing him to fall on the floor. That would leave far more than a bruise. That was not the deal. He had agreed to only bruise him...

"Might be true most a the time. Not in this case." he icily remarked.

The baby wriggled in her arms, innocently reaching out to Carter.

"Yeah? Why not?" she demanded. "Why don't he belong with me?"

By pure coincidence a picture on the wall behind her caught his attention. It was of the three of them, Lara, Carter and Tom, at their wedding. Yet there she was in front of him, barely a trace left of the bride on that glossy paper. Too thin from the stress of all that had transpired. A look of weariness as if she'd lived a century in what had only been a brief two years since she and Tom had danced, smeared cake on each other's faces and toasted to their future. This disgusted him. It made him question his agreement. It made him consider wrapping his hands around her throat and taking her out of her misery.

The baby giggled loudly, unaware of the events that teetered on the brink of happening or not. This pure sound jolted Carter back to attend to the matter at hand - the purpose of his visit. Most of all, the untimely interruption reminded him of what Tom knew. There was that... the matter of Tom knowing about what he'd done to the girl. Yes... he firmed up his resolve to see the thing through.

"Itn't a judge in the county that'd give you custody. Not with you bein in A.A. and not once they see what you've done." he stated, the calm certainty of his tone dissipating to a harsh sternness.

Her phone went off signaling she had a text. In an effort to demonstrate how little he intimidated her, she walked over to the counter, picked up the phone, looking it over.

"Yeah well, I just got another chip. I'm doin real good. Best I been in a long time. Go to meetins least three times a week over at First Presbyterian. So you can tell him that right there won't tread water. What the hell else is he sayin I done?"

A smile formed on his lips. The type of smile that if he had been sitting up to a bar, might have fooled an inebriated girl into thinking he'd be just the kind of guy to take home. Though it was the kind of smile that in his best friend's house, with him on the brink of doing what he'd been sent to do, exposed his sinister nature.

"You grabbed him, shook him, bruised him up good." he told her, in an eerie monotone.

Her phone dropped to the counter. Glaring up at him, she foolishly sauntered over.

"How long you know me, Carter?"

He crossed his arms, remaining silent, composure in tact.

"I'll tell you how long. Forever! You known me since we was knee high. An you know full well I wouldn't never hurt my boy. No judge'll believe that neither. You tell him he's crazy if he thinks..."

With swift precision he reached out, snatching the baby by one arm, at first, jerking him away from her. Instinctively, she lunged. He stuck out his free hand, blocking her with a quick jab to the windpipe, sending her backwards to the floor. The baby's scream climaxed into ear piercing squalls. Carter now gripped both tiny arms in his hands. He made sure to squeeze one more tightly than the other. The baby's cheeks turned bright red.

Lara cowered beneath him, demanding he give her back her child, then cursing him when he did not instantly comply. Done with the task he'd come to perform, he obliged her. Leaning down, he handed the baby over. She cradled her child to her chest. His shrill crying persisted. Their eyes never left Carter as he walked to the door.

"He better see the papers by mornin." he threatened, making sure not to look at her, not to fold in the last few seconds and do far more than he'd been sent to.

Their cries would've turned any other soul soft. Not him. No, he stood proudly as he ran his hand over his .45, just the hard, cool feel of it against his skin prompting him to remain *on point*, as they had called it back in the academy.

" If not, I know a social worker who'll be chompin at the bit to pay you a visit." he persisted. "Got one who owes me a favor. Cain't stand young ones bein mistreated. Be a shame. A shame for em to get pictures a that arm. Specially in the next couple days or so. An when me an Tom tell em you been back on the bottle, hell, might make it so you wouldn't see hide nor hair of him til he turned 18."

With that, he turned, stepping out the door and onto the porch. Clutching the baby tighter, she jumped up, darting over slamming the door in his face. He let it lie. Though he knew he could make her night much worse than it had been already. He instead strutted back to his vehicle.

" 350 in progress. A 350 in progress. Over..." Dispatch sounded off over the radio.

As he situated himself back in the driver's seat, he pressed a button to answer. The light on Lara's porch went off, her lone act of defiance in the face of what he'd done. For some reason, this caused him to chuckle. The thought of her thinking that he minded the dark. His radio sounded off once more.

"350 in progress."

He finally answered.

"I'm on my way."

The Tranny

My brother's always said he thanks the Lord above that our momma died without ever layin eyes on me the way I am now. "Long fore she woulda ever had to see her baby boy turned into a girl at the hands of some money grubbin surgeon." as he likes to put it. This is one a the few thangs me an Jarvis ever have agreed on, the part about momma anyways. Probly the only thang we ever will.

Bless momma's heart. Bet she's up there thankin the good Lord for herself that she never witnessed, any a my transformation. My metamorphosis from her lil' baby boy, Jermaine Nathaniel Braxton to Queen. Queen Mae Braxton to be exact. Cause you know royalty's got to be called by its rightful name. Mmmm hmmm, thas right, baby.

There's a part of me that knows momma was well aware a more than she let on. How much more, I'll never be sure, but she was a perceptive woman. Sometimes, I swear, she knew what I was gonna say fore the words ever left my mouth.

When I brought girls home for dinner, she never once asked me if we were datin or what my intentions were. She'd be sweet as pie to em an treat em nothin but good, but she knew the deal. On the other hand, soon as Jarvis walked in with a cute thang on his arm, well, now that was a whole nother story. Then it'd be "What's her family like?" an "Is she a church goin girl?"

Then there was that one time. That time we never dared speak about when she caught me in the dress I'd borrowed from a friend. I know she saw me. Opened that bathroom door an there I was plain as day. A blue velvet spandex mini dress huggin every curve I was ever born with an some I whatin. She pulled that door shut quick as she could an flew down the stairs fast as her little bird feet could carry her.

Stayed hold up in my room as long as I could that night. A million thangs runnin through my mind. Like whether or not it'd be best to jus go on ahead an end it all. Wrote a letter to that affect. Laid it out on my desk. Draped the dress over my chair beside it. Got halfway cross the room to the bathroom to run a tub full a water so I could soak for a while, make my wrists tender enough to slit, fore my thoughts got the better of me.

Stopped me in my tracks imaginin momma's face if she was the one to find me, an more than likely she woulda been. How she'd wail an carry on when she read my note. The more I pictured it, I knew I couldn't do it. There was also the knowledge that I'd be buried in a suit. That was right up there on the list a thangs that kept me grounded to this world. Imagined myself laid in that black box without a stitch a the makeup I'd taken to experimentin with or one a the dresses I kept hidden under my dresser, an I caved.

Whatin long til my appetite got the better of me. Slunk down to the kitchen. When I tiptoed in I was sure I'd get an earful. She never said a word, not one word. Jus smiled as she took my plate out of the fridge, warmed it up an slid it to me. Went on to tell me bout how the youth group was goin on a retreat that next month. She'd already signed me an Jarvis up.

She always did say Jesus was the answer for anythang ailin a person. Guess she figured the more a him I got the less I'd need that dress. There were times I wished she was right. Woulda made life a lot easier.

"Itn't bein a black man in this here world hard enough without your addin all 'that' to your load?" *Jarvis asks me from time to time, like I got some choice in the matter.*

Like I woke up one mornin an it suddenly came to me that shavin my head an my legs every day, buyin women's clothes, havin everybody an their brother includin my own kin thinkin I'm a freak a nature, an eventually gettin my balls whacked off was somethin to aspire to. Never ceases to amaze me how people assume by lookin at you that you're the incarnation a all your hopes an dreams. If it itn't true for the fat housewife who's ended up with four kids an a husband who spends all his wakin hours at the office, then chil', why would it be true for me? We all do the best we can with the hand we're dealt. Sometimes we do the dealin. Sometimes I swear the devil his self's shufflin the deck fore he passes those cards out. Mm hmmm, he sure is.

The only answer I ever give Jarvis when he gets to askin fool-headed shit like that is silence. My only intention is to keep on keepin on. "When you ain't got the words, you got your actions" was what momma used to drill into us. Jarvis always was the one to have a way with words.

That blue spandex get-up was the last time I dared wear anythang but my manliest a outfits in momma's house. The last time while she was livin anyway. Til that night a her funeral when Jarvis gave me the task a gettin a head start on sortin through what she'd left behind.

He'd headed on back to Shreveport for a work meetin. Said there whatin no way around it an seein as how I didn't have a "real" job, it'd be a good use of my time. My singin an callin out bingo numbers in bars while I "gallivanted around in women's under thangs", as he liked tell it, didn't qualify. Thas how he is, wouldn't dream a takin a break to grieve our mother. Mmmm hmmm. An to hear him tell it, I'm the one who needs their head shrunk.

There I was all alone in the house we come up in. The house where I'd sat on my mother's lap while she shucked corn. The house where I'd climbed the stairs on those balmy Florida nights to lay with her when the nightmares pried their way into my peaceful sleep. My feet walkin on the same floors where me an Jarvis played cops an robbers an army men. Movin those plastic figures around, all the while, knowin I whatin much for it. Feelin, even then, that I'd missed the day when the good Lord gave out that man's handbook Jarvis seemed to know by heart.

I always was a momma's boy. Helped her out in the kitchen an tagged along with her to church. When you're different you're gonna get singled out. Ain't but a matter of time. How my older cousin sensed those differences I'm not sure, but he did. It was his noticin that made him ask me if we could go up to my room to play one day.

It led him to take the opportunity to show me what men liked the same way his uncle had showed him. Right there in my room it went on with the whole Braxton family settin outside my window eatin fried chicken from cardboard buckets at the annual reunion. Lickin that grease off their fingers while I lay there on that hardwood floor havin my first sexual encounter. To this day, I still can't so much as drive by a KFC or a Popeye's without my mind goin back there.

These are the thangs that lingered as I made my way through each room of momma's house. Some of em resided there without momma knowin or givin her permission, these thangs Jarvis left me to sort through. The thangs that reached out like ghosts lightly grazin my arms with their wispy fingers tryin like anythang not to be forgotten. Lord knows I wish I could forget.

That night, I lay in my old bed in my old room. Closed my eyes tight an prayed for sleep. Hadn't talked to God in years, but I figured he might remember me even if I had gone an gotten myself a vagina. Sleep didn't come. The man upstairs never showed up. He was as silent as the grave.

I lay still, acceptin the thang I feared most - that he was done with me. That he'd been done with me for a long time. Pulled the covers up around me, reminded myself I'd be alright jus like I had to every other time the Almighty crossed my mind. After a while, I got up an wandered down the hallway to momma's room. I stood at the end a her bed, ran my hands over her pretty spread.

I'd been with her the day she bought it at the consignment store. Mmmm that woman loved to go thriftin! We went by this one place least once a week after school. Jarvis always made sure she dropped him off at the house first. He whatin much for shoppin but me, I was always game. I'd act like I was doin momma a favor by goin with her when really I loved it every bit as much as she did.

I'd let her do her lookin, while I roamed around. The back room was full a vintage dresses. It'd never fail. Didn't take long fore I'd make my way on back to that room, rubbin the silky fabric a those dresses between my fingers til momma'd call for me.

Layin down on that pink floral spread, I reached out for her. Took me a minute to recall she was in the grave. That I'd seen her lowered down in the dirt that very afternoon. Imaginin her holdin the hand a her Lord was of little comfort. I wanted her there with me! I was mad as hell! God couldn't have her yet, specially if I was doomed be burnin in hellfire an never see her again. I needed more time!

Rollin over, I caught sight of a nightie hangin on the back a her bathroom door. A white lacy nightgown she got from Aunt Lynn couple Christmases ago. I remembered thinkin when she opened it that it was awful bawdy. Seemed like a strange gift to give an elderly woman who hadn't dated in years an, to hear her tell it, didn't plan on ever doin so again.

Said our daddy had done her in far as men went. That the day he died a part a her died too. Always tol' us boys we were the only men that had any space left in her heart. Tol' us we were all she needed.

She'd commented to me later that evenin, when Aunt Lynn was out of earshot, an we were washin up dishes that she was gonna donate that nightgown to the Salvation Army. She was gonna be sure an slip it in their drop box. Wouldn't want a soul to see her with it she'd said, yet there it was, still on the back a her door.

I walked over, took it down from the hook. Holdin it up to my nose, I breathed in her perfume. She'd been wearin it! The fact that my mother had paraded around in such a garment made me smile. I took off my t-shirt, let it fall to the floor. Her nightgown felt like a soft baby blanket slidin against my skin as I pulled it on over my head.

Standin in front a the mirrored door a her armoire, I couldn't help but cry as I looked at myself. If I'd had my wig on, I'd a been the spittin image a momma when she was about my age. I cried not jus cause I felt so outta place, there in momma's room, not barely an ounce a the man she'd known, but because I didn't have my wig to complete the picture. I cried that I'd given in to Jarvis's request to wear a suit an tie to the funeral an leave all a what he refers to as my "tranny junk" back at home.

Under those other dark reasons for all my blubberin, I unearthed an unexpectedly glittery one. Like a quarter down in the pocket of an old pair a jeans. A swan elegantly glidin its way across a pond a gray goslins. I was cryin cause I felt beautiful.

Up to that point, I could've counted on one hand the times I'd felt that way. The first, was the day I got the balls, even though I wouldn't keep em long, mmm hmmm honey, to strut my stuff up on stage an spin that wheel, call out those bingo numbers in my fuscia sequined jumpsuit. I'd taken the surgical tape I'd nabbed at one a my doctors appointments an wrapped my package up tight. I was the hottest Miss Thang to ever step out on the jimmy rigged stage a that little hole in the wall bar, mmm hmmm, I was.

The second time was when I went to buy my first pair a hot pants. It was right after my reassignment. I'd always been partial to dresses, most gals like me are, specially if they don't have the dyin need or the money for surgery. I'd slipped on those tight black pants an zipped em right up without havin to worry bout catchin em on a thang. Felt right. Felt like a place I'd always wanted to travel to an finally I'd arrived.

Once Jarvis got back to momma's, he relieved me a my sortin duties. He whatin gonna hear a the two of us bein shut up together with all those leftovers from our past. Said he'd finish it up an I whatin about to argue. I took the first bus back to Lisa. When I unpacked, I held up the nightgown for her. Gave her an earful about wearin it an how pretty I'd felt in it. How close it'd made me feel to momma.

Lisa listened. She made over it some, but she didn't understand. I could see it in the way she went on with her cookin while I was talkin. This happened a lot when I spoke about thangs that had more to do with me as Queen an less to do with me as Jermaine.

She always reminds me she'll stick with me long as I'll have her. Tells me she loves me to the end a this earth an back again. Cain't imagine life without her. She's the only person to ever accept me as Queen an Jermaine. Only person cept Jarvis who's known us both. At the end a the day, when I think about what it'd be like to be with a man, I know I could never bring myself to betray my Lisa. Wouldn't never be worth it.

I don't get my panties in a wad about it. Shit, spent way too many years not bein able to wear panties. Sure as hell ain't gonna wad em up now that I can. Please, honey, mmm hmmm, you know thas right.

No blame can be put on her for missin Jermaine though. She knew the better parts a him. Met him when he was still able to peek his head out, prop himself up an play "man" with the best of em.

She didn't know the Jermaine who got teased all growin up. The one who outran the boys in fifth grade when they threw rocks at him jus cause he was the best dancer in music class. The one who'd sucked his cousin's cock an let him return the favor at first because he had to, but later because he took a likin to it. The one who couldn't remember what it felt like to walk around without feelin ashamed a jus about everything he was or wanted to be.

No, Lisa whatin real acquainted with that Jermaine, but I was. Had been for too long. Thas why when I got my chance to let the other part a me, the *funnier, sweeter, prouder part a me come out, I took it. Unlocked the door a that closet, let her right out an named her Queen.*

Got that name cause I felt partly like royalty, an partly cause momma's favorite Bible story was about a lady named Queen Esther. She'd held fast to what she believed an God worked it all out in her favor. Used to look at Esther's picture in momma's Bible. One page showed her in an old brown robe out in a field an the next one had her in a glamorous gown with a crown on her head.

Now I knew the minute I put on a dress, God whatin gonna be interested in workin thangs out for me. I knew I whatin gonna have no Boaz come along an redeem me like Esther did. I knew I was gonna have to be my own knight in shinin armor. Knew I was gonna have to work thangs out for myself. That it was me against the whole heterosexual world. I figured with name like Queen, I couldn't lose, an if I did, at least I'd make an impression.

The other part a why I'm who I am now is the fact that my idol, Miss Tina Turner, is called the Queen a Rock. Lord, that woman sure went through the ringer an came out shinin! Saw her on T.V. for the first time over at my Auntie Geneva's house, singin on a lit up stage in a big concert on HBO. I couldn't a been no more than ten at the time. Back fore even half a all the bad that was headed my way had peeked out from under my bed.

I can still see Tina up there sportin that short white mini dress, her big hair wavin around. She was beltin out "Proud Mary". First time I'd ever seen a black woman doin what she was doin. Struttin her stuff, actin like she whatin even black, like it didn't make a hill a beans difference that she was. I didn't jus want to be like her. I wanted to be her.

The name set well with Lisa when I told her. She said when we decided it was time to adopt a child they'd blow their teacher's socks off at school talkin bout their daddy who got himself turned into a momma an named herself Queen. I laughed when she said it.

There we were standin in line at the county clerk's office waitin to get my name changed legal. I'd laughed at the time, but down deep I felt a sadness creep in. It made me wonder if Lisa'd be on the first bus outta town when I finally confessed I whatin never gonna want to adopt nobody.

Shit, somebody needed to adopt me. Specially after momma passed. Didn't need to be takin on another livin soul. Sides, we were gettin ready to move back to her hometown. Stuffy ol' Murfeesboro Tennessee. Mmm hmm, ain't a place I ever saw myself. Not in a million years, an I whatin about to drag some poor chil' there either.

I threw her off the scent by tellin her if we were gonna be livin in her daddy's ol' place, tryin to put his restaurant back on the map, we didn't need to be havin any kids tyin up our time jus yet. Hell, I hadn't seen but one person a my "persuasion" in that town. One dyke in the grocery store with a husband trailin behind her, a chil' in a stroller, an a baby on the way. The way she looked Lisa up one side an down the other, I knew she whatin battin for the right team. Mmmm hmmm. Some people can sure keep up those facades. Rest of us gotta live honest. All this to say, I knew from the get go we'd have our work cut out for us there.

But I spoke too soon. Went an ran my mouth fore we'd laid eyes on Lil' Miss Thang. That day Rodrigo, our Chihuahua, the only macho one in our anythang but conventional family, got it in his mind he was sick an tired a mine an Lisa's bein the only two faces he hardly ever got to see. I left him out a touch too long while I was unpackin, an that was when he saw his self a chance an took it.

It was like he made up his mind he wanted to find a girl to dote on his lil' ass an poof! She appeared outta thin air. Jus settin out on her porch eatin candy that her size two momma'd tan her hide fore even takin a whiff of never mind puttin in her mouth. All dressed in black like one a them goth, vampire lovin kids. Downright pitiful an depressin, mmm hmmm, honey. There she was...an who coulda known then that sadsackin lil' white girl'd be the closest thang to a daughter me an Lisa'd ever have.

The Girl

Freshman year of college, my creative writing teacher gave us a list of topics to write about. Upon first glance, I wasn't enthused about any of them. However, upon reconsideration, two of them stood out as though they were placed there just for me. I asked my teacher if I could weave them together as I couldn't see how to adequately write about one without writing about the other.

The first was *the most beautiful thing you ever saw* and second, *the worst thing you ever did*. The words instantly flooded my mind. I saw her clearly and all at once - the most beautiful person I've ever seen to this day and how just her knowing me nearly sent her to her grave. That first image of her has never lost its vibrance. It's stayed with me, always accessible, like a compact mirror you carry in your purse. One you hardly ever pull out, but that you know is there waiting for the right occasion.

 Sitting down to write the essay, I looked out my dorm window. Even though I was miles away from my childhood home, there she was all those years later, unaltered. The same as she was when I'd seen her that very first time. She'd stood in the middle of our subdivision, a skin tight pink dress that barely covered her shiny black thighs. Hair blowing in waves around her face. She frantically called her Chihuahua, Rodrigo, like the world would end if he ran past the end of their driveway.

 I had never seen anyone like her. Skin dark as night, showgirl makeup, and an athletic figure that, upon meeting her, likely made any other woman secretly wish she'd drop dead. I blinked long and hard to make sure I hadn't conjured her up out of sheer boredom. When I opened my eyes, there she was - the woman I would come to know as Queen Mae Braxton.

 Before this sighting, I could've counted on my hand the number of black people I'd even seen in our whitebread Murfeesboro. None of them had been men trying to be women, which I wouldn't have realized about her til mother so quickly pointed it out the minute she caught me gaping from our living room window. I couldn't take my eyes off them as she and Mr.

Lawson's daughter, Lisa, unloaded their car. The way she navigated the sidewalk in her stilettos, every move like that of a movie star, sure of every step.

"You're not to go anywhere near there!" mother cautioned as she tried to pick her jaw up off the floor. "And you're most certainly not to talk to him!"

"But we always take cookies to new neighbors." I reminded her.

"That's when we want to get to know them. I already know *his* kind." she retorted storming off to start dinner. "Now come away from there!"

I obliged her, yet shortly after, snuck up to my bedroom where I could get a better view. Questions whizzed through my brain, colliding into each other like bumper cars at a carnival. How could my mother, of all people, know him already? How in God's green earth had she even known that striking person was a man? Had she met many men in dresses, and if so, where? He had certainly fooled me.

As I parted my curtains, and peered down, I hoped for the clues that had come to mother so easily. Queen took the last bag from her trunk and lifted up her little Chihuahua. She rose just in time to catch me gawking, all wide eyed with shock. Her hot pink lips simply broke into a smile. With full arms, she managed to raise her dog's paw in a wave. I ducked down, huddling against the wall.

"You can always tell by their hands." My mother informed us once we were seated at the table.

We tried not to frown as she spooned one of her latest Weight Watcher concoctions onto our plates.

"They can wear what they will and have whatever they want *added* or *removed*, but they still have a man's hands."

I looked over at my Daddy's hands as he lifted his fork and then his glass. I had never noticed how big they were compared to mother's. It started right then and there. Queen's presence alone, causing us to notice things we never had.

Much to mother's chagrin, I picked at my food while I waited for Daddy's response regarding this undesired interruption on our normally picturesque street.

"Charlotte Grace! You will eat those Brussels sprouts. You cannot just eat carbs, and leave the rest. Baby fat will not drop off all by itself. Now stop your playing and finish up." mother ordered.

Daddy nodded in my direction, petitioning me to comply for the good of the both of us so she would move onto other business. I popped one of the putrid, green things into my mouth and grinned at them.

Though Daddy was seldom home, I was his girl. Mother had served only as the vessel by which he and I had been united. I worshipped him the way most Southern girls tend to worship their fathers, placing him on an impenetrable throne of my own design.

At that time, he was the D.A. for our county. This caused him to spend much of his day at his office working hard to lock up the *dejected* and *degenerate*, as he often referred to them. His attendance at dinner was only a once or twice a week occurrence. For this reason, it was evident that he was withholding his opinion in hopes that the conversation wouldn't continue to revolve around a man who wasn't a man any more and the extra baby fat that had long been my archenemy.

"If Mr. Lawson knew his daughter would move a man like that into his house, he'd have rather seen it burned to the ground. Wouldn't you agree, Bill?" mother persisted.

Clearing his throat, Daddy sipped his water, looked at his plate, and breathed deeply before weighing in.

" I can't say what the man would've wanted. In all the years he lived over there, barely two or three words passed between us."

This didn't set well with mother. She went on to further prove her position as she regularly felt she must - a side effect of marrying a lawyer.

"That's a shame. Why I, myself, had a very nice chat with him one afternoon last fall while he was raking. It wasn't long before he passed. I got the distinct impression he was a conservative sort of gentleman and most definitely a Republican." she stated with the eloquence and poise of a political candidate.

I took it all in, choking down a couple more Brussels sprouts. Mother went on to slice her steak into tiny bites. This was, as she'd reminded me on numerous occasions, one of her tricks for keeping her figure: small, digestible bites.

"I'm curious, Melanie, exactly how does a Republican go about raking?" Daddy asked struggling to keep a straight face. "Short, quick strokes?" he snickered.

Though I wasn't altogether sure what was funny about his remark, I snickered along with him out of solidarity. Mother didn't dignify his comment with a response, but proceeded onto another subject, one particularly *near and dear* to my heart...the subject of the Miss Gaffney Peach pageant. She, herself, had been runner up two years in a row before finally, at seventeen, achieving her life's accomplishment of being crowned Peach Princess.

As was custom for all former Princesses, mother continued to serve on the board for all further pageants. It was understood she'd do so until she died, or disappeared off the face of the earth. I found myself praying for either to happen; whichever would serve to deliver me from the hell that came with competing.

"If you stick to your diet, I think you'll be able to get into that purple dress in no time." she rallied like it was easy as pie.

"Why'd Ms. Leery have to take it in so much?" I mumbled, mouthful of prescribed green sludge.

"I told her it would be a good incentive. Besides, you have more than enough time, miss." she chided.

I glanced at Daddy off and on for the remainder of the meal in hopes that he'd finally break the news to her. Explain to her that I was a different sort of girl. The kind of girl who loved to read, and write stories. The kind of girl who was far too smart and possessed far too many skills to be wasting time on frivolous pursuits like pageants, but he'd only sat there. Likely he was preoccupied, sorting through case files in his mind.

This was the nature of things in our house. From an early age, I accepted that I was the sacrificial lamb on mother's altar. Daddy, grateful to me though he was, would never intervene on my behalf as he knew full well that mother was the type of woman who demanded a sacrifice. If it wasn't me, he'd have been next in line.

At times, I found myself hoping for a sibling, someone to share the abundant *wealth* of my privileged Southern aristocracy. Then at other times, slumped on a bench in the dressing room of one of the dress shops mother frequented for example, I'd be grateful that I was to be the only victim of her obsessive whims. Daddy hardly had time for me as it was. There was no question he'd have ignored any successor of mine altogether.

The longer I live, the more I see that this is the way of it in most families. The parent who would have the best effect on the child has the least time. The parent who should've never been put in charge of anyone but themselves has ample time. The better candidate thinks that the other must be doing a good job purely out of time devoted. The worst one agrees that they're superior for the very same reason. Everyone suffers under the weight of all these trumped-up delusions.

That night after dinner, I found myself again peering out my bedroom window. It was pitch dark out, and I don't know what I thought I'd see, but I was hopeful. That in and of itself was enough for me. Before spotting Queen, I couldn't remember the last time I'd been truly curious or hopeful about anything.

I had ceased being hopeful that mother would let me forego the Peach Princess sham, or that Daddy would select another birthday gift for me on his own. He'd managed to do it one time that I knew of, yet it'd been so memorable it ignited an anxious spark that carried over every year after.

It was a journal, a light gray one. On the cover, there were teal butterflies flying away from a black tree. Part of me knew there had been little thought to the purchase of it, that he'd simply picked it up in an airport on his way home from interviewing a witness for one of his many cases. This fact was of no consequence. It hadn't stopped me from talking myself into believing he'd looked at it on the shelf and been reminded of me. That as he ran his fingers over it, he'd felt those butterflies represented us both. Two pent up souls dying to get away from our finely decorated cage.

The front door of their house opened slightly. I pressed my face to the glass, hoping...hoping...only to see the Chihuahua scratching his paws against the welcome mat before wriggling back inside. The door shut again.

All the lights went out. That was to be it for the night.

Lying back on my bed, I closed my eyes and listened to the familiar sounds coming from within my own house. Daddy turning off the television downstairs. Mother's muffled voice as she mistook this as her cue to begin her list of demands for the following day. The heavy steps against our wooden stairs as Daddy climbed them to turn in. The light quick steps of my mother fast on his heels. Their door shutting. The creaking of floor boards as they readied for bed.

For the first night in a long while, I found it hard to sleep. My heart raced with the anticipation of what might transpire. The questions of when, where, and how all warbling around in a swarm of unprecedented thoughts. I lay there envisioning it. Seeing myself, Charlotte Grace Danby, walking right up to the new neighbor that very next day, sticking out my hand and saying "Hi."

The Cop

It was the kind of place where men came on their lunch hour. Not because the cuisine was anything to write home about, but rather out of pure nostalgia. Men whose fathers had been brought there by their fathers, then they'd brought their sons in turn. A mom and pop establishment on the verge of extinction.

It was as busy as could be expected at that time of day with only a couple tables still open. The new McDonalds out on the bypass had hurt them. There were still enough loyal customers and enough tips to keep the waitresses employed. Yet not enough to silence the grumblings among them about needing to look for other work.

Tom sat across from him perusing through the Pennysaver with a borderline girlish excitement. Of late, his partner had made this a habit in order to find the best deals on baby furniture for his new bachelor pad. He wanted to snatch the paper from Tom's hands. Tell him to forget all this and run back to his family, back to Lara and the baby. Maybe then all of them could get back to life the way it had been, back to his routine.

He knew it would be pointless. The once idolized union of his friends had become irreparable. The one relationship he'd looked to as a constant, like the very North Star, had disentigrated. Plummeted to the earth in a blaze of flames. He knew this because of the part he'd played in it. Between sips his coffee, and watching Tom circle ads to follow up on, he slowly stepped into the knowledge that this was a pattern of his. This pattern he had of idolizing a thing, or a person only to tear it down, and glory in its demise.

He'd done it with his own mother whom he'd cherished, as much as he could cherish anyone, until his father decided to leave not long after his sixth birthday. A father who'd barely known he existed until that day. The day that he'd opened their front door, suitcase in hand and called, "Carter!"

His mother had stood at the opposite end of the hallway, tears trickling down her hollow cheeks. She'd yelled with a guttural rage.

"He stays!"

He'd never heard its equal come from her nor would he during the brief visits they shared in the months that followed. And in that second, the one second it took for him to look up at his beckoning father and glance back at his sorrowful mother, he made his choice.

He moved forward, gripping the hand of the man he hoped would finally pay attention to him. The man he was shocked had even remembered his name. A hope wriggled its way into his heart. A hope that this act of sacrifice would show his loyalty, making him noteworthy and the two of them inseparable.

They'd walked out the front door leaving his mother a wilted mass on the freshly mopped hardwood - a rose snipped too early from its stem. There'd been something powerful in their departure. That day for the first time he felt it: the power that comes from rejecting someone, to be the one holding all the cards.

This embedded itself inside him, made itself comfortable more than any other feeling had before. More than the twinges of pleasure that resulted from the sweet adoration his mother lathered him with when she'd thrown her arms around him. More than the inklings of pride in response to praise she'd hastily dish out when she'd introduced him to people.

"This is my Carter." she'd say all smiles. "He's so smart for his age. Hadn't even been to school yet an knows his ABC's. He can count clear up to a hundred too!"

He'd looked back at her briefly from his seat that day as he sat on the passenger's side of this father's Cadillac.

"Ready?" his father had asked as if they were going out to eat or to a ball game.

He'd turned to face him, and nodded. As he'd watched his father put the car into gear then pull away with a disconcerting ease, he knew then that they were cut from the same cloth. That, in fact, he had much more of his father in him than he'd ever thought possible. Feeling the leather seat underneath his small hands, he'd dismissed that and reveled instead in the opportunity he'd been given to ride up front for the very first time.

Tom stood up to get a refill of coffee bringing him back to their lunch, to his adulthood. Not all the way back, but far enough so as to escape the clutches of his tragic, melancholy past. He nodded a *go ahead* as Tom held up the pot, showing that he was about to pour what was left of the coffee into his own cup.

"I gotta drive over to Atlanta tonight an check on a crib. Ain't got a thang for the boy to sleep on at my place. Lara's gonna be all over that." Tom complained as he returned to his seat. "Cain't see no need. Told her he can sleep with me. Hell, I slept with my momma an daddy til I was in grade school. Didn't think a thang of it, but nowadays social services'll be on your ass checkin that off on their list when they come to inspect. Makin sure you're *competent* enough to give him his own bed. Shit, ain't any wonder why the world's gettin overrun with spoiled mother fuckers."

He swigged down the last of his coffee.

"How old were you when you got a bed a your own?" he asked Carter as they paid Mary at the register then headed for the exit.

Carter held the door open for an elderly couple on his way out, tipping his deputy's hat to them before trailing after Tom towards their cruiser.

"Cain't say as I recall ever not havin one." he answered him.

They got in their patrol car, putting on their seat belts.

"See, now that right there says it all." Tom jabbed.

He looked at him wondering what exactly *it all* entailed.

"Spoiled." Tom sniped before he broke into full-bellied laughter. "Privileged, spoiled mother fucker."

His response to this was only to look straight ahead, mouth forming into a smirk. They drove a block when he reached into his shirt pocket for a toothpick. The pocket that customarily also housed his wallet that he then discovered was missing. Tom griped as he circled back to the restaurant grunting that he'd return as soon as he had gotten cash out of the ATM for his Atlanta excursion. No sooner had he walked back into the restaurant when Mary ducked behind the counter re-emerging with his wallet.

"Knew you'd be back." she said as he took it from her, putting it in its rightful pocket. "If you're anythang like I am with my purse, you got your whole life in there."

He nodded then turned to go.

"Hey Carter, you hear bout the new boss?"

Mary's inflection indicated this news was to be of particular interest to him - a thing of note that stood out from the usual gossip and distinctly repeated for his benefit. He shook his head. She leaned on the counter. He stepped closer, propped his elbow near the register.

"They'll be here next week." she said.

"What happed to Old Man Lawson?" he questioned.

"You don't know? Lord, must be goin on a month ago now. Sprised you ain't heard. Had a heart attack. Whole town was tore up over it. He'd been runnin this place since I was a baby." she went on.

"Who bought it?" he queried further.

Another customer approached. He moved aside momentarily as Mary took their money. Continuing to keep him in suspense, she smiled and thanked them as they left and went about needlessly straightening her apron before saying anymore.

"Nobody. His daughter inherited it. She's comin to claim it any day now. Might already be in town."

His mouth went dry. Hands instantly sweating. His daughter...his daughter...

"Lord knows I hate workin for a woman even if it is Lisa."

There it was. A bullet piercing the dull, overall predictability of what he'd come to call living. He hadn't heard it for years. Sure, there'd been the mention of her here and there in the restaurant, but those had been nothing more than murmurings among the staff. They were not directed towards him in any way, and there'd never been any talk of her return.

His chest pounded, it was hard for him to get his breath. A metamorphosis was taking place at the mere mention of her homecoming. A certain joy and anxiety simultaneously surfacing all at once.

"She'll be livin at her daddy's. Her an some *roommate* she's draggin with her." Mary continued.

"Roomate?" he inquired.

A bell sounded from behind the grill causing Mary to snap too, coming around to deliver an order to it's rightful owner.

"Don't know much more that what I tol' you." she called over her shoulder. "Rhetta's the only one who got a good look at em when they came for the funeral last month. They checked the place out afterwards fore the wake got started then hightailed it back to Florida to pack up. All she said was that the roommate had on enough make up for all the girl's in the county pageant. Said neither of em talked much, just wanted a look around. Seemed in a hurry to get back on the road."

He looked down at the floor, gathered himself then lifted his head taking in the restaurant with new eyes. His imagination got the better of him as he conjured Lisa out of thin air. She stood by the register talking to customers, appearance unaltered since the day of their high school graduation. The customers chatted and joked with her, and there he was coming out of the back. He kissed her cheek as if the interaction was as natural a thing as putting on clothes or brushing his teeth. His arm found its way around her shoulders as if he'd always had a passport into that country, a place not so foreign, a land where they were in love.

His eyes closed to that world and opened again to the reality of the one in which he lived. Mary, not Lisa, hurried past the register, arms filled with plates. An odd notion came to him. A dark, evil, and thorn marred rabbit trail veered off from that romantic pebbled path that had first come to mind at the mention of Lisa's arrival. The notion that he wouldn't be cast aside again as he had been that day so long ago by the slide. No, he would win her over, make her love him only to be the one to do the dashing of the hopes, the trampling on the heart.

He took to this idea. It sat well with him, like the way a helping of your favorite comfort food sits with you when at last you indulge in it. This idea didn't allow for any unwanted feelings, any miscalculations as so many other ideas had before. This idea gave him the very end result he'd grown to want out of most endeavors: control.

The toothpick hanging from the side of his mouth had grown soft. He discarded it as he walked out. Tom was parked up front. His feet felt as if the steps they made to the car counted for something, that more purpose was in them than there'd ever been prior.

There was a silent knowledge that these events, this death of Old Man Lawson and the return of his *treasured* daughter, had been the very thing he'd been waiting for. A small drop of gasoline at the bottom of his contorted heart had been ignited with these newfound revelations. He felt somehow that in the coming months, the seducing, the pretending, then the long awaited betrayal would be just what he needed.

"What's gotten into you?" Tom asked. "Look like you won the fuckin lotto."

Carter chuckled.

"Naw," he replied. "Nothin like that."

The Tranny

Rodrigo shakes himself off soon as I set his lil' ass out on the porch. I laugh at the way he stops short like he's tryin to get his wits about him. He's a sassy lil' thang, has been since the day we found him all scrawny an starved this one summer out back a this cabana restaurant where me an Lisa was both workin at the time.

Crazy Cuban ran that place. He was hell bent on callin Animal Control soon as he saw Rodrigo rootin around behind the dumpster.

"He's no dog! He's a rat!" he'd carried on.

Didn't take no thought atall for me to intervene. I told him it didn't matter what he looked like, he was one a God's creatures an had a use like anythang else. Minute I walked in the house with him, Lisa made it known she whatin thrilled. Said we did well enough to take care a ourselves, but he ran right over to her, hopped up on the couch an went to lickin her cheek. It was like he knew she was the one to win over. Hell, nowadays I gotta put in a petition to get any time with him.

Goin back to unpackin, I plum forgot all about how long he's been outside when there's a knock. Bein the social butterfly that I am, I don't think twice about waltzin right over an throwin open the door. When I see the startled face of a lil' girl in front of me, I'm reminded that not only am I a long way from Florida, but I got on my hot pink daisy dukes with a crop top T to boot.

What's done is done. I look behind her, ain't nobody else out there. Street's dead as a doornail. One in this welcoming party. We stand here takin each other in. Don't know which one a us is more an alien on this here planet seein as we're both bout equally as strange.

It's got to be 90 degrees an here this chil' stands decked out head to toe in black. She's got pudge on her too. Sweatin like a whore in church. Got a studded leather cuff on her wrist like she's hopin a biker gang's gonna ride through here any minute an ask her to join up.

"Hi." *I finally say seein as the cat's sure 'nough got her tongue.*

She holds Rodrigo out to me.

"Is this your dog?" *she asks with a Southern drawl that makes me seem more like a native New Yorker than the Florida belle I like to think I am.*

I take him off her hands, set him down behind me, an he scurries on inside.

"Rodrigo, you know better." *I scold.* "Hope he didn't tear up nothin. I tell you, most days he's nothin but a hot mess."

She looks past me, curious as all get out as to what someone like myself's got in their house.

"Come on in." *I offer, standin aside.*

Her head shakes no so hard I think it's gonna up an snap her off her lil' white neck.

"No thank you ma'am. My Momma'd have my Daddy wear me out if I was to go into a stranger's house."

I put a hand on a hip.

"Hmmm. That there is a problem." I tell her.

She looks down the street like she's watchin for her momma to catch her for makin it even this far.

"I'm Queen Mae Braxton." I announce, puttin my hand out.

Her chubby pale hand reaches up an shakes mine. I see her lookin at my long purple nails. I'm guessin it's the first time she's seen acrylics like these.

"Charlotte Grace Danby." she replies, smooth as maple syrup over hot cakes.

"Mmm chil'! I envy you that. Now, that there is a name!" I exclaim.

Her pudgy cheeks get red as Julia Robert's dress. That one she wore in Pretty Woman in that scene where she's waitin on Richard Gere up at the bar. Got to be my favorite of all time. Mmm hmm. Julia put everybody to shame in that dress. Yes she did.

Rodrigo runs back out right between my legs an sets on Charlotte Grace's shoes. He paws at her feet, lookin up at her. He's wantin to be picked up.

"Now see there, see Rodrigo's done gone an invited you in too an ya'll already acquainted. You known each other fifteen minutes at least. Where I come from that makes you a far cry from bein strangers." I laugh.

She picks him up, stands there like a statue thinkin it over.

"Chil', you ever hear tell of a serial killer or a kidnapper who had em some acrylic nails an a Chihuahua with Swarsky crystals on his collar to boot?"

Her mouth drops, but she's finally able to shake her head.

"Well then come on in here. You can tell me your story while I unpack. Bout to be bored outta my mind up in this joint."

I move a few boxes. She comes in real slow, sits down even slower like the couch's gonna come to life an bite her.

"Somethin wrong?" I ask.

"No ma'am, I just, it's just that I haven't seen an orange sofa before."

"Neither had I fore this one, honey. Thas why I had to have it. Velvet too. Ain't it somethin?"

She nods.

Rodrigo gets real comfy on her lap an she takes to strokin his back.

"You got a dog?" I ask.

She shakes her head.

"You should. You real good with em." *I say.*

"We don't have time for dogs, and they're very dirty." *she schools me with this line she's rehearsed an got down pat.*

Kids got a lot a those lines. Lord knows I did. "Pretty is as pretty does. Cleanliness is next to Godliness." *Jus a couple a the ones my momma drilled into us. Not in any mean way, but jus by sayin em every time we turned around.*

"Hmm, well Rodrigo don't get too dirty. He's a bonified 'gentleman'. An when he does get a wild hair an rolls in somethin nasty, well I jus march his lil' ass in to the kitchen sink an spray him off jus like I'm cleanin a skillet."

Her eyes get big as plates an those Pretty Woman cheeks come back. I realize I've gone an said serial killer, kidnapper an now ass to this chil' in the last ten minutes. Lord above! This is exactly why I tell Lisa adoption ain't in the cards. I couldn't have no filter if I tried. Had one all growin up an eversince I used a crow bar an popped that thang off it's been broke beyond all recognition.

"I like your picture." *she says lookin over at my framed poster a Miss Tina Turner.*

"Is she famous?"

I strut right over an hold it up so she can get a better look. Clear as day to me this chil' ain't had a lick a learnin about anythang worth two cents.

"Honey, this here is Tina Turner on stage at Caesar's Palace in Vegas! Only one a the greatest voices a our time. She whatin jus a singer. No! Mmm mmm. She's what they call a world-class icon. Why I'll go as far as to say she's the black Marilyn Monroe. Always been ahead a her time, set the style for every soul sista."

Charlotte Grace keeps on strokin Rodrigo jus a listenin. I can tell she's eager to hear about somethin so important.

"Started out as a back up singer for a no good man, Ike, who later became her husband. Mmm, he was a fool, a woman beater, an a bad dresser on top of it."

"Why'd she marry him?" *Charlotte Grace pipes up.*

"Good question, chil'. Good question. Why's any good woman marry a fool? History's chalk full a ones that has though. Like every good woman's got to have her a bad boy phase. I mean jus look at Whitney Houston an Bobby Brown, an O.J. an Nicole." *I keep goin.*

From the confused look on her face I can tell that I jus threw out a whole lot more information she ain't got clue one about.

"Any how, Tina, now Tina's a different story. She wised up an left her fool.

Set out, made her own way, her own mark on the world. An wouldn't you know, don't nobody know who the hell Ike is anymore. Only thang everybody know is how he beat her an how she left his sorry ass. Thas all everybody in this whole wide world remembers bout him."

Rodrigo jumps off her lap an scurries on over to his water bowl. She watches him lap it up, then she turns her eyes to the bowl a candy settin on the end table. She goes to eyein it with the kind a longin I have when I'm at the mall lookin at a dress I know full well I cain't afford.

"Help yourself." I offer, reachin over pushin it closer to her.

She's froze up, cain't make up her mind, but then her hand reaches in the bowl pullin out a Hershey's kiss.

"Don't know about you, but I cain't go a day without chocolate." I confess.

Unwrappin it like it's the best thang since sliced bread, she puts it in her mouth real slow-like then rolls it around. Closin her eyes, it's like she thinks it might be the last bit a sugar she'll have in her life.

"What grade you in?" I ask her.

"I'm starting seventh next week." she says real proud.

"Mmm, thas gonna be fun. Ain't gonna be on the bottom no more. Yeah,

seventh grade's a good grade. People start carin more bout what they're wearin, work gets harder, an the boys start growin. Mmm hmmm. Seventh grade I had my first true crush." I reminisce, stoppin my unpackin puttin my hands on my hips. *"What was his name? Cute lil' fella always wearin Timberlan boots with jeans. Thought he was the shit, an he was."*

Her cheeks blaze red, but she cain't take her eyes off me, lappin up every word flowin outta my mouth.

"Ryan! Yep, his name was Ryan Clark. Mmmm wonder what he's up to now? Boy sure could get my motor started."

Her eyes look down at the floor, an I know she knows what I'm talkin bout.

"You got you a boy like that?" I want to know.

I sit down next to her like we're jus two girlfriends dishin dirt at a sleepover. She don't answer right off.

"Come on now, I tol' you mine." I say battin at her arm playful like.

"Donnie." she whispers.

"I didn't catch it, honey."

"Donnie Phelps." she says all prouder an louder.

"Mmm! Sounds like he's a looker with a name like that." I tease.

She nods her head.

"Well, I'm guessin you got yourself the perfect outfit for the first day a school so you can impress the hell outta Mr. Donnie."

She shakes her head.

"Chil' you got to get on that!" I exclaim, poppin up, lookin round the room for my box a dresses, but it ain't nowhere to be found. "Lord! I cain't put my finger on my box a clothes right now, but I'm gonna make it my mission fore you go walkin down the halls a that school. You'll see, we're gonna get you ready. We're gonna make it so the only thang that Donnie Phelps can think about is you!"

Her mouth widens into a big smile. I can tell this sets real well with her. Rodrigo jumps up in her lap again. She takes to rubbin behind his ears. He licks her hand.

"Mmm, now hadn't he gone an taken to you." I remark watchin the two of em together like they's separated at birth.

"Hey, startin next week, I'm gonna be workin at the restaurant all day. Be lucky if I darken this door fore supper. He'll be here all on his lonesome."

She holds him to her chest, scratchin his belly.

"You think you might have time to stop by here after school an let him out, *maybe walk him a few minutes?" I ask.*

Her smile gets even bigger, but jus as quick as it came, it falls to a frown.

"My momma keeps me busy with chores and there's this pageant..."

"Thas alright. I was jus thinkin that the two a you gettin on so good an all it might work, but don't worry none. Lisa gave me the number a this kennel an they got a list a dog walkers. He's picky but he'll get used to em."

"I better get goin. Can't be late for dinner." she says all nervous.

Pickin Rodrigo up, she hands him to me an walks over to the door. I see that I jus may have gone an overstepped my bounds askin her for a favor first time we met. As she walks, she looks all around, takin in everythang she can like she thinks she might never travel back this way. I open the door for her, tuck Rodrigo under my arm. He's jus a squirmin to go with her.

"Bye Miss Charlotte Grace." I say, wavin Rodrigo's lil' paw at her.

She touches his head one last time fore she turns an goes on down the sidewalk. Chil' only gets halfway fore she stops dead in her tracks, looks up an down the street checkin for that momma a hers or nosy neighbors who might tell on her. Coast is clear. She whips around, nearly knocks us over bouncin back up on the steps.

"If it's alright, ma'am, I think I can find some time to stop by an walk Rodrigo."

I smile wide an hand him to her to hold for a second.

"I'll owe you big time, an he'll love it! Let me go get you a key." I tell her.

I dart back inside an hunt under the papers on the counter for the extra keys Lisa bought a couple days ago. Findin one, I grab my own set off a my purse. I take my snazzy high heeled key chain off em an attach it her to key then I grab me a handful a Hershey kisses outta the bowl. I walk over an trade her the key an the candy for Rodrigo.

"Can you start Monday? His leash hangs on that hook right there. All you gotta do is open that back door an he'll be rarin to go."

She nods rubbin her fingers over that shiny shoe in her hand.

"Ain't a chance you'll lose it with that thang on it." I laugh.

"Ten dollars a week sound good?" I offer.

Her eyes get big. She shakes her head up an down so hard I think it's liable to pop right off an roll on down the driveway. Puttin the candy an the key in her pocket she smiles up at us.

"It's been a pleasure to meet you, Miss Braxton." she says all proper like *she's Jackie Kennedy herself.*

"The pleasure's been ours Miss Charlotte Grace, an it's Queen chil'. Jus call me Queen."

Me an Rodrigo watch her scurry across the street. In all that black, she looks like a burglar hurryin to rob that big fine house a hers. When she gets to her door, she takes one more look around fore she waves. I wave back smilin for all I'm worth. I shut the door an set Rodrigo down. He hops up on the couch, whinin as he goes.

"You're smitten, ain't you?" I accuse him. "I like her too. Sure do. Somethin about her, Lil' Man. Jus somethin about her."

The Girl

That pink and gold heel burned in my palm as I turned it over and over. I made sure to do it slowly so that the key dangling from it didn't alert mother to its presence when we sat at the dinner table. It felt as though I was engaged in a mortifying act of defiance. There she sat across from me, obliviously going on about how the plans for the pageant were coming along, and the mind-numbing details of the committee meeting she'd attended that day.

Every now and again I'd nod. A meager acknowledgement was sufficient, a response I'd learned from an early age by mimicking Daddy. It was how interactions between mother and anyone else went. Even friends of hers who came over could be observed attempting to speak at intervals. Trying to wedge any words they could in between her long drawn out sentences, only to end up retreating by nodding and nibbling bites of her famous chicken salad finger sandwiches.

As I looked at her carving a turkey cutlet into little pieces on her plate, I knew that there was a loneliness in being as beautiful as she was. That when you're that gorgeous, no one cares what you have to say. You are a trophy sitting on a mantle. An object given for one day, one crowning moment, yet having no real relevance to day-to-day life except to create fodder for the occasional story, or serve as an arm ornament at a party. A pang of sorrow crept in, but it was short lived.

"Did you try your dress on?" she asked, instantly putting a stop to any bliss the keychain shoe had brought on.

"Yes." I lied.

"Did it fit any better?" she interrogated.

I nodded thinking that if I didn't speak, it wouldn't be a full out lie.

"Charlotte Grace, that's wonderful! See you've set your mind to it and now it's happening. That's how life works." she admonished.

She cleared the table. Her hands delicately picked up each plate and carried them to the kitchen. I stood, collecting napkins and utensils. Walking in after her, I wondered what she'd set her mind to. Being Peach Princess? Marrying a lawyer? Having a baby? The first two I was sure were on her list of things she'd wanted to accomplish, but motherhood, I was convinced, had come only as a repercussion of being a wife.

No matter how I tried, I could never picture my mother daydreaming about having a baby. Not like those mothers who came and volunteered at our school during lunch. The ones who always sent cupcakes on their kid's birthdays, and were sure to be chaperones on field trips. My mother always came on the first day of school to sign all my registration papers and did not darken the door again until the next year when it was time to do the same.

I'm not sure the PTA made it on my mother's radar. Again, another concession made due to her beauty: not having to stoop so low as to do any of the typical stay-at-home mom responsibilities. She was likely saving such things for middle age, when her looks would be waning so she'd have to compensate by proving herself in other arenas.

I helped her wash the dishes taking note of her occasional glances out the window. This was the most vulnerable thing she did. This looking out at the driveway, watching and anticipating Daddy's return. It was as though when he was not around, she had less purpose, like an oven with nothing to be baked on it's racks.

We finished and headed out into the living room. She sat on the couch; a thoroughbred resting on a bed of fresh hay. I headed towards the stairs.

"I thought I'd see what movies are on." she said so as not to come right out and invite me or seem too needy.

"I got a new book at the library. I'm just gonna read a while." I told her.

"Alright." she conceded, sighing, reaching for the remote.

I didn't make it to the top step before she called to me.

"Charlotte Grace, I'd like to see that dress on you in the morning."

"Okay." I answered though I knew full well it was anything but.

Shutting the door to my room, I didn't turn on the lights, but instead walked over and looked out across at Queen's. Her front room lights shone brightly through her thin pink drapes. I pictured her there on that velvet couch, eating her chocolate, petting Rodrigo, telling Lisa how she'd found a dog walker. She'd go on to explain that it was to be the neighbor girl they'd met and how much Rodrigo had liked me.

An odd yearning came over me. Not jealousy exactly, but more of an envy. I didn't want to be her. No, I was fully satisfied with the gender I'd been given in my mother's womb. I wanted to be like her - to be just fine with me as me, even proud of myself. I wanted to do what I wanted when I wanted. I wanted to feel as if I was the *queen* of the world in which I lived.

Turning my lamp on, I tried to read, to immerse myself, as I often did, in a book I'd checked out, Anne of Greene Gables. I'd taken the initiative to go to the library and put it on hold so that I'd be ahead for my seventh grade literature class. It was interesting enough. All about a girl who'd been adopted by an older couple. She was a girl not unlike myself. A girl with quirks, an oddball in all the places she found herself.

My mind drifted with each turn of the page back to Queen and the new job I'd been given. How I wanted to wake up and have it be Monday. I rose and took off my jeans and t-shirt, letting them fall to the floor. Putting on my nightshirt, I laid back down. Before I could get situated, I hopped back up jerking my pants off the floor, and recovering the key from a pocket. I stuffed it in the zipper pouch of my backpack then returned to bed.

Below my room, the front door opened and closed. Daddy had arrived. Usually, I'd have snuck down to hug him and give him a kiss goodnight, but on that particular night I left him to my mother. I figured he could fend for himself. He'd left me to do so more times than I could count. I wasn't angry with him, just preoccupied.

I fell asleep to thoughts about how it would be to walk Rodrigo down the streets behind Queen's house. I knew without a doubt we couldn't be seen in our own subdivision. There was a shortcut through the woods I knew that he'd enjoy. I'd get to show him off in the neighborhood that adjoined ours, and I knew exactly where we would go first.

We were going to walk right past the Phelps, right past Donnie's. And if I was lucky, because he'd never have seen me over that way before, he'd come out to see Rodrigo. He might even talk to me. This was the best thought I'd fallen asleep to in ages.

My mother's irate voice woke me as the sun's rays barely cracked their way through the trees. She stood by my bed, my clothes from the day before in her one hand, and a handful of silver Hershey kiss wrappers in the other.

"Where did these come from?" she demanded.

I looked at them wadded in her fist, my mouth watered as I remembered how their savory goodness.

"Ms. Terrell's." I fibbed. "She gave them to me for helping her with some boxes."

She stomped over to the door. I could tell she was composing herself, thinking of what would be the most *ladylike* thing to say.

"Just because something is offered, it doesn't mean you have to accept it."

With that she scampered off down the stairs. I slung my legs over the side of the bed dangling my feet. As I ran my toes over the shag rug, I wondered if everybody who knew Queen had to lie. If knowing a person such as herself was possible without it. Without having to lie to all the people who couldn't bring themselves to know her. Standing and stretching, I caught sight of Rodrigo across the street, sunning himself on the porch. I decided that this was probably true, but I also decided it didn't matter. It was so very worth it.

The Cop

Tom had told him that he wouldn't believe his eyes when he saw Lisa Lawson now that she was all grown up. He'd told him she was hotter than she ever was in high school, but he'd also made sure not to leave out that he'd be shocked when he met the roommate. When he had pressed for more, Tom only laughed and told him, "Just wait. Just you wait."

Of course, this had the desired effect. It made him get up early the next morning, put on his uniform, though he had no need of it on his day off, and head right over to the restaurant. He strode in, alert, ready to re-introduce himself, though somehow, he knew there'd be no need.

His usual booth was occupied. This put him off kilter, threw him off his game, but he adapted, as he always did, finding an empty one next to it. It wasn't long before Mary bounced over.

"Took you longer than I thought it would." She joked with a satisfied grin.

He looked up at her, handing her the menu that had been waiting for him on the table. She nodded, stalking off to the kitchen. She knew him backwards and forwards. He was a man of habit.

There were only the usual suspects to be found before him. Carl the line cook flipping flapjacks on the griddle. Mary delivering plates as fast as she could. There was Nan the aged cashier who wouldn't have been able to obtain employment anywhere else. She remained a staple there however, due to the fact that, at one time, she and old man Lawson had carried on quite a fling. Once he'd decided she had no place in his bed, his sympathy had prompted him to give her a permanent position at the register. There appeared to be no sign of Lisa or the roommate yet.

"Here you go, hon." Mary said as she plopped the plate of eggs and sausage in front of him.

He picked up his fork and dived in. Unable to help herself, she lingered by his table.

"I reckon they'll be in any minute now." she whispered.

"Who?" he replied without looking up.

"Lisa and that *friend* a hers."

His knife scraped the plate making a nails-on-chalkboard sound. He winced, yet only grunted that he'd heard her. Mary's heels clicked in a happy, rhythmic, dancelike manner as she made her way to tend to other customers. The glee over dangling the carrot of Lisa's arrival had made her morning, possibly her week.

Friend... hung in the air like a gray cloud over his head. How had she meant that? Her putting emphasis on that one word had been peculiar. If her intent had been to pique his curiosity, she had succeeded.

Questions stared him in the face from the seat across from him where Tom usually sat. Were she and the roomate only *friends* or were they more than that? Could they be that odd term that he still didn't fully understand the meaning of, *friends with benefits*?

More than an hour passed. Nan occasionally glanced at him as the dining room was starting to fill up. She undoubtedly hoped her eyeballing would encourage him to relinquish his seat.

At one point she brought him a Sunday paper. He'd thanked her, taken it, pretending to read. Near lunchtime, he fought the urge to get up, walk out and make better use of the only day off he'd gotten in the last month and a half, but then it happened. His waiting had not been in vain.

"Thanks for holding down the fort, Mary." Lisa's voice trickled in from the back. "Can't recall the last time I got to sleep in."

He froze not daring to turn and take her in just yet. He held off to heighten the enjoyment of the experience, this clandestine reunion.

"Whew, chil'! You know you everybody needs their beauty rest, baby." An unfamiliar voice weighed in.

This voice must belong to the *friend*, though it was not what he'd expected, a strange quality to it's tone. Heels clunked against the tile floor towards Nan's register.

"How you doin this morning, Nan? Rarin an kickin?" the friend boomed.

The back of her came into view. She was six foot if she was an inch and her skin was as black as night. He'd never seen a woman so tall or so black. In actuality, he'd seen very few black people on this side of town at all. Nan smiled politely proceeding to show her the receipt tape, demonstrating how busy they'd been.

It was apparent to him that Nan was being classically *Southern*. She wore the kind of tight lipped smile that all Southern ladies don when they're highly uncomfortable, yet want to maintain their manners. Having been on the receiving end of this look on many occasions, he'd become an expert in identifying it.

Blending in did not seem to be of concern to this *friend*. With tight jeans and a silver tank top, she looked ready for a night on the town. She turned to the side, revealing a face thickly slathered with makeup. It caused him to ponder if she was a showgirl of some kind.

In no way was she the sort of *friend* he'd imagined his Lisa Lawson associating with. She possessed a certain beauty; there was no doubt about that. Strong features and a slender physique with curves in all the right places. Yet there was something off, something he dared to label abnormal. He couldn't quite put his finger on it. A hand lightly grazed his shoulder. He looked up. His ability to breathe in and out nearly forgotten in that one second.

"Carter Dade?" Lisa said with the same Tennessee drawl she'd had since childhood. "Thought that was you. Wasn't sure with the uniform and all."

This was not how he'd wanted it to play out. No, he'd wanted to be the initiator. He'd wanted to be the one to take her off guard, be standing with perfect posture before her, uniform and all. Instead there he was cowering from his seat below her, taken aback by the *friend*, by Lisa herself touching his shoulder. He was speechless.

Lisa smiled, not with that Southern- pursing-of-the-lips kind of smile, but with another type he knew all too well: one of sympathy. Once again, she had the upper hand. Having spotted him there all alone on a Sunday morning. She likely assumed he was single, and she was right. No doubt she'd proceeded to sum him up as a man who had little control over his life, over his relationships. She'd taken one look at his uniform and surmised that he'd then gone on to choose a career that had rendered him an ultimate sense of power.

"Heard you inherited the place." he managed to utter.

"Sure did. Got into town last week. Quite a change for us, but I couldn't bear for it to be sold off, and to be honest, the older you get the more home seems like a place to get back to instead of run away from. You know?"

He nodded, yet in reality, he had no idea what she was talking about. He'd had no real home what with being jockeyed back and forth between his mother and father until third grade. Until that day she didn't come out of the bathroom, and the numerous apartments he and his father had gone on to occupy all over the county after that, had never earned the name of *home*. A customer called to Lisa waving hello. She smiled and waved back.

"I was real sorry to hear about your daddy. He was a good man." Carter offered her the customary condolences trying to keep her by his side.

The smile she'd given the other customer dissipated into a look of confusion.

"Was he?" she stated more than asked.

Before he could organize his thoughts enough to answer, as he'd not known Old Man Lawson anymore than he knew anyone else, the *friend* stalked over, heels clicking as she came, water pitcher in tow. At the mere sight of her, a patron at the table adjacent him, took to choking on the bite of grits he'd just taken. The *friend* picked up his cup, refilling it. The patron drank it down, wiped his mouth and continued to eat his grits not taking his eyes off of her for a second.

"Mornin officer." she then greeted Carter with her unnaturally plump, pink lips.

"Carter, this is my friend, Queen. She came up here from Florida with me to help out. Queen this is Carter. We came up in school together." Lisa performed an obligatory introduction.

Queen put the pitcher in her left hand, sticking out her right.

"*Officer* Dade." Carter corrected gruffly shaking her hand.

There it was. The thing he hadn't readily been able to put his finger on. Her grip was firm. Her hand was enormous! The bones in it far bigger than a real womans would have been. Though the long fingernails on it were an elegant shade of mint green with white jeweled tips, it was unmistakably a man's hand. He found himself holding on a bit longer just to make sure.

Finally withdrawing his hand, he could not help but to take a quick survey of her person. First off, her chest with protrusions that certainly qualified as breasts. Secondly, her crotch - flat across and having no visible bulge. It was a full indication that the hands were her only manly quality.

As he edged out of his seat, he then took notice of her ankles. They proved to be the only other evidence needed to convince him that she had indeed, at one time or another, been a man.

"Better be heading on." he barked.

The two moved aside, Queen clearing his plate as she did so, and Lisa taking up his newspaper.

"Good to see you, Carter." Lisa called.

He nodded, turned, and walked up to the register. Nan was nowhere to be found. Queen bustled around behind the counter. As Carter dug for his wallet, he discovered it was stuck in his shirt pocket. Queen's big black hand reached over the register, yanking it out, then handed it to him.

"You need you a bigger pocket or a smaller wallet." she joked.

The thick, iron taste of blood filled his mouth. He became aware that he'd bitten into the side of his cheek hard enough to tear it open. He already had a permanent scar on the other side of his mouth from doing this as a means, a barrier jarring him to pause before committing a deed that could serve to bring him to ruin. One that could easily take away what little he'd been able to construct out of the scraps he'd had tossed down to him from life's banquet table.

"That'll be $5.50. Big spender huh?" Queen went on.

Pulling a ten from his wallet, he plunked it down on the counter. *That Nan!* He thought to himself. *Why couldn't she have waited to take a break? Lazy good for nothing...*

The front door opened letting in the sun's blinding rays. Queen shielded her eyes with his ten dollar bill.

"Chil' get on in an shut that door." she greeted the incoming customer. "I'm gonna have to get some sunglasses if I'm gonna be workin up here, mmm hmmm."

Her large hands opened the register, retrieved his change from the drawer, and handed it to him. With an undeniable awkwardness, he snatched the change, stuffing it in the pocket of his pants rather than taking the time to put it back in his wallet. She withdrew her hand, a child who just dared touch the burner after their mother had warned them not to.

"Have a good one, Mr. Dade." she exuberantly ended their encounter as he rushed out the door.

On the drive home his stomach churned. A rumbling, gurgling anxiety boiling inside. Hands on the wheel, he was determined to get back to the safety of his house. The place where everything was how he wanted it - organized and in its place. Where he and he alone was all he had to deal with. Most days this was sufficient.

Not able to keep his foot on the gas pedal, Carter tasted the acid first, then felt the vomit rise in his throat. He pulled the car over. Flinging open his door, he clamored out into a field. Hunching over, he watched helplessly as everything he'd eaten that morning and a bit from the previous night came spewing out onto the ground.

Stumbling back to his car, he realized he couldn't put a name on what it was that had caused such an episode. Though he sensed that it was the conglomeration of the events of the morning. Carter was uncertain, however, if it had been his unsatisfactory reunion with Lisa or meeting Queen that had been the onset of a full-fledged panic attack.

Just last month, the doctor he visited a twice yearly for his prescription that was supposed to keep such things at bay had suggested he no longer needed to take the pills. He'd told him that he was doing better and so he'd not taken one since. He'd, in fact, let his last bottle expire. However, on that afternoon, there in that hot field, his chest pounded out its own conflicting opinion.

His fingers quivered as he gripped his keys. Re-starting his car, he continued down the road. He came into the sickening awareness, the ungodly realization that it wasn't just meeting Queen or the shaking of her hand that had done it. No, it was the horrifying fact that he hadn't really minded looking at her. He hadn't minded it at all.

The Tranny

Layin in my bed, listenin to the sound a Charlotte Grace openin up the back door so she can walk Rodrigo, I look at the clock an cain't believe I done slept most a my day off away. Had a million thangs I wanted to do like get my nails filled in, catch up on my Real Housewives. Hope Lisa hadn't gone an erased my Tivo.

"We'll be back in a little while." Charlotte Grace calls down the hall.

"See you then." I holla back.

Sure picked a winner when I snagged her to help out with Lil' Man. Come 3:30 every afternoon, he's waitin at that back door. How he knows what time it is. I ain't got no idea, but I spect he knows a whole lot more than I give him credit for. That chil' ain't missed a single day that I know of. She puts the "R" in responsible.

Now, she went an let me know right off that she'd have to be sneaky an take him walkin in that neighborhood behind ours. Said there was plenty a nosy neighbors on our street who'd love nothin better than to run an tell her momma all about her associatin with us. She seemed real embarrassed to have to tell me that. I jus patted her shoulder an tol' her I understood. I tol' that chil' most a my friends hadn't ever been much for usin the front door an it don't make no difference to me. A friend's a friend no matter which door they use.

I lay here a little longer. Mmm, restaurant work ain't no joke. Lord knows it'll break you if you don't know what you gettin yourself into. Even if you do know, it'll still cause you a world a pain. All the fetchin, carryin, totin, heat from that grill, mmm hmm. Only perk you get is that free facial what with all the sweatin. My skin's smoother than a newborn's powdered ass.

There's a whole lotta the job you can train for, practice so's you're good an prepared. Thangs like followin somebody around, takin orders, clearin dishes, where to put em. You can get all that down to a science, but then there's thangs you cain't never prepare for an thas customers. They'll damn near shock the hell outta a you.

In Florida, you had the tourists to tangle with. Snowbirds we called em. Northerners who'd swoop their J. Crew, L.L. Bean wearin selves down to our neck a the woods every winter so they wouldn't freeze up their way. Locals saw you all the time. They were used to you. Once you proved yourself, kissed their behind, gave em good service, they didn't care if you was a man, woman or chimp, but those Snowbirds, mmm, they always had to school you.

Had this one ol' woman who commenced to prayin over me right there in the dinin room fore I could even take her order. Didn't do it in no discreet way neither. Called out loud for the Lord to deliver me from the "oppression of homosexuality". Seemed like Jesus was listenin to me that day cause the only deliverin he did was to deliver me from havin to put up with her judgmental ol' ass. Soon as she finished her prayin, she got right up an walked out.

Lisa says all my bad experiences have made me "agist", always hatin on ol' people. She says how am I gonna like it when I start headin down the road towards my golden years. I tell her "agist" ain't even a real word. I jus don't like ol' people an when I'm ol' the young people can hate me too. I'm sure I'll deserve it. On occasion, I'm sure to remind her not to let me get too ol'. If I'm sixty an thangs are saggin in places that don't another soul want to see, then she should take me out to the woods an turn me loose.

She laughs when I say this, thinks I'm jokin, but I'm serious as a heart attack. Thas what momma did with Boots. That big ol' smelly dog lived to be thirteen. Lord, we loved him, but he started gettin tumors. Momma didn't have two dimes to rub together. Couldn't get em tested. Vet said they were more than likely benign an we could keep an eye on him, but you could take one look at him an tell he was miserable.

One day I come home from school an momma was loadin him in the car. She'd been sure to do it when Jarvis was at ball practice. He wouldn't a stood for it. I swear, he's softer for animals than he is for people, so it was jus me an her an Boots.

Drove out to the middle a somewhere I'd never been an hope I'll never go again. Boots sat in the back right by me, happy as a clam. I stroked his fur, tol' him my goodbyes. Thanked him for being such a good dog, for not chewin up too many a my thangs, for keepin watch over us, for listenin to my cryin an belly achin. Momma didn't say much. She had her hands glued on that wheel, jus kept drivin.

Once she thought we'd gone far enough, she pulled over an I got out an walked out in a field with him. She stayed in the car, watched us out the winda. I'll never forget how he looked when he went runnin off in that tall grass. It was like he was a puppy again, runnin for all he was worth, like he knew right where he was goin.

He got further an further ahead a me. I called out, he turned back one time jus a pantin, eyes raised like he was sayin "Bye now, Jermaine. You behave yourself. I'm gone." An jus like that he ran off into the woods. That was the last time we ever saw hide nor hair of him.

I imagine he found himself a cool spot under a tree where he lay down, went to sleep, an didn't wake up. Thas how I want it too. Ain't gonna be put in no retirement home to rot. Gonna go out in my prime, eyes raised an happy like ol' Boots.

Fore I know it, it's 4:00. Charlotte Grace ain't back yet. Strange for her cause her momma usually gets home by 4:30 an she likes to be sittin in her bedroom by then lookin like she's been tendin to her homework. I go out into the livin room, part the back curtain. No sign of em.

Decidin not to get all stressed yet, I sit on the couch, thumb through my magazine. Ain't long til the back door opens an here comes Rodrigo staggerin to his water bowl, Charlotte Grace behind him, sweat jus drippin off her.

"Chil' I know you an black got you a love affair goin on, but cain't you wear you a tank top, or a miniskirt or something lighter fore you up an die a heat stroke?"

She lifts her black ball hat an wipes her forehead.

"Come on in here an get somethin to drink." I tell her.

She shakes her head.

"No thank you. Mother'll be late today. Thought I'd head over to Ms. Terrell's. I told her I'd help her get her packages in off the porch." she says pattin Rodrigo fore she heads out the door.

"Thas real nice a you." I say walkin upstairs. "I sure preciate all you doin for Lil' Man. He loves you. If he runs off, I know right where I'll find him, all snuggled up at your house. Oh, an don't go hurryin out an forget your money on the counter."

I hear her usin her key to lock the door after her. I start runnin my bathwater. Don't get even half a tub full or any clothin off, when I happen to walk by the winda. There's the chil' an that ol' woman next door tryin to lift a box the size of a casket off a her porch. Lord above! Cain't let that pass. Won't be able to lay my head down at night, well, might be able to lay it down but won't get a wink a sleep knowin I let them do that all on they own.

I slip on some presentables, tell Rodrigo I'll be right back an head out over across the yard. Don't get ten feet fore Charlotte Grace sees me comin. From the look on her face I know how we gonna have to play it. I played it this way a thousand times. We got to pretend like we ain't already acquainted.

"How ya'll doin?" I say.

I stop at the edge of the yard, not knowin if this lady's one a those ol' school Southerners. The kind with a shotgun by the door jus waitin for an occasion when a young black "queer" ventures onto their property.

Charlotte Grace turns her Pretty Woman red, an eyeballs the lady.

"We're havin us a time." the lady admits.

"I can see that. Thought you might need some help." I reply sweet as candy.

The lady stands up tall, squints, looks me over.

"I jus moved in over there at the Lawson place a few week's back. My name's Queen. Queen Braxton."

I take a step closer.

"I've seen you." the lady answers.

Cain't tell how she feels about that, an neither can Charlotte Grace.

"I'm Charlotte Grace. I live over there." Charlotte Grace re-introduces herself pointin over to her house. "And this is Ms. Terrell."

Lookin at me one more time, then at Charlotte Grace, then down at that big ol' wood crate, Ms. Terrell makes up her mind she's gonna have to accept any help thas bein offered in this here situation she's gone an got herself into.

"I reckon we could use an extra hand." she finally says.

I walk up an get on one side. Charlotte Grace gets on the other. Ms. Terrell holds the door for us. Now I can't rightly tell you how, but we get that box into her livin room. Like to pop off all my nails off doin it. They were due to be re- done anyhow. Standin up, takin a breath, I look around. Cain't believe my eyes. Place is full up with crates, some half open, some with their contents spillin out.

"I'm a collector." Ms. Terrell confesses.

"You sure are, honey." I laugh. "Takes one to know one. I collect shoes myself. Got close to a hundred an fifty pair now."

"My!" she exclaims. "How do you wear all those?"

"Not at the same time, I'll tell you that." I tease.

The three of us chuckle. I lean against the back a her couch, catchin my breath.

"What you got in this thang, honey?" I cain't help but ask.

"This is...well this is..." she stutters lookin down at the label. "Would you believe I don't know what this one is? Sometimes I've got so many comin in I can't keep track."

I refrain from tellin her I've seen enough in my short life to believe damn near anythang she wants to tell me. Charlotte Grace an me shoot each other a smile. From the looks a the rest a her "collection" it looks like this one's probly another big ol' vase or gaudy statue. This one sure was heavy, though. Long as it ain't her dead husband, I'm good. Don't need to be gettin wrapped up in nobody else's drama, mmm mmm.

She invites us to sit on her couch, have some ice tea, but Charlotte Grace makes it known she's got to get on cause her momma's due back any minute. I follow her out on the porch not really wantin to overstay my welcome. Didn't see no shotgun, but don't mean Ms. Terrell ain't got one. Things still might go further south when we alone.

"Thank you kindly for your help, Ms. Queen." Ms. Terrell thanks as she walks us out.

"Ain't no thang, honey. Anytime. Lisa an me are up at the diner a whole lot, but you see our car over there, you jus holler. We'll come runnin." I tell her.

She nods, shuts her door. Me an Charlotte Grace head on. We're walkin through the yard. She's jus about to go her way, an leave me to mine when a gang a lil' boys tryin they hand at lookin all big an bad come tearin down the street on they bikes. The way Charlotte Grace cain't take her eyes off the one in the lead, I know right off who he is. Got to be Donnie Phelps.

"Is that who I think it is?" I soflty tease, elbowin her.

She giggles.

"It is! Well, chil' you can pick em cain't you?"

We watch as he circles around eyein us as he goes. He don't smile, he don't frown, jus takes stock a thangs then leads his lil' entourage on down the road outta sight.

"Talk to him yet?" I want to know.

She shakes her head.

"Mmm, well Lil' Miss Thang, you better get on it. That one's gonna have his pick if he don't already. You got to make your impression." I advise.

I watch as she scampers off, lets herself in her house. Latch key kid. Cain't imagine what she did with her time fore I came along an gave her somethin to do. Says her momma's got her in some pageant, but you can take one look at that girl an know she ain't no beauty queen contestant. Poor thang. Another square peg somebody's tryin to squeeze in a round hole.

My own momma used to go on an on about how sometimes you find yourself somewhere you didn't never want to be, in some kinna predicament you didn't never wanna get all mixed up in, but then fore you know it, the sky opens up an a dove flys down - a sign to show you exactly why it all happened. Never did really know what she was goin on about. Thought it was one a them thangs Bible thumpers need to think so they don't go crazy in the face a all the evil in this here world.

As I cross the street, walk over to my place, I think the meanin of it finally hits me. No dove came down, only Rodrigo who goes to lickin my toes soon as I open the door, but I think I see now I didn't come here jus cause Lisa wanted it. Naw, I'm certain I landed right here in this backwards, uptight town time's done gone an forgot so that lil' girl don't plum up an lose her damn mind.

The Girl

All these years later, there's no compliment, no crumb of male attention that rates as high as that look. The one that Donnie Phelps gave me that day as I stood out there next to Queen on Ms. Terrell's lawn. I'd seen him coming. I would've recognized that bike anywhere. A dark purple BMX bike he and his high school brother, T.J., built. At least that's what I'd heard. That's what everyone had heard.

We all knew everything there was to know about the Phelps boys. They were the icons, the celebrities of Rutherford County. Daddy attended school with their daddy, and from what he recounted, it had been that way for him as well. In our neck of the woods, the Phelps inherited their fame much like a Kennedy or a Rockefeller.

Every small town has these idols, these golden calves they make their shrines to, that they look up to, and aspire to be like. They're as much a part of our culture as the drawl we speak with or the Confederate flag itself. Maintaining their status takes little to no effort. They simply wake up each morning and make an appearance.

By the time I saw him ride past, I had already walked by his house every day for two weeks. He hadn't once looked up, even with Rodrigo prancing out in front of me, he hadn't noticed. One afternoon, he'd even been out by the road working on a car with his father. Rodrigo came close to lifting a leg to the hem of his jeans before I jerked him away, and even then, we had not warranted a glance.

Though now in hindsight, I am painfully aware why he chose to finally look my way that day as I came out of Ms. Terrell's. At the time, I was naïve enough to think it had anything at all to do with me. I was so enthralled, that I didn't entertain the thought that it could have had to do with the fact that I was standing beside the only woman who hadn't always been a woman that Murfeesboro had ever seen. As it turned out, it was neither me nor Queen that garnered his attention. Unfortunately, however, that fact wouldn't rear it's head in time to save either her or me from a world of trouble.

That afternoon as I walked up the steps to my room, I felt like one of those astronauts who'd touched down on the moon. My feet bounced with every step. It was as if I'd entered a place where all the things that usually weighed me down, the pageant, my baby weight, my mother's constant hovering, couldn't affect me. That I'd touched down on a planet that existed for me and Donnie Phelps alone to inhabit.

I determined to follow Queen's advice, and walk up to him the very next day either at school, or when I was out with Rodrigo and talk to him. As luck would have it, I didn't have to. There he was, at a standstill on his bike at the end of the path Lil' Man and I always took through the woods to get to his neighborhood.

I gulped, and froze where I was. My throat felt swollen like the year before when I'd caught strep from Mandy Reynolds because I'd used her pen in science class after she chewed on it. My hands immediately pulled my t-shirt down to ensure my pale, pudgy belly wouldn't blind him and ruin the whole thing.

"That your dog?" he asked slightly rocking back and forth on his bike.

I shook my head.

"Didn't think so. Saw that queer with it over at Wal-mart last week."

Noticing his absence, several boys circled back. He looked behind him, motioning for his posse to leave, proceed on without him. They lingered briefly before pedaling off, peasants at a loss without their king. He pulled a pack of cigarettes from his pocket, brought one to his mouth, lit it then held one out to me. I stepped forward, Rodrigo tugged me in the other direction as if even he was aware of what my mother would do to me if she detected the faintest hint of smoke on my clothes.

Taking one, I watched as he lit it then put it up to my mouth. This was the first time I'd done anything so unseemly, so rebellious. It felt like with that one motion he'd ignited my whole invisible existence, all it had taken was an Ed Hardy lighter. Reluctantly, my nostrils inhaled the smoke. I tried like anything not to cough, but before I knew it, I was hacking and hacking. The cigarette hit the pavement narrowly missing Rodrigo. Donnie smiled and lightly slapped my back.

"A virgin, huh?" he chuckled.

I regained my breath, and stood upright. Rodrigo looked up at me scornfully from where he sat by my feet. My cheeks involuntarily turned bright red over hearing the *V* word. Even though I knew he was talking about the cigarettes, I had been around long enough to know that the accusation was likely two fold and meant to extend to other areas of my sheltered little life.

"I was a hell of a lot younger than you when my brother gave me one a his." he bragged.

My hands tightened around Rodrigo's leash. I leaned over picking him up, tucking him under my arm in hopes of taking the attention off my failure.

"How old are you?" Donnie questioned.

"Thirteen." I managed hoarsely.

"Man! Just a baby." he snickered.

I didn't let on that I knew he wasn't more than a year or two older than I was. He dismounted his bike, walked it a few steps down the street. I followed alongside him, mentally screaming at my feet to step as casually as possible.

"You got Ms. Delray's class with me right?" he inquired.

"Mmm hmmm." I mumbled.

It was only the good graces of God in heaven that I didn't blurt out the fact that we'd been together in one class or another since elementary. That I didn't go into how since junior high began we'd been in at least two classes together, a math and science, and now Ms. Delray's literature class as well as Mr. Thomas's world history class. I knew his records, if he had any, were much less meticulous than mine. Few people have the same knack for detail as a lawyer's daughter.

I told myself none of that mattered. Convinced myself to live in the moment, but that was wrong to do. Misleading myself in that way began long before Donnie and went on to evolve into a pattern that has plagued me on into adulthood. Even still it rears its head at the most inconvenient of times.

As my feet stepped one in front of the other, I secretly prayed to act normal. For those few moments, to act like anyone but me. So determined was I not to blow the opportunity fate had seen fit to bestow, that I slipped a hand into one pocket. I tamed my overly excited strut into an indifferent, makeshift sort of stroll.

As we progressed further down his street, every kid we saw waved to us or shouted a greeting. An overzealous fifth grader jumped on his bike and sped towards us, an obvious, and pitiful attempt to gain audience, even if for only a few seconds. All Donnie had to do was nod his way, and administer his signature look. I had seen it many times, though it had never been directed at me. The look all the *fans* knew; the one that said *not right now*.

The boy stopped in his tracks, retreating to his own driveway. He then dejectedly took to riding around in circles. A cat emerged from the bushes ahead of us. Rodrigo darted towards it, but I easily restrained him, tightening my grip on his leash.

"Feisty, ain't he?" Donny laughed.

I laughed too, but also focused on keeping my giddiness in check. We stopped in front of his house. His brother, T.J., sat on the front porch with a couple of scantily clad girls. All of them flagrantly smoking for all to see. He was every bit as handsome as Donnie. I imagined myself sitting there on that very stoop in a few short years. I'd be skinnier, if mother had anything to do with it. If I still knew Queen by then, I'd have on a lot more make up.

Only when I saw them there doing whatever they wanted right out in the open did it occur to me that his neighborhood was a few rungs below mine. During the walks I'd taken there in the weeks prior, I'd been so concentrated on spotting Donnie, that I hadn't registered how much smaller the houses were, or how many of them had shingles dangling, ready to fall off, or paint peeling. There were more unkempt yards than kempt ones. Many of the cars parked in the driveways were old, and dirty. Some with deflated tires, or dented fenders. Scruffy kids littered front yards like trash that the garbage truck had missed.

In my neighborhood, I had to make a concerted effort to find any children playing outside alone even in the summertime. If I'd have taken time to really look around before that day, really digest what I was seeing, I'd have been scared. I'd have surmised that this was the sort of neighborhood where a girl and a Chihuahua could easily go missing, but by the time I stood there with Donnie it was too late for any healthy fear to take root.

"Dad's lookin for you, man." T.J. called to his brother.

The ugliest of the girls cut her eyes at me. I surprised myself by glaring back at her. She looked away.

"I'll find him when I'm good an ready." Donnie shot back as he looked at me rather than at T.J.

Pulling out his lighter, and his last cigarette, he lit it. He charmingly made sure to blow the smoke to the side, away from my face. This foolishly struck me as a sign that he held me in some regard, though I'd come to discover it was just one of the things he did for anyone. He held no one but himself in any kind of esteem.

"See ya." he said as he turned, pushing his bike up his driveway.

My heart pounded. My brain shouted all the things I should say at once. None of them made it to my mouth. The idea that my fifteen minutes of fame was to be hacked down to a premature five was unbearable. I willed myself to fight my usual irritating passivity and speak.

"See ya tomorrow!" I called a bit too loudly.

It wasn't my intention for it to come out so frantic and squeaky. T.J. smirked and the girls giggled. Donnie only smiled as he laid his bike down and stepped around them. Rodrigo pulled me onward. I gave way to the whims of his search for the next optimal sniffing spot.

"Wish I had a dog like that." I heard one of the girls say to the other as I walked off. "I'd dress him up real cute, put him right in my purse."

"Shit, you're doing good to dress yourself." her friend retorted.

I wondered if this was how all teenagers were. Cursing when they wanted, smoking where they wanted, wearing what they wanted, or if it was how just they were in this neighborhood. I rolled around the idea that your class, or rather the lack of it, gave you a license to be whoever you wanted to be. I decided they were lucky. They never had to try on pageant dresses or eat at the dinner table.

A jealousy crept in. A feeling that the world I lived in, the world where your future was set in stone, wasn't the only one available. An abrupt realization accosted me. A realization that the stoic, plastic kingdom I'd been born into was foreign to most people. The minute I let Rodrigo in the door, I shared this with Queen. She strutted over in her red pumps, placed one of her large hands on my shoulder.

"Now don't get yourself all in a knot, chil'. The important thang is you talked to your man, right?"

I thought about it and nodded.

"I gotta head on an help Lisa. Got some stuffy retirement dinner we're caterin tonight. Mmmm, you know theys gonna be a whole mess a ol' people.

Sure ain't my idea of a good time, but it'll get us some paper to pay those bills. You mind feedin Lil' Man?"

"Sure." I agreed.

"You a lifesaver. Be sure an lock up. Cain't have no body makin off with my shoes." she stated with a wink before she waltzed out the door.

I fed Rodrigo, readied to go, but hesitated. I hadn't been alone in someone else's house before. When letting him out, and letting him back in, I'd never ventured past the back kitchen area. Maybe it was the way the whole afternoon had seemed to present me with new experiences that compelled me to explore. Maybe it was the fact that I knew Queen wouldn't care. I didn't know about Lisa. We'd only met once, but if she was how Queen described her, I couldn't imagine her caring.

From the look of it, Queen had certainly been working hard to make it look like home. Tina Turner was hung in her rightful place of prestige above the orange velvet couch. A hot pink leather chair sat to the right of it. I had no idea where such furniture was purchased. Running my hands along the back of the couch, I envisioned one like it in my own apartment someday.

Rodrigo ran ahead of me as if enticing me to check out the bedroom. My feet didn't make a sound as I walked down the shag carpeted hall and lightly pushed open the door at the end. The bed was draped with a satin Turquoise spread. At the head of it was a silver headboard with enough red pillows leaning against it for five heads to rest on. It didn't look like a place where anyone actually slept. More a room that served as a set for one of those old sixties T.V. shows. One of the ones Daddy liked to watch on Nick at Night.

On the wall by her closet was a framed movie poster of a man and woman dancing together very closely. *Dirty Dancing* was printed in neon, cursive font at the bottom. I made a mental note to ask Queen if she owned that movie. I'd always wanted to watch it, but as to how I'd bring it up, I was uncertain because then she'd wonder how I'd seen the poster in the first place.

Her closet was open. An array of heels lined the floor. I'd never worn any women's shoes, certainly not any heels. Mother had bought me a pair of shoes with only a slightly raised heel to wear with my pageant dress. They'd had childish buckles, Mary Janes she'd called them - definitely little girl shoes in my book. I crouched down and picked up a black stiletto. Rodrigo scampered over, and batted at it with his paw like he'd been the appointed guardian of the prized footwear collection.

"I won't hurt them. I promise." I assured him.

He jumped up on the bed, keeping a watchful eye on me as I sat on the edge. Taking my shoes off, I slipped my feet into the designer stilts to find they were much too big. I tried to walk across the room, but one of the heels lodged into the long threads of shag carpeting. I made it far enough to steal a glimpse of myself in the mirror by the closet door.

Sucking in my stomach, hands on my hips, I couldn't believe how much taller and thinner the shoes made me look. It was as if they magically corrected my slouchy posture and enhanced my beauty more than I'd hoped possible. I turned this way and that enjoying this new me to the fullest. Determined to soak it in as I had no idea when I'd be afforded such an opportunity again.

"Hi," I said to my reflection, trying my hand at Queen's distinct accent. "I'm Charlotte. Charlotte Grace Danby. I'm a sexy Lil' Miss Thang."

The bright purple clock on the nightstand caught my eye. 4:30! "Mother!" was all I thought. I'd forgotten all about getting home before her! As quickly as I could, I returned the shoes to their rightful place. I didn't even bother to put mine on. I tucked them under my arm, patted Rodrigo goodbye, locked up the back door and by some miracle sprinted barefoot across the street.

This incident of bad luck jabbed its way into an otherwise blissful afternoon. Mother's car turned onto our street as my feet touched our yard. I could only pray she hadn't seen me. Unfortunately, Ms. Terrell was sweeping her porch as I tore through our grass to the front door. I fumbled in my pocket for my house key.

"Sure is a hot one, today." I nervously acknowledged her, giving her one of my best smiles.

"Sure is." was all she replied as mother pulled in the drive way.

Leaving the door locked, I quickly sat down on the front stoop, and pocketed my key.

"What are you doing out here?" mother asked getting out, lifting a shopping bag from the back seat.

"Locked out." I lied.

"Did you check the hide-a-key?" she reminded.

Hopping up, I turned over the small stone rabbit beside the step.

"And here you've been waiting out here all this time? Charlotte Grace, My goodness, I do believe you'd lose your head if it wasn't attached." She scolded as I used the extra key to unlock the door for us.

"Afternoon." mother called out to Ms. Terrell.

"Afternoon." Ms. Terrell returned.

Once mother was inside, I briefly glanced at Ms. Terrell as she swept the last bit of dirt from her steps. She winked at me before opening her door and stepping inside. I knew I had nothing to worry about. Though I didn't know her very well, I'd always made an effort to be nice, and it appeared that my occasional help with her packages had gleaned her loyalty.

"You'll let all the cold air out." mother chastised me all the way from the kitchen.

I sat up to the counter observing as she unpacked what was to be our dinner. She'd purchased a few new Weight Watcher's microwave meals, and proceeded to educate me about their low calorie content. I performed my duty of periodic nodding, and polite smiling, as I let my mind drift.

It drifted all the way back down the wooded path to Donnie's street. There, a perfected image of me emerged in one of Queen's dresses and a pair of her heels. An image that walked right up the Phelp's driveway, and knocked on the front door. I looked down at my lap, rubbed my sweaty palms on the legs of my jeans as mother rambled on.

An odd stirring overtook my body. A stirring I'd only experienced a few other times when sitting in class staring a hole through the back of Donnie while he leaned his head on his elbow trying unsuccessfully to catch up on his sleep. Rather than be embarrassed, or ashamed, I embraced this stirring that was conjured so easily by just the thought of him opening his door to me.

It struck me that I could ask my mother if she'd ever felt that way. That possibly she'd regale me with the tale of how Daddy had awakened such feelings in her. Yet watching her flit around in her neatly pressed Talbot's dress putting away food, I felt it was a conversation that would inevitably go badly and that somehow it would end with her being troubled by the idea that I would even have such *carnal* thoughts.

Instead I resolved to talk to the right person. The person I felt sure would not be appalled but had posters on her wall of the very things I longed to do with my Donnie. The person who, I was certain, had experienced more than their fair shair of new and unusual stirrings. The person who I somehow sensed I could talk to about anything…

The Cop

The streetlight illuminated the sequins on *its* t-shirt. The flickering display they created was nearly blinding. He slunk down further in the driver's seat as he watched *it* dispose of several large trash bags hoisting them up, one by one, into the dumpster behind the restaurant. The notion that his spying was crossing a line of some kind didn't register. It didn't dawn on him in the same way musings about what it would be like to walk with two legs wouldn't dawn on a fish as it circles the bottom of a lake.

In *its* high heels, taking aim, and tossing garbage, *it* looked to him as if *it* could've played for the NBA. *Its* arms and legs equally muscular. He envisioned *it* as an African native, without *its* wig, manicured nails, and breasts. *It* was a hunter running barefoot through the jungle - a dark streak trampling vines, spear in hand.

He'd been careful to borrow Tom's truck for his unsanctioned surveillance. The keys had been handed over without question while Tom bounced his squalling son on a knee in a feeble attempt to quiet him. Only as he'd exited, made his way down the hallway outside the apartment, did the baby's cries cease. On some intrinsic level he felt the baby remembered the *arm incident*, and that perhaps his little arm even quivered whenever he was nearby. When he'd said as much to Tom, his partner had scoffed saying, "Nah, their resilient little fuckers."

With the job completed, he expected the *Queen* to go back inside, yet *it* didn't. Instead, *it* sat on a crate by the door and looked around to ensure *it* was alone. Sliding one of *its* large hands down the front of *its* flashy top, *it* recovered a cigarette from *its* bra. *It* lit the cig then leaned against the wall slowly inhaling the smoke. In the distance a car door slammed. *It* sat up, holding the cigarette down beside *it*. Once no one emerged from around the side of the building, *it* resumed a more relaxed pose.

With the binoculars he'd brought along, he studied *its* face closely for some sign, a hint of evidence that would spell out for him what it was that Lisa saw in this *thing*. If he could understand, unwrap what it was that attracted them to each other, then possibly he could recreate it in some way. He'd store it in his arsenal of weapons; the kind he accumulated for everyone and anyone. They were the ones he unveiled at precise moments, ideal opportunities he deemed fit to enact long awaited punishments.

An unavoidable fact threatened to shatter his calculated procedures as he acknowledged that Queen had done nothing to him. It was simply a case of the wrong place at the wrong time. *She, he,* whatever *it* was, could only be accused of being misplaced. It was Lisa alone with whom he had his regretful history. He didn't dwell on this, however, dismissing it as he always did anything that would take him off course or thwart his brand of fun.

Queen leaned forward on the crate, stamping out what remained of the cigarette with *its* heel. Propping *its* hands under *its* chin, *it* looked out at the eerily, stagnant night. There was a glance in the direction of his truck. An inconvenient pang of fear, on his part, at the thought that *it* had discovered him, yet before any real anxiety could sink its teeth in, *it* went back to looking out at the empty field across from *it*.

Bringing the binoculars into focus, he saw *its* face more clearly. Tears trickled down its chiseled cheekbones. It wasn't in Carter to feel sympathy or anything close to pity. Indeed, these were not emotions that had ever earned a place in his day-to-day goings on.

Pain traveled from the inside of his mouth to his waking consciousness alerting him that he was biting his cheek again. His behavior often mitigated by his environment, he immediately stopped. Rolling his tongue along the wound, he remembered he was alone with no one to appease and gloried in the lack of need for such camouflaging techniques. A full and satisfied smile formed across his face.

The Tranny

"It takes time." Is all Lisa has to say when I tell her Murfeesboro's turnin out jus like I'd tol' her it would: borin an beige. Ain't a thang to do in this town cept eat an go to Walmart. Don't get me wrong, I love that store much as everybody else. Hell, where else you gonna get your dog food, your hair products an a gun all in the same place? But I didn't never walk in one an think it was the closest thang I was gonna come to a social club like they do here. In Florida, you only went there cause you needed something. Mmm hmm, hard up I tell you. Hard up round here.

I say borin an beige on account a thas what color damn near every house is every which way you turn, an if the women sure nough don't dress to match, honey. Frightful amount a kaki's an over the shoulder cardigans. Which came first? It's like the chicken an the egg. Was it the beige or the backwards ways? Don't think you could ever know for sure. Gonna be one a them thangs right up there with how in hell Ike ever snagged Tina to begin with…a mystery.

Now I ain't about to tell a livin soul that Florida didn't have problems cause it did. The problems were of a different nature. There, we had so many "gals" you had to fight tooth an nail to stand out. Here I'm all on my own. Knew from the get go I'd have to tone it down.

Lisa tells me the south requires subtlety. They like to be taken to dinner first, is how she likes to put it. Exactly how she expects me to do that I ain't got a clue. I ain't never done "dinner" in my whole life. Always lay it out there, get right to the dessert, baby, mmm hmmm, thas right.

For her sake, I'm tryin to give it time. Workin helps. The thang I love about workin at the restraunt is regulars. There's Mr. Donaldson who's waitin at the door bright an early every mornin for his pancakes an bout every evenin for his chicken salad sandwich followed by a cake slice. Lisa said his wife died last year. Man ain't got a clue how to cook for himself. She said she's jus about sure that the food he orders at our place are the only real meals that man gets all day. Pitiful. He sets up to the counter on that stool goin on about his wife an how cain't nobody cooks like she could, but how we damn near come close.

Bein born an bred right here, he nearly liked to swalla his dentures first time he laid eyes on me. I jus kept bein my sweet self. Didn't let his wide eyes get to me. Now I do believe he sits in my section on purpose. Took to callin me

Queeny last week. I like the sound of it, but he's the only one who can use it. Somethin kind about the way he says it. Anybody else takes to sayin it an we gonna have words.

There's Tammy who comes in least three or four times a week round lunch. Mmm I'd like to get a hol' a her! Give that chil' a make over. Works at the library an you sure can tell it. Looks like a lil' ol' bookworm who spends most a her time with papers an words. Lisa laughed when I asked her how she thought Tammy might take to me offerin to do her nails. She said it couldn't hurt to ask, but she didn't think nothin would ever come of it. Said that girl was the same way back in high school, plain Jane an quiet as a mouse.

Lisa reckons thas how Tammy wants to keep it, but I cain't believe that. Mmm mmm. I think it's on account a how nobody's taken a interest in her. An honey, ain't a man who's goin to if she keeps that up. One a these days, after she's known me long enough, I'm gonna pop that question. Gonna walk right over an give her my number, see if I can lure her to our house so I can shake up that wardrobe.

If she's feelin real liberated, hell, we'll burn her beige corduroys an one a those frumpy blouses she wears. I'll kindly instruct her that there ain't a soul under fifty wears a button up blouse. Even then the ones who do only doin it to keep the sun from givin em age spots or causin the melanoma.

Right on time every Friday night we got Frank Hartford an his girl a the minute, usually some young thang on his arm straight from law school or gettin ready to start. He'll flirt with any thang with legs an a skirt. Tol' Lisa first few times I waited on him I thought he didn't have no clue as to who he was really talkin to, winked at me whenever I'd walk off to get his drink. She patted my back an told me it whatin that, it was jus that he don't give a rat's ass one way or the other.

He's one a them divorcee cliché's, but Lord knows, he sure is a handsome man. Left his wife a few years back after their kids went off to school, now he's sewin his oats. One night he didn't have a girl with him. Came in with some other lawyers instead. Lil' Miss Thang's daddy was with em.

He acted like he didn't know who I was from Adam. Didn't let on in front a his coworkers that he sees me nearly every other day settin out on my porch when he's gettin home. Then there was that one time he nearly ran over Rodrigo in his Mercedes. Soon as he spotted him, he stomped on the brakes so hard his foot like to broke off. I screamed an ran over scoopin up Lil' Man. Mmm, now I know he got himself a case a whiplash that day. I'd a good mind to go over in front a his law buddies an thank him, but I didn't. Naw, I whatin about to let on we're neighbors.

Halfway through me servin em, he slid his glass over to me without even a word. Not a "Could I please have more Coke" or "Refill" jus nothing, like we was back in the 1800's an his daddy owned my momma. Right then an there I thought I might have a case a verbal diarrhea, tell him how much I appreciated his daughter comin over an takin my dog out. Go on about how sweet she was an how good a friends we are, but I knew better. Knew that be the end a Lil' Miss Thang ever darkenin my door. I jus poured it for him, smiled real sweet.

Couldn't tell much about him with him jus settin there. Seemed real serious, but they were probly talkin bout a case. Charlotte Grace always talks like the world ends an begins with him. She loves him to death. Says she wishes he could come home more, wants em to get more time to theirselves.

I jus listen. Ain't got no frame a reference. Always wished my daddy woulda lived long enough to have jus one more day with me. Always thought kids with a daddy who was alive had it easier, but hearin her, I see that havin a momma an a daddy at home's got it's own problems. Reckon everybody's always thinkin everybody else has it easier.

Two sides to regulars, like a snake's forked tongue, cause they ain't all like Mr. Emory, an Tammy or Mr. Hartford, Lord, no! Some of em are wretched, full a piss an vinegar an ain't got enough people to share all that with at home so they got to come up in our place an let it out. Any time you got a place open to the public at large, you gonna have em. Haters who are so ate up with hatin theirselves their hate cain't help but spill out onto the rest of us.

That cop Lisa went to school with cain't stay away. Comes in here with his partner every weekday on his lunch break. "Mr. Big Stuff" I call him when he itn't anywhere in sight. Him an that fool partner. Two of em full a theirselves, think they're the shit. Mmm hmm. Ain't it always those kind signin up to get a badge an weapons? The kind who love rules an regulations, an like totin a gun so you gotta snap to whenever they come round.

Lisa's tol' me more more times than I can count to watch out for him. Tol' me he never did set right with her an she made sure she's steered clear a him ever since they was in grade school. I laughed an tol' her he couldn't hurt a fly. Might want to, but couldn't if he tried. He's jus a lil' boy who didn't get cops an robbers outta his system. Another one a them who cain't get a date an went out an found himself a outlet for all his pent up frustration.

Partner's the same way. Cuts his eyes at me every chance he gets. I never have understood their kind. Oh, I got ideas about why they are the way they are, but I don't understand em on a level a really knowin where they're comin from. Best I can figure, they're the sorry type who take to hatin anybody who don't fit this mold they got it in their head that everybody's sposed to fit into. One a them Type A assholes who cain't stand if you don't have the need to adhere to the same rules everybody else does. Rules like stickin with the hand you been dealt in the gender department. They ain't kept up with modern science. Ain't got no clue that nowadays where there's cash there's a way. Stuck in the dark ages. Mmm hmm they are.

People like em want everythang in a neat little package so they can label it right or wrong. If you don't fit that, they take to the idea that you need to be done away with. That you plain de-fective. They may not want you dead, but they gonna cause you trouble sure enough an they damn sure don't want to see your ass in their town.

Here I go thinkin about em an here they are walkin right in. You'd think I'd learn. Thinkin bout people can be the same as conjurin em outta thin air. I look over to see if Mary's gonna tear herself away from filin her nails to tend to their mean asses. She don't look up. I've tol' Lisa she's a lazy, triflin lil' thang, but Lisa ain't wantin to make too many changes yet. Says we got to get settled, establish ourselves for we go cuttin anybody loose.

Shit! Usually hadn't had to do more than take their cash on their way out an thas been "pleasant" enough. I look Mary's way one more time. Come on, now I know damn well she sees them! Alright. I'm takin this here situation by the cajones. I got this. Takes a hell of a lot more than two big headed cops to intimidate this here gal.

I ease out from behind the counter, grab a couple menus. Lord, if my feet don't feel like cinderblocks draggin me to the bottom a the ocean.

"Mornin gentlemen." I say, sweet as pie, puttin the menus on the table.

The partner pushes em back to me without lookin up.

"They know what we want." he barks motionin to the kitchen crew.

I pick the menus up an tuck em under my arm. Standin real strong an proud, I take out my pad an pen like I didn't hear him.

Mr. Big Stuff sits back against the booth, looks at the partner for he starts in.

"Seems like we usually get offered coffee don't it?" he asks.

I look down at him, a anger wellin up in me. A anger that after all I got through, I'm still goin through more a the same. Takin a deep breath, I look up to see Lisa starin at me from behind the line where she's helpin fill orders. She shakes her head then winks at me.

"Comin up." Is all I say.

I strut off to the coffee pot like I'm walkin a cat walk. Like ain't a thang they can say thas gonna rattle my cage. Mmm hmm. Crosses my mind to turn my back an spit in both their cups, but the lady in me gets the upper hand. I pour, stuff a few creams in my apron pocket an head on back. I set their coffee down in front of em, then take out the creams. The partner watches like he's supervisin.

"*We don't want those.*" *he sneers.*

"*You one a them that takes it straight. I got you.*" *I reply with a smile.*

Reachin down, I go to scoop the creams back up, but he knocks em further away.

"*No. We just don't want 'those'.*" *He shoots off at the mouth like a spoiled toddler.*

Mr. Big Stuff steady watchin him while he's already sippin on his cup.

"*I'd be happy to bring you some milk out the cooler in the back if you…*"

"*No need.*" *he grunts.*

"*Well, then…*"

"Have Mary bring us more a these." he orders real sweet, like he's changin his tune.

"I thought you don't want that kind?" I say like an idiot, jus askin for it.

"No. I didn't say we don't want this kind, we just don't want anythang outta your pocket." He clears that up, then smiles up at me battin those redneck eyes.

There's that hate. A hate I thought I done exorcised an done got rid of. I feel it comin up from my stomach right up through my throat. My fists clench all on they own. Fore I know it, Lisa's right beside me puttin a handful a creams on the table.

"Got your orders started fellas." she says, her free hand touchin the small a my back.

Mr. Big Stuff nods, still sippin that coffee. He looks out from under that cop hat like a wolf peekin out from its cave.

"Thanks, hon." The partner says touchin Lisa's arm.

God! We gonna wash that spot extra hard when we get home! Son of a bitch!

"Ya'll enjoy." Lisa says as she nods for me to head to the back with her.

I know as I'm doin it that I shouldn't. I got no business doin it, but I don't even try to help myself. Turnin my head around, I look back at em. The partner smiles up at me. Mr. Big Stuff lifts his coffee cup to me like he's toastin to my good health. God damn motherfuckers!

Once we're outta sight, Lisa sets me down on the stool by the grill an lets me go off. She flips those sausages an listens to me tell her how we should kick em out. Tell em we don't need their kind in here. I go over every other idiot we had to deal with in Florida an how they's jus like em. How we done traveled all this way to have nothin but reruns.

When I'm all wore out, an as near as I get to cryin, she crouches down in front a me. She takes both my hands in hers. Don't even pay any mind to Mary who's gawkin from the doorway as she's grabbin orders off the line. Lisa does what she does best; she reminds me a what I know is true.

Reminds me we outnumbered, an bein so we got to do what we got to do. That we're jus tryin to survive in this here world, a world that ain't ours. That we cain't let their hate get in us or we're no better. We're jus like em if we do that, an I know right off that she's right. She hugs me. I lean in to kiss her, but catch myself. Murfeesboro ain't ever gonna be ready for that no matter how good a burger we make.

I stand up, smooth out my apron an take my fine ass right past those assholes to the register. Sure nough gonna take their money when they're done. Ain't gonna bat an eye. Show em I ain't one bit bothered. Gonna come out shinin on the other side a this lil' situation.

Don't take long fore the partner's up to settle the bill. He takes extra long diggin the money out a his pocket. I stand there waitin grinnin like I ain't seen a rainy day in my whole damn life.

"Hope ya'll enjoyed everythang." I say.

He finally plunks his money down, walks out to meet Mr. Big Stuff who's already out startin up their cruiser. I count out his money. Wouldn't you know that pig's a dollar short. Sure as I'm standin here, ,whatin no accident. Pullin a dollar outta my own pocket, I decide it ain't worth it. Ain't worth wastin any more a my mind on.

On my drive home, I roll all this around. Did I think it'd be different? That I wouldn't have the same kinna regulars I had in Tallahassee? The good, the bad an the worse? Hell, when I tol' the gals back home we were movin to Tennessee they like to come unglued. Said I was crazy to come up in the Bible belt with my big ass Jimmy Choos. Said I might as well slap a bullseye on my face, jus askin to get myself shot.

Tol' em it was real important to Lisa that her daddy's restraunt didn't get sold off. Said we could hold our own. Didn't have no real clue what we was in for. Hell, I'm about to forget what it was like to be able to go to the grocery story without causin some ol' church lady to up an fall out right in the parkin lot.

Lisa tol' me it whatin gonna be easy. She warned me about doin how I always do. I tend to overestimate jus how thick a skin I got an underestimate how sharp a knife everybody else is totin. She says the world is more like a garbage bag we gotta sift through than some treasure chest full a gold an jewels like I like to think it is.

She's right about me. Cain't recall a time I ain't been this way, but I cain't change it. Cain't see the world through any other glasses. Somethin in me's always seein the better, or at least the chance of it. There's a part a me that won't be painted gray like the rest a this here world.

I pull in our driveway, put the car in park. Rodrigo pops his head up in the winda lookin out at me. Walkin in, I see Lil' Miss Thang asleep on the couch. Her face all streaked. She's been cryin up a storm. Sittin down in the chair across from her, I see she's got on a pair a my heels, her big white socks tucked in em.

I slide the shoes off real slow so I don't wake her. Cain't help but laugh to myself. I know I got to get her up pretty soon. Her momma'll throw a hissy fit wonderin where she is, if she itn't already over there right this second blowin a gasket, but I like watchin her sleep. Makes me think about when I was her age. Takes me back to that time when you got the whole world waitin for you to find it. More doors you hadn't opened than ones you've already seen an slammed shut behind you.

Her pale face squished up against my sofa gets me to thinkin Lisa's wrong. Everythang's more like I see it. Watchin Lil' Miss Thang here all peaceful, I get the feelin that there's a mess a ruby's an gold jus waitin to be uncovered in this here life. They're jus waitin for the right person to lean down, dip their hand in the dirt an pull em out. Rodrigo hops up on her back an it don't even make her stir. I giggle watchin him circle, an make himself comfy. I know for a fact if this here girl's the only treasure I find in this town, she'll be enough for me.

The Girl

I'm convinced that most of life comes down to geography. If Murfeesboro had been further away from Atlanta, most of my less than idyllic youth would not have been overshadowed by a series of embarrassing vignettes, many of which revolved around the Miss Georgia Peach Pageant. Even now, when I try on a dress, I hear my mother's voice, plain as day as if she's right next to me. Though I've had a flat stomach for some years now, I still cringe.

"Suck it in!" mother hissed as she tried to zip up the dress she'd paid to have let out. I stood there trying with all that was in me to get the upperhand on my gut. A few of my fellow contestants couldn't help but watch. Clearly they'd never seen such a disgusting display of flesh. Few of them ever got their hands on so much as a Tootsie Roll and even then only on Halloween.

Unsuccessful, mother sat back letting the zipper slowly descend, unleashing my rolls in all their glory.

"I don't understand this." she huffed exasperated.

I looked up as Danita Witherspoon's mother helped her zip up her bright fuscia dress without a single hitch. Her waist was so small she could've easily fit through a basketball hoop hips and all. She was the reigning princess and far from ready to relinquish her title. The rules clearly stated she could not be crowned two years in a row, however. I smiled as I imagined her and that year's winner on stage for all to see, playing tug of war with the crown.

"You find this funny?" mother scoffed.

"No ma'am." I muttered.

"I sincerely hope not! I'm not having this let out again. We are going to get your rear end into high gear, miss. I will just tell your father to have all his sweets at the office. There'll be no more sneaking food. No, siree. " she said very matter of fact, getting herself all worked up then talking herself down in the same conversation.

She then gruffly tugged at the dress. I took this as my cue to assist her, so I pulled it down and stepped out of it.

"You'll have to practice walking in your clothes." she instructed, shoving them at me before storming off.

Having given everyone enough of a free show for the day, I re-dressed behind a divider. As I emerged, I noticed the others were taking their places in line. Bossy Amy Saunders snapped her fingers at me, pointing for me to fill my customary slot behind her. All of them had on their dresses. I was the only one in jeans and a t-shirt.

"Where's your dress?" Amy demanded as if she was my mother's minion.

"It doesn't fit yet." Hannah White commented.

She had all too nosily been taking in the exchange between mother and me while putting her own dress on.

"God Almighty!" Amy declared. "You know the pageant's less than a month away, right?"

I nodded.

"What're you gonna do if you can't get skinnier, Charlotte Grace? You'll be fit to be tied!" she continued.

Reaching up, I did something that served to surprise myself as much as it did her. I took both of her shoulders in my hands and turned her in the other direction in hopes I would forego anymore of her berating.

"Hmmph. I'm just saying." she mumbled.

My turn was fast approaching. I imagined my mother out front standing amongst her friends, frustrated, and ashamed. I knew she was likely making excuses. Blaming my eating on Daddy's inability to leave his snacks out of reach when all the while the fault lay at my doorstep, mine and mine alone.

I was the one who chose of my own free will to take extra helpings from that bowl of chocolate on Queen's coffee table. She had left explicit instructions for me to feel free to have as much as I wanted whenever I was there. I alone was the one who snuck with Donnie into the corner store near his house any chance we got for soda, chips and cookies.

As often as finances would allow, we'd use the change I found in the couch cushions, and the money I earned by walking Rodrigo, but when that was gone, we'd steal. This was not something I had done before I took up with him, though his cunning ability to make it out with well over twenty dollars worth of junk food revealed it as a regular habit he'd refined over time. He had never been caught, or so he said, and it was easy to believe him when I watched the casual ease with which he executed his craft.

The music became louder as I stepped forward. I waited to hear my name. My mother nodded to me. She put her fingers up to her mouth demonstrating the kind of smile I should have. I mimicked her, holding it until my turn.

"Here we have Miss Charlotte Grace Danby!" the announcer exclaimed.

Jeans and all, I put one foot in front of the other. The bright lights in my eyes, reminded me of the ones that illuminated the corner store freezer. The freezer I had opened ever so slowly only the previous day, had then slipped my hand inside to pocket two drumstick cones. One for Donnie and one for myself. Looking down at my mother, her mannequin-like pals, perfectly dressed paper dolls encircling her, I grinned at the thought of how that plastic smile she donned would instantly turn into a frown if she ever knew I'd done such things.

Turning the corner at the end of the stage, I foolishly let myself get lost. So enraptured was I with glee over having this secret double life that she was not aware of - a life where I walked gay people's dogs through the rougher part of town with a boy who was anything but respectable right before we'd steal food. I was unexpectedly glad to have been born to who I was born to, to be living in our crummy town, because it had all led up to that precise moment, a moment of sheer, undeniable happiness.

Before I knew what was happening, I bumped right into Amy, who'd paused too long to wave one too many times. She flapped her arms like one of the penguins we'd watched last year in science class on a video. Not as if she'd actually take flight, but as if she was preparing to swim, or out of excitement, readying to fall from it's rock into icy water. In a flash, she lost her balance on her high heels falling over face first onto the stage. I barely stopped short of landing right on top of her. The shrieks of her mother piercing the air could be heard over the music.

The skirt of her taffeta dress was hiked all the way up to her waist in the hubbub so that there, visible to all, were her Hello Kitty underpants. Giggles went up from some of the girls. With one fell swoop, her mother hopped up beside her, yanked her dress down, grabbing her up so that she would avert any further humiliation. Amy only starred into space with a look of bewilderment, unable to process an event of such horrifically epic proportions.

"Charlotte Grace, you are a clutz!" Mrs. Saunders screeched up at me.

"I...I...I'm sorry. I ..." I stammered.

"Sorry! Sorry?" she raged. "That won't cut it! This dress cost more than your whole wardrobe put together and it's not your fault she didn't break an arm or a leg falling like that!"

Amy turned her gaze to me before inhaling deeply. The whole world seemed to come to a stand still, waiting to see if she would indeed again exhale. When she finally did, she burst into tears, running her hands over her dress, checking that it hadn't been marred by my clumsiness. Her mother coddled her in her arms, stroking her hair.

"You're alright, honey." she cooed to Amy then glared up at me. "I really think you should decide if you really want to be in this pageant *Miss Danby*. Seems your mind is elsewhere and God knows you don't fit the bill."

Everyone froze. The music ceased. I stood in a stupor. The instinctive cub in me waited on my own mother bear to barrel over and fend for me, but there I remained. Alone under the bright lights, the focus of insurmountable scorn. I did not even turn to see where my mother was. There was no point.

"Let's call it a day, shall we?" Ms. Everly, the hallowed pageant choreographer proclaimed. "I think we're all a bit fatigued."

Everyone shuffled out, single file back to the dressing room from whence we'd come. The door at the back of the auditorium opened, revealing mother with a look on her face that would've stopped Hitler in his tracks. She held the door for me signifying that it was time to go. We did not speak on the walk to the car. She unlocked the trunk, flung it open, shoved the garment bag that held my dress into it then slammed it shut.

As she drove us home, I was mute, hands in my lap, looking out the window. Her quick, jerky turns, and the heaviness of her foot on the gas reminded me of Cruella Deville in her yellow towncar, chasing down Dalmation puppies. Biting my lip, I knew my only job was to maintain a somber mood. I had to pretend that I understood the full weight of what I'd done.

She fumed about how I always found a way to make things difficult. About how the onlt thing she was guilty of was trying to give me the kind of life she'd had, all charmed and wonderful. She wailed about how she couldn't help it if I threw it all away, and that she was through. Done trying to give me anything. I could go on and wear my black and be depressed up in my room if that's what I wanted.

This would've been grand news, except that I'd heard it all before. I knew she couldn't follow through with it if she tried. She couldn't resign herself to such negligence. Not because she was a caring mother, yet purely out of fear of how it would look to her innumerable acquaintances and also out of boredom and monotony.

Tuning her out, I counted the trees as we whizzed past them, discreetly twiddling my thumbs in my lap. When this lost its charm, I closed my eyes, soaking up the sun and thinking of the cover of my journal. I transformed myself into the largest of the butterflies flying higher than the rest. My wings a bright orange, I was a monarch among monarchs, admired by all.

"Did you hear me?" mother's voice penetrated my flight.

Opening my eyes, I saw that we were home. I nodded though I hadn't heard a word for the last few minutes.

"Go on upstairs and finish up your homework." she instructed.

"Where are you going?" I grumbled.

"I'm going to go and get a manicure or something relaxing." she retorted.

"I don't mind waiting. I ..."

"No." she commanded. "Please! Just go inside."

I meandered up to the porch, turning in time to wave as she pulled out. She did not wave back or even look at me. Her car tore off down our street. I sat on the front steps looking at Queen's house. It was supposed to have been my day off. Queen had told me she would be home early from work and I didn't need to bother walking Lil' Man, but no one's car was there. Hopping up, I looked up and down the street then crossed.

Hurrying over, I took my key from my backpack and let myself in the back. Rodrigo was his usual giddy self running circles around my feet as soon as I walked in.

"Hey there Lil' Man." I greeted.

He cuddled up against me on the couch. I stroked his back, and breathed a sigh of relief. It didn't take long before I made up my mind to dart back to Queen's bedroom. I wanted to feel pretty in her shoes again, pretend I was a tall and elegant lady.

I'd earned his trust by that point so Rodrigo waited in the living room. Picking out the perfect pair of cheetah stilettos, I made my way out to show them off.

"You like?" I asked.

He cocked his head to one side as if to say *yes*. I flopped back down beside him, lifting him onto my lap. Relaxing against the pillows, I looked at Tina Turner hanging on the wall. I thought of how beautiful she looked, how powerful, and glamorous. I looked down at the rolls of fat threatening to peek out from under my shirt, my pale skin and bitten fingernails. I knew I'd never be anything close to as spectacular as Tina.

That whole day came to a head. The way I'd felt like a piglet my mother had tried to roll up inside of a tiny blanket when she struggled to zip up my dress. The casualness with which the other girls had talked to each other about my dilemma as if it were commonplace, as if they had discussed it before at some slumber party I hadn't been invited to. All of it culminated into one big reason to have a pity party. There seemed no better place to have such an outburst.

I leaned over, letting my body collapse on the couch. Rodrigo nuzzled up close to me, and then my tears came. He licked my cheeks as a deer would a salt block. The slick, yet rough feel of his tongue against my skin lulled me to sleep.

It wasn't in me to care if my mother returned home to an empty house. I almost hoped she would. I prayed she would search all over only to panic when I was nowhere to be found. Then and only then would she know what it felt like to be me.

The Cop

He'd been responding to a call just as he'd always done every day of every week, though he'd been ill prepared for what he found. He'd assumed from the details dispatch had given that it would be like any quarrel between lovers, a routine domestic violence altercation. That assumption had been his undoing.

When he knocked, a man cracked the door without peeking through the blinds beforehand or yelling to demand who was there. If he'd been at his best, these things would've been clues. However, it was a Tuesday. He and Tom had drunk more than usual while watching their Monday night football game only hours earlier. Tom had the day off, and was likely still in bed while he'd reported for duty bright and early. He cleared his throat. The man preempted him.

"Can I help you, officer?" the man asked smiling too wide to be up to any good.

Carter gave him a once over more to make him squirm than to assess the situation. His dirty appearance, odd twitchings, missing teeth, and then the stereotypically long nail on his left pinky finger were all very incriminating. All the tell-tale signs that Carter was not addressing a person, but an addict. He knew all too well that there was a big difference in the two.

"Sir, I'm responding to a call." Carter informed him.

"Didn't nobody here call you." the man mouthed off.

Carter stared right through him. He held back from lambasting him with a number of verbal accelerants knowing it would only serve to ignite the pile of invisible kindling now wedged between them into a full-blown fire. He quieted these perfect comments that could only be used in a situation like the one he found himself in. Later on, when he was alone, he knew he would regret that they'd remained unsaid.

"There's been complaints of shouting, and rough housing." Carter accused.

The man looked up, his gaze shifted across the street to the neighbor's trailer. He squinted to see if he could spot them peeking out from behind their front curtains.

"Rough housin?" he laughed "Hell, people don't know good fuckin when they hear it do they? "

Taking a step back, Carter took notice of the small windows pock marking the front of the shack. All conspicuously covered from the inside with newsprint.

"Hmmm." Cater grunted. "Guess not."

"Thas all it was, man. Scouts honor."

The man held up his right hand as if taking an oath.

As Carter shifted his weight to one side, out of pure happenstance he glanced down at the man's feet. There it was, the dead give away: a smear of blood on the toe of his shoe. It could've been his own, there was that chance, but the things Carter had witnessed caused him to think otherwise.

" Well, I'll just talk to her, then I'll be on my way." he stated.

This immediately put the man on edge. He stepped out, pulled the door too. Though the smell of the suspect was enough to make most people gag, Carter maintained his position.

"Awe well now ain't exactly a good time. She's sleepin, man. She's got to be at work for the crack a dawn an she's plum wore out." he made excuses, his smirk widening.

The kind of morning he'd had so far, he thought of letting this one lie. He'd already taken in two drunk drivers and withstood a ruckus caused by two homeless bums when he'd issued citations to them for sleeping in the park. Neither had been any too cooperative. His pager buzzed giving him further permission to leave the scene, yet he pressed a button silencing it. A shout erupted from inside the house.

The man froze. His eyes met Carter's whose hands simultaneously reached for his cuffs. Without stopping to second guess himself, he shoved the man up against the porch railing.

"Fuck man! I ain't done nothin! Ain't done a damn thang!"

The handcuffs fastened, one to the railing and one to the man's wrist, gun drawn, Carter opened the door enough to see inside.

"Bitch! Don't you fuckin say a word! I know where your momma lives. Don't you forget that! I know - "

Carter swiftly whacked him in the mouth with the butt of his weapon. Unable to see anything, he pushed the door open further with his other hand. There on the couch sat a girl. Her lip was bloody, and she tugged at her short skirt in an attempt to cover the bruises and scrapes scattered like sadistic confetti over her skinny legs. He stood still, gun pointed towards the dark hallway.

"It's just me in here." the girl reassured him.

"You sure?"

She nodded continuing to pull at her skirt. Her sniffling and quick breaths persisted. Tears trickled in black eye liner defined streams down her youthful cheeks. From the look of her, he estimated she could be no more than fifteen if she was a day. A feeling resembling empathy coupled with surprise overtook him. They caught him off guard as he'd long ago given up on ever feeling anything for anyone but himself. It dawned on him that this could be a sign that weakness was taking hold.

"You live here?" he questioned her.

" She sure as hell does! " the redneck from the porch bellowed. "She's my daughter!"

Carter looked at her. She only shook her head. The man glared at her, teeth gritted in warning.

" You cunt! You cunt bitch! I - "

Slamming the door in his face, Carter turned to her.

"You don't live here or you ain't his daughter?"

"Both." she whimpered.

He sat across from her. Her skimpy clothes had no doubt been borrowed from someone a good deal older. The makeup caked on her face also alerted him that she was a *working girl*.

"Wanna tell me what you're doing here?" he said softening slightly, lowering his guard.

Taking her hands from her skirt, she absentmindedly used one of them to lift her shirt, enough to wipe her face, and give him a slight preview of her bra.

"I guess you already got that part figured out." she said.

He nodded.

"I've been known to be wrong."

This caused her to laugh, choke back tears. For some reason unbeknownst to him, this opened up the floodgates. She spilled her guts about how she was just supposed to deliver something for her boyfriend, and then get on back across town. Said she'd been to that same house a dozen times at least and had always been able to hold her own with that fella, but how on that day he'd gotten out of hand.

He tried to listen while she talked, but the unladylike way she sat sidetracked him. He caught sight of her panties, which excited him more than it should have. It'd been forever and a day since he'd gotten laid. Even with her age and her bruises, he found himself imagining the two of them engaged in number of physical acts. Only when she quit talking and stared at him did he refocus himself on the matter at hand.

"I think it's best if you come on with me. " he told her. "We'll get you home."

This seemed to suit her. She nodded then gathered her purse and jacket. He opened the door being sure to use his body as a barrier as he led her past the still handcuffed criminal. That didn't stop the idiot from trying to get in a few kicks as the girl scurried by.

She situated herself in the front seat. Carter turned to go back for the man, but she touched his arm. Her tiny fingers sent bolts of electricity throughout his entire body.

"Cain't you just leave him?" she proposed.

He stared at her, unable to comprehend this kind of mercy.

"You don't want to press charges?" he clarified.

She shook her head.

"Let's just get goin."

He looked back at the wriggling, writhing hillbilly, and suddenly understood her sentiments. Who would want to spend one minute longer with him? The man cursed them, hissing and spitting as Carter took large confident steps towards him. He unlocked his handcuffs then seized him by the collar of his shirt. He pushed him up against the wall, threatening that he better not ever lay eyes on him again.

As he returned to the patrol car, he was sure he could see the girl through the windshield smiling with satisfaction.

"Go on an take her!" the man yelled. " She's the devil that one!"

They rode in silence for a few blocks. He felt like he did his sophomore year in high school on his first date with Wendy Nolan. The sneaking suspicion that this was inappropriate hovered, but his loneliness, his debased needs, reduced these apprehensions to barely audible background noise.

"Where do you live? " he asked in a feeble attempt to set himself on the right path.

She didn't answer, only slid a hand down casually pulling her skirt up just enough to show off her thighs. He couldn't help but notice. She smiled as this was the result she'd been wanting. Again, he tried to do the noble thing. The thing that people presumed he'd gone into his profession for.

"Are you over on the east side, or closer to the high school?" he re-appealed, including more detail in hopes it would bring a response.

Arms out in front of her, she stretched, yawning. Her chest arched to show off the beginnings of breasts she'd already learned to accentuate.

" You hungry? I'm starved. " she said.

He looked over at her. She winked.

As he drove them to the Sonic, he reminded himself that it couldn't go the way he hoped it would, that few things ever could, but he was not in control. With each turn of the wheel and acceleration of the gas, he surrendered himself more and more over to the idea. By the time they pulled in to order food, he'd relinquished any control to the singular belief that he was well on his way to getting something he deserved. Something that had been a long time coming.

The Tranny

Me an Tina have coffee every mornin. Yes, chil', I sit right across from her on my sofa an tell her about how life here in Tennessee is goin. Strange, I'd end up in her home state. She looks so lively, an dynamic up there on that Vegas stage. One a these days she might jus pop right off that wall an tell me all about how it was when she came up.

She whatin born Tina Turner, uh uh honey. She was born Anna Mae

Bullock. Mmm now who woulda thought? Ike was the one who give her the name Tina. Said at the time that it was more fittin for a stage name, but wouldn't you know years later he told some reporter it was so her old boyfriends wouldn't be able to come sniffin around so easy?

A new name was probly the best thang she got outta that relationship. That an learnin how to sing better, have some stage presence. Got to find the best outta any bad situation. Figure thas the way it is with anybody. Hell, thas how I got Lisa. Met her when I was workin for my ex named Manny. Manny Vitalle. Now itn't that a name?

He liked bein the man carryin the biggest stick, if you know what I mean, an if you don't then it ain't no thang. All that to say he liked bein "top dog". Don't know what it was that did it for me. Have to confess it was nothin but animal attraction. He could do thangs I'd never heard tell of, thangs most people on this earth ain't heard of neither, but man, he made me feel good!

Round the time I met him, I'd gotten real comfortable wearin dresses. Would even take myself down to the clubs in one now an then. Up to that time, I'd mainly been wearin em in the privacy of my own apartment an every now an then at a party where other gals would strut their stuff. Thas where Manny first laid eyes on me.

His "Lady Godiva" he called me cause I'm the color of Godiva chocolate an cause I didn't seem like I cared what anybody thought a me. He was a good fifteen years older, but it didn't matter. Lisa calls him my "daddy" phase. Man had taste though. Bought me designer shit, paraded me around on the weekends.

Whatever he was, he was a hot mess. Mmm hmmm. Had a temper on him! Walked around like a volcano ready to go off anytime he pleased over any lil' thang. I swear that man was so fine! He could knock you to the floor an soon as you got yourself up an looked in his eyes, you'd already forgiven him.

He owned the swankiest restraunt in Miami named Manny's. Everybody who was anybody went there specially on Friday an Saturday nights. Thas where Lisa came in. She started waitressin there while she was in college. We was real good friends right from the get go. Jus somethin about her. She was funny as hell even then, an cute as a button.

She didn't get too nosy, but I think she knew somethin was goin on. The secrecy of it got Manny all hot an bothered, an I have to admit, it was a draw for me too. I hadn't made up my mind at the time which "team" I was exactly gonna play for. Dated girls when I could. Sampled those goods. Snuck around with guys, an got my kicks with them too. Always kept my dresses in the closet less I knew the club or party I was goin to whatin gonna be a place I'd see anybody I knew. I guess you could say I was confused as they come.

Lisa hadn't been workin there long when she happened to come into the office right after me an Manny had one a our World War three fights. There I was laid out on the rug. Fore I knew it, Lisa was standin over me pullin me up. I looked over an there was Manny knocked out next to me. She'd done gone an clocked him over the head with the lava lamp from off his desk.

In that second, seein her tuggin on my arm, I loved her. Not in the way I loved Manny, not with that physical kinna madness. More like the same sweet kinna love I'd had for momma, that loyal kinna endebted love. She was my Wonder Woman swoopin in to save the day. An I knew we would do that for each other forever. I jus knew.

"Tell Tina you cain't be late for work." Lisa teases, then kisses my forehead.

She walks to the door balancin her to go cup a coffee an her bag like a real workin girl.

"Awe now, it ain't ever her fault. If I'm late it's cause beauty cain't be rushed. Mmm hmm." I tell her.

I get up an walk over, open up the door for her. Fore she gets out, I hug her to me, an kiss her with a "Do you really have to go?" kiss, but I know she does.

"Bye now." she says hustlin out, catchin her breath.

I shut the door an head on back to take a shower. I'm dryin off, when I hear the back door creakin open.

"That you, Lil' Miss Thang?" I holler.

"Yes, ma'am." she calls back.

I slip on my robe, stick on my wig an walk out to the livin room. She's sittin on the floor happy as can be, Rodrigo in her lap.

"How many times we go over this ma'am business? Makes me feel ol' as dirt chil'."

"Sorry, Miss Queen." she giggles.

"Thas on the right track but how bout we drop the miss an jus go with Queen." I suggest.

She nods.

"You early ain't you?"

"Early release today. Teacher's in workshops or something."

"Your momma know?" I ask.

Her face turns all shades a that Julia Roberts red she's famous for.

"I'm not sure."

"Well, alright. Now, what you gonna do with all this time to yourself?" I pry.

"I'm just gonna walk Lil' Man and then…well then I'm goin to the mantinee with Donnie."

"You got you a date?" I shout nearly scarin her outta her britches.

"Not really. We're just friends." she explains.

I jump up, put my hands on my hips.

"Anybody else goin?" I demand.

She shakes her head.

"Mmm, Lil' Miss Thang, let me tell you then, that right there is a date. Man asks you to go to a dark theatre with him all by your lonesome, ain't nothing else it can be."

She stands up real slow, thinkin this over as she goes. She scoops Rodrigo up, takes his leash off the back of the door an puts it on him.

"You really think so?" she asks.

"Chil', don't question the Queen! Now put that dog down. I'll walk him. I got time. You got to get yourself on back to my closet an get presentable. You cain't go on no date in all that black. Lord knows! I love you, but I swear it's like you livin in a re-run a the Adam's Family every damn day. Now come on!"

I point towards my bedroom. She freezes where she is, but then she sets Rodrigo on a chair, hangs his leash back up an obeys. Now I know full well as I walk behind her down the hall, this makeover ain't gonna be no easy task cause she ain't come into her figure yet. Ain't no way I'm gonna breathe a word a that to her though. Lord knows her momma tells her enough. We get to work an find jus the right combination a skirt an top to help her cause.

When she finally comes out a the bathroom, she's all cute in my jean mini, which happens to be jus the right length on her, an a sweet jean jacket over a tank top. Helps disguise the lil' bit a baby fat she's got hangin on. I ain't got a pair a shoes she wouldn't break her neck in so we ain't go no choice but to leave her black high top tennis shoes on. Turns out they don't look too bad with it.

"Mmm hmmm! There you go!" I exclaim, movin her in front of the mirror to take a look for herself.

She turns every which a way, pullin at the skirt, scrunchin up her face.

"I don't know." she whines.

"You don't need to know. I know, an I say you look good Lil' Miss Thang. Real good. Now get on back in there. We're gonna take off that hat, an do somethin with that hair."

I remove her hat real quick fore she can argue, an fling it on the bed. She opens her mouth, starts to say somethin, but I wag my finger in her face.

"Uh uh. No you don't. Lisa can testify to this chil'. Ain't a soul who wins when they argue with me."

She laughs an we set to brushin the knots outta her hair, puttin it up in a sweet lil' ponytail. Standin in that bathroom, brushin that rat's nest, takes me back to when momma used to have me put the relaxer on her hair fore I'd braid it. We'd talk over what was goin on. She'd tell me bout when she was a girl an how her grandma showed her how to do hair too.

Times like this, I think a how whether she meant to or not, momma treated me an Jarvis more like daughter an son. I get the notion that momma recognized the "queen" in me way fore I did.

I put a little mascara on Charlotte Grace for a finishin touch. I pull one a my lipsticks outta my purse an put some on her lips. She's too young to be paintin that barn too much, but every girl can do with a little color. I turn her around in the mirror to behold my handiwork!

"There you go, chil'. Go on with your bad self!" I proclaim.

Her eyes get big. Tears start comin. I grab a wad a toilet paper an dab under her eyes.

"Oh no no no! Lil' Miss Thang, don't you go gettin all Tammy Faye Baker right fore you bout to leave."

She blinks the tears away, then stares at me with that "I ain't got a clue who that is" look she gives me nearly every other time we talk.

"Good Lord, you ain't heard a her neither? Nevermind. We'll save her for another day. Come on. You don't want to keep your fella waitin."

She looks in the mirror one more time.

"This is pretty." she says touchin her lips, smackin em together.

"It should be. It's my signature color. Designed it myself. Got my name right there on the bottom. Order myself new tubes every few months from this company back in Miami. You can be sure ain't nobody else gonna have Queen's Quintiscential Pink. Mmm mmm, not another livin soul." I school her.

Pickin up the gold tube, she looks it over. I do somethin I ain't never done.

"*You want it?*" *I ask.*

She nods her head. I stick in her pocket. She smiles wide, smearin lipstick on her top teeth. I give her a demonstration a how she can be real sly, slide her tonge over her teeth real quick to lick it off. Chil' ain't got a clue about nothin to do with bein a woman. Her momma's been fallin down on job. Bein in pageants an bein a real lady day in day out are worlds apart.

I walk her to the back door. Pride wells up in me. It's like I'm sendin one a my own on their first date. Tears come to me, but it's alright cause I ain't even begun to paint my own barn for work yet. Rodrigo runs to catch up to her, but I snag him.

"*Not today Lil' Man. Lil' Miss Thangs' got places to go an people to see.*" *I announce.*

Steppin down off the back porch, she turns back an looks up at me.

"*I've been wonderin something.*" *she says.*

"*Whas that, chil'?*"

"*How come you call me Lil' Miss Thang?*"

The way she says it, all proper with that drawl a hers, strikes me funny, makes me laugh so hard, I nearly drop Lil' Man on the ground. Tuckin him under my arm real tight, I look down at her. I try to think of a better way to say it a way without usin obsceneties, but it don't come an I figure she'll survive. Figure she's old enough to a heard most a what I could think up an if she hadn't, well then there's a first time for everythang.

"I call you that cause thas the only name there can be for somebody as fabulous as you. Thas what me an my gals back in Florida call anybody who's the 'shit'." I tell her.

A big ol' grin takes over her flashy lips. I jus made her year, maybe her whole lil' life.

"Go on, now. Get goin." I command.

As she skips down the trail through the back yard that she an Lil' Man done worn down through the grass, I find myself prayin it goes good. I pray to God, first an foremost that he'll open up his ears an listen since it ain't for me this time. Specially cause it ain't Lil' Miss Thang's fault I went an got myself reassigned, he can go back to holdin that against me later.

I beg him to make that boy be a real gentleman. Make him tell her she's pretty. Most importantly, to make sure he makes her feel real special, like there's *nobody else compares to her. I pray extra hard for that last part. Mainly cause I can tell by the way she hates goin home, by the way her daddy's away more than he's there, by the way she wears all that black that she don't feel special half as much as she deserves to. Hell, guess most of us never really do.*

The Girl

Aside from Daddy taking me to the movies one Christmas to see Prancer, a movie all about one of Santa's reindeer that gets lost then found by a girl, I hadn't been to the movies with a man. Going with Daddy had been a whole different scenario than sitting beside Donnie. He was so relaxed that he propped his feet up on the seat in front of us. He'd been to a lot of movies, and I was sure I wasn't the first girl he'd been with.

I sat hugging the arm of my chair in that movie theatre as if it was the only life raft left to be hoisted off the Titanic and down into the icy ocean. I don't even remember what movie Donnie and I watched. I was in such a daze through it all. If you had asked me how we'd gotten there, I wouldn't have been able to tell you.

We hadn't even paid for tickets. He'd educated me as to the ins and outs of getting free seats. All we had to do was hang around the back exit and duck inside when another movie let out. It was just that simple. It reminded me of this one movie I watched one night after mother went to bed. I'd wanted to wait up for Daddy, and I'd snuck downstairs to watch T.V. The late film was all about this couple who robbed people during the depression: Bonnie and Clyde.

As I looked over at Donnie, I wondered if this was how Bonnie had felt, an exhilarating feeling of doing something forbidden. Something no one else you knew would even contemplate. Sneaking in had felt more criminal than taking food from the corner store. The theatre manager had a harsh reputation and everybody knew he wouldn't hesitate to call the police if he caught you. I cringed at the thought of Daddy getting that phone call at the D.A.'s office.

"Wanna share?" Donnie offered, tilting a tub of popcorn towards me.

There'd been no way to get around paying for that, and I hadn't minded paying for it since I'd saved up some of the money I'd gotten for walking Rodrigo. I shook my head no and silently informed my growling stomach to keep quiet or I'd never feed it again. I didn't want to get butter on Queen's outfit. It would've been just like me to grab a big handful and drop most of it right in my lap before it ever reached my mouth.

A group of girls from our school walked in, collectively sashaying down the aisle. One of them spotted us. They proceeded to elbow each other, like dominoes going down the row until each and every one of them looked up.

"What's he doin with her?" one of them audibly chided.

Out of nervous habit I reached up for my hat to pull it down, take comfort in hiding under it's brim, then I remembered that Queen had talked me into leaving it behind. Donny looked over. He must have sensed my embarrassment. His arm slid behind my shoulders.

"Ya'll go on an sit your asses down!" he yelled. "It's about to start!"

They scrambled to their seats like chickens huddling together, clucking as they went, in hopes the big bad wolf wouldn't gobble them up. At first, his arm behind me had felt like being hit in the back by Daddy's Mercedes, but then, as I settled in, it felt like the first time I swam in a pool, all cool and tingly. I could've sat there forever. I imagined the two of us turning old there. Never moving from that exact spot.

He left his arm behind me, going on to explain that he couldn't stand nosy bitches like his brother's girlfriends who were always in his business. He went on to say they bossed him around like he was their kid brother. He told them all that he already had a mother and they weren't half as pretty as her either. I laughed at the thought of him sassing them out on his front porch.

"I like your laugh." he flattered, looking right into my eyes.

I just smiled. he leaned over, his lips grazing my ear.

"I bet I'm the only one that makes you laugh like that." he softly whispered.

I nodded even though it wasn't true. Daddy made me laugh. Then there was Queen. She definitely made me laugh my head off, but I let him think this. I was in no position to argue. I couldn't even bring myself to speak.

The movie started and I remember a few images of Jennifer Aniston and some guy talking. It seemed like she couldn't get to the guy she really wanted, but some other guy was trying to help her get him. I was surprised Donnie picked a movie like it, such a girlie movie.

Halfway through, he leaned over and asked if I was enjoying it. I nodded. He said he knew I would because girls liked romances. Again, this was a misconception as I also liked mysteries, westerns and most anything Daddy liked, but I only batted my Maybelline coated eyelashes at him and grinned.

When it was nearly the end, one of the girls a few rows in front of us, one of the hens who ran the roost, turned and glared at me. A pure, unadulterated jealousy had taken hold of her. She stared a hole straight through me as if she was praying to God or the devil or whoever was listening that her look would kill me right then and there. Donny caught her. He put his arm back around me tightening his hold, pulling me closer.

I felt his breath on my face. The smell of the butter from the popcorn wafted up into my nostrils. Shutting my eyes, I prayed to God that I didn't smell bad and that my shoulders didn't seem fat. Before I could pray anything else, Donnie turned my face towards his and kissed me right on the mouth!

My heart had served to pump blood before that second, its sole function only to keep me alive. When he did that, however, my heart took on a life of its own. It expanded, making me feel like it would never shrink back to it's original size.

The snotty girl whipped her head around in disgust. Mission accomplished! We showed her! Donnie and I laughed as he pulled his arm out from behind me. He slid a hand into mine. It was the first time and the last time anything that magical happened to me. I felt fortunate. That it had occurred at all made me the luckiest girl that ever lived.

When the movie let out, he asked if I wanted to sneak into another one. I told him I'd love to, but I had to get home. Mother had been at the auditorium decorating for the ever-looming Miss Peach *extravaganza*. All the former crown cronies had to do their part to make it ready.

Donnie said he'd walk with me as far as the entrance of my subdivision. I told him he didn't have to and he could stay there to watch another movie if he wanted, but he insisted. Even when a few of his usual gang raced by us on their way in to see a blood and guts flick, he turned down their invite. We walked hand in hand down the sidewalk.

I tried to look like I was paying attention as he pointed out various Phelps landmarks. If it wasn't a place he'd burglarized with T.J. it was a street where he'd gotten into a fistfight or helped a friend who'd gotten into a jam. I wondered if this was what boys bragged about, if I should be impressed or worried. It was a world so foreign to me that I didn't dare to speculate on the normalcy of it.

As I listened, I felt like mother must've as she listend to Daddy talk about his cases. It seemed that's what women did - listened to things they had no idea or care in the world about. Secretly, I found myself hoping that would change as I got older, but there was a sneaking suspicion it would only get worse from there on out.

Donnie's hand clasped in mine felt so good. He could've told me gory tales of killing cats out in a field, and I'd have likely nodded, only smiling the same congenial smile. I never wanted him to let go, and I so craved even one more little kiss.

"Better stop here." he said as we came to a halt under my street sign. "Don't think I'm exactly who your momma wants to see comin down the driveway with." he muttered.

This was true. We both knew it. I let my hand go limp, and turned to head home. His hand lingered in mine, and I paused.

"I uh...I saw you a few weeks back over there, at your neighbors." he said.

"Queen's?" I asked.

"Naw, not that faggot. Over there, at the other one's. At that old lady's." he clarified.

It crossed my mind to correct him about the whole faggot thing and tell him Queen was as much a woman as any woman I knew, but then again, she did live with Lisa and in Donnie's world, most people's world, that still made her only a *faggot*; a fact that made me profoundly disappointed in the whole human race.

"Oh, Ms. Terrell's? Yeah, she's pretty nice. I help her carry in packages sometimes, and check on her now and then. She loves the home shopping channel. This one time she - "

"Yeah, thas her." he agreed.

A car drove by. He instantly let go of my hand, putting both hands in his pockets.

"How well you know her?" he dug a bit deeper.

"We've been neighbors for a while. I guess I know her about as well as I know anybody." I replied not sure at all where the line of questioning was going.

Seeing the confusion on my face, he began walking backwards towards his own street.

"Good to know. Good to know." he commented, giving me a wink. "See you tomorrow."

I watched as he turned and jogged off. My hand was still numb with the ecstasy of being held. I didn't give much thought as to why he wondered how well I knew Ms. Terrell. The tube of lipstick Queen had given me rubbed against my leg from it's hiding place inside my pocket. I retrieved it applying a bit more. I'd never worn lipstick before, and I couldn't get enough of the slippery, soft feel of it on my newly-kissed lips.

Walking down my street, I replayed the afternoon. His arm around me, the scorn of the jealous girl, our kiss. I savored these things like the sweet chocolate bar mother let me have every year on my birthday, or the Russell Stovers that Aunt Claudia mailed with a card.

Once home, I turned the key, unlocked the door, and all but floated up the stairs to my room. Laying back on my bed, I looked up at my ceiling - a stark white canvas on which I painted my imaginary masterpieces. Ones where I was beautiful. Where Daddy and I took walks, and he'd stand idly by, watching as I burned my pageant dress with a lighter.

A dark spot caught my eye. A chip had crusted off to reveal where the former owner of our house had slathered my room with a hideous brown. I sat up, scrutinizing it. Had it always been there?

Then a question crept in, much like that brown spot there against the white. The question Donny had asked, *How well did I know her?* and with it came the recollection of the strange and jaded tour he'd given on our way home. I recognized that no matter how good his hand felt or how tenderly his lips had pressed against mine, he was more than likely to be feared. More than that, I knew it didn't really matter. It was too late. I already loved him.

The Cop

"You owe me big time." Was all that Tom had to say as he shoveled the last of the dirt.

There'd been no choice but to call him. They'd been getting each other out of scrapes for as long as Carter could remember. Their schoolyard dilemmas had been simple; nothing more than who would start or end a skirmish. Afterwards, in quick whispers in the lobby of the school office, there would be the inevitable collaboration to decide whose rendition of the day's events would be told to the principal.

As they'd grown older, the tight spots between the rocks and hard places had become even tighter. There'd been the burglarizing of a stereo store so Tom could put a new sound system into his car, and then there was the pawn store they'd broken into several times without repercussions. There was also the time Carter had driven out to a hospital one state over after Tom crashed his car while he'd been drag racing.

Even after all these, the only event that came close to the one at hand was when Tom had driven them to Atlanta for Carter's sixteenth birthday. There he presented him with the gift of an hour with a hooker to *pop his cherry*, as his comrad had so eloquently phrased it. Though Carter was in no way ready, they went to the trouble of borrowing a car from Tom's uncle, picking up a woman who was lingering on a street corner, and following her directions to a seedy motel. Once there, they discovered that they were a hundred dollars short for her full *works*, and the best he could afford was a blow job.

Rather than retreat with their tails tucked between their legs or settle for mediocrity, the two used their typical *powers of persuasion* to convince her to give them a discount. For weeks after that when he lay down to sleep and shut his eyes, he'd see the woman whimpering, bloody lipped and black eyed under him on the hotel bed. As time passed, he found he had to try, with some effort, to call it to mind, but he always managed to. It relaxed him in an unexplicable way.

Sitting against the tree trunk, he watched as his cohort put the finishing touches on the makeshift grave. Tom was right. He knew he would indeed owe him from that day forth. Only if Tom slipped up and did something of the same caliber, only if Carter had to bring out the shovels and drive to Timbuktu with an unidentified person in the trunk, could they call it even.

·

As they trekked through the woods back to Tom's car, he'd expected an interrogation as to what he'd been thinking when he'd done such a thing, but no questions, no rebuke came. This served to both ease his anxiety while simultaneously heightening it. It seemed only natural that Tom would want to know, yet they were cut from the same cloth - the one woven from very few things that could qualify as natural. They loaded the shovels into the trunk then stood back staring at the sod-covered metal.

"It's kinna like Goodfellas ain't it?" Tom jovially summed it up as he slammed it shut.

Carter looked at him. He recognized that this statement was indicitive of what made Tom an ideal accomplice, but knew it made him a wretched human being. He also knew this was the only type of friend he could ever hope to have. The two of them, living proof of the catechism he'd learned as a child: *birds of a feather flock together.*

As they took the winding back roads home to Murfeesboro, he glanced down at his hands. A strand of the girl's long greasy hair was coiled around his thumb. Holding it up, he rubbed it between his fingers, savoring the stringy feel of it. He then rolled down the window, stuck out his arm, letting it fly off and disappear into the dark.

The stereo blared out one of Tom's prized Nirvana CDs, and though Carter had heard this same one many times over the course of their adolescence and then adulthood, he found himself actually ingesting the lyrics for the first time. *"I've been drawn into your magnet tar pit trap. I wish I could eat your cancer when you turn black..."*

This struck him as beautiful and sick. He'd never felt that much love for someone. Worse than that, he was sure no one had felt that much love for him. He'd wanted them to. Oh there were times he'd longed for someone to reach inside and rip out the dark rooted hate, the indifference, the outright evil that had indeed matasticized like cancer throughout his body, mind, and soul. The thought of this made him wonder if someone could do that. If any person could accomplish such a feat. And if they could, what, if anything, would be left of him? When it came right down to it, he sensed he'd rather not know.

"You hungry?" Tom interrupted. ""I'm fuckin starvin. I'll tell you one thang for sure, this here boy whatin made for manual labor. No siree."

It was the second time in the last twenty- four hours that Carter had been asked if he wanted food. How fitting that the whole ordeal should begin and end with such a basic need as eating.

"Naw, I'm fine." Carter replied.

As they pulled into the Sonic, Carter listened as Tom unknowingly ordered the same meal that the girl had only hours before. He bit his cheek in order to keep from crying as they waited for the food to come. The threatening tears were not ones of remorse. No, they were not for what he'd done, not out of any heartfelt emotion. They were over the fact that he'd committed the heinous deed before having obtained any real objective, before having satisfied even half of the devious urges that surged through him.

The Tranny

Some thangs ain't meant for women. Thangs like construction, or heavy liftin, an cars. Ain't no way to look your best doin any a those, an Lord knows I always tell Lisa you got to look your best jus to ride down the road. Cain't go out a the house wearin your pajamas an hadn't even combed your hair.

You never know when you're gonna have a flat an need to get some fella who comes along to help you out or if you're gonna have to put your thumb out for a ride. Thas one a the perks about bein a woman. If I look good enough, in certain circumstances, I don't have to lift a finger.

As I'm puttin oil in my car in this damn heat out here in the driveway, it crosses my mind that if I was back in Florida I wouldn't be gettin any oil under my nails. Mmm mmm. I'd put me on a pair a Daisy Dukes. Wouldn't take no time at all til I'd have ample help. I keep telling Lisa we got to get us a new car, but she don't want to spend the money til we see how the diner's gonna do. She says we can go to usin one car if we have to.

She's the cautious one a the two. Cain't fault her for it. Kept us outta the gutter so far. Ain't my department. She always says if it was up to me we'd be livin on government cheese in a cardboard box in a alley somewhere. I tell her thas probly true but with my fashion sense, that box would still be the most stylish thang on the block.

By the time I put the cap on an shut the hood, one a my nails is fallin off an the rest of em's tar baby black. Mmmm, ain't fittin I tell you jus ain't fittin. I look up to see a U.P.S. man draggin another one a them big ol' packages up on Ms. Terrell's porch. Nother one a them body sized deliveries. If I didn't know better, I'd be wonderin if she's in some kina organized crime family, but thas silly cause she's got way too much junk in her place to ever be part of a organized anythang.

She comes toddlin out on her porch, puts her hands on her hips, looks it over. I look down at my nails. Why not? Hell, I already got to get a full set put on again as it is. Ain't no heavy liftin gonna make em worse.

"Hey." I call to her as I walk over. "Need some help?"

She nods. I walk up the steps an see it's a whole lot bigger than it looked from across the street.

"I'd sure be grateful, if it's not too much trouble, Ms. Queen." she says nervous as an alley cat who's jut spotted a animal control truck.

"Naw, I'm glad to help. Jus gotta see exactly how we gonna get it done." I tell her.

We stand on the porch workin out a solution. She says she don't want it dragged. Says it's fragile. I don't dare tell her that U.P.S. moron dragged it all the way to where it sets now. I'm dyin to ask what's in it, but I don't want to pry. Ain't no air holes so cain't be nothin livin, least not anymore.

Fore we can make up our minds, Lil' Miss Thang's school bus drops her off. She sets her back pack down on her own steps, an runs right over.

"Ya'll need some help?" she asks goin ahead an gettin on one side a the thang.

"Whew, you got good timin chil'." I exclaim.

I get on the opposite side an in no time we hoist it up. She's strong for her age. While we're finaglin that box, I take a good look at her. Well, look at that.

She's got her hair in a ponytail. Got on some a the lipstick I give her. Mmm hmm. She's resortin to prettyin up for her man. I nearly bust out cryin right here an now!

Ms. T. directs us where to put it. We do our best not to break nothin around us as we follow orders. Got to be twice as many thangs as there were last time linin these walls. Do-dads an play pretties, thas what momma used to call ricky racky settin around that don't have a purpose. Ain't got no idea how she can keep track a what she's got.

Me an Lil' Miss Thang both stand there in a stupor takin in the conglomeration a junk. Ms. T. disappears into the kitchen. We figure she's finished with us an we get ready to leave, but then she calls after us.

"Come on in here an have some cake for your trouble."

When it comes to free sugar, you don't got to ask Lil' Miss Thang twice. She zips on across an through that door fore I can blink. I chuckle to myself. Watchin my step, I navigate my way through the maze to join em. Sure is a nightmare of an obstacle course specially in my nine inch Jessica Simpsons.

Pushin open the door a the kitchen, I see right off she's got cats. Ladies like Ms. T., ladies that got more stuff than they know what to do with, always *got cats. There's two of em settin right up on the counter bout to swipe their paw across the cake she's cuttin. Don't bother Lil' Miss Thang none. She's already settin up there jus pettin the fattest one, all ready to get her some sugar. Ms. T. puts a slice on a plate an starts to slide it to Lil' Miss, but she stops herself.*

"Now your momma's not gonna be over here givin me an earful is she?" she wants to know.

Lil' Miss Thang shakes her head no, an gently scoots the plate over right in front a herself.

"I surely hope not. Couple weeks ago she was over here askin me not to give you any chocolate. I jus waited her out. Didn't see no point. Don't think she'd believe me if I told her I haven't had chocolate in this house for God knows how long." Ms. T says with a wink.

I sit on the bar stool an watch as she puts a hunk a that cake on a plate for me. Now, I ain't one to be rude, but regardless a the fact that I'm watchin my figure, I cain't help but wonder those cats been lickin on that cake when nobody was lookin an if they up to date on they shots. I look over at Lil' Miss Thang jus chowin down. Takin a big gulp, I get up my courage an pick up my fork. Here goes nothin.

"Mmm mmm! Ms. T., now I hadn't had cake this good since my momma passed." I say shocked to pieces it tastes so good an not a bit like Kibbles an Bits.

"Well thank you, Ms. Queen. I take that as the highest of compliments. It's mighty hard to measure up to a mother's cooking." she replies as she lets one a the cats lick icin off her finger.

We all sit eatin, lettin that sugar seep in, an take hold. Lil' Miss finishes first, an Ms. T. slices her another small piece.

"Might as well go all out." she tells her.

Lil' Miss smiles big forgettin about her fork an diggin in with her fingers the second go round. Ms. T. goes to put another piece on my plate an I shake my head no.

"Thas got to be it for me, thanks. My waist don't stay like this all by itself." I gracefully decline.

"I should be working harder." Lil' Miss Thang says real embarrassed, mouth half full a the last bite.

"Oh now, you look just fine." Ms. T. offers. "You're a growin girl."

"I've really been tryin. The last two weeks I've been having Slimfast for breakfast and lunch then broccoli with brown rice for dinner. This one treat *shouldn't hurt too much. I think I'll still fit in that dress."* Lil' Miss convinces herself.

"Thas right. You got that pageant comin up soon don't you?" I ask.

"Tomorrow." she mumbles.

"Well that sure snuck up quick. Your man gonna go?" I tease.

"God no!" she nearly shouts.

"Alright. Alright. Jus askin."

I pat her leg fore she blows a gasket.

"Charlotte Grace, you have a beau?" Ms. T. gushes.

Lil' Miss nods.

"Young love is wonderful!" Ms. T. exclaims like the mention of it's takin her back to another time.

I sneak a peek over at Lil' Miss. She's lookin at me too. We try not to laugh.

"You remember your first love, Ms. T.?" I pry.

She picks up the tiniest a the cats an takes to strokin his head. We're jus about to think she didn't hear the question when she really gets goin.

"Sammy Pesagno." she starts in all starry eyed. "He would come into my father's hardware store with his brother. He was several years older. He had this skin, this skin that wasn't brown, but it certainly wasn't pale, and he had this dark curly hair. When he'd pay the bill, he'd always say 'Keepin everything here in order Thelma?' and I couldn't speak if I wanted to. I'd just giggle."

We listen as she goes on to explain that he started walkin her home from the store. How their walks took longer an longer each time. How he finally asked her to a school dance, but her father had a hissy fit sayin as long as he was alive, his daughter would never date a Wop. She said she didn't even know what a Wop was. All she knew was that bein with Sammy was as close as she'd ever come to flyin.

Lil' Miss sits takin it all in like it's better than the good book bein read on a Sunday mornin. Like hearin about how other people felt the same way she's feelin is medicine to her soul. When Ms. T. stops to take a breath, I tell her I know exactly what Italian's are like. That mine's name was Manny.

"Once you go Wop, it's hard to stop." I joke fore I remember I'm in a proper lady's house an not shootin the shit with one a my gals back in Tallahassee.

Ms. T.'s face freezes up. I think for sure I've gone an done it now, but then

Lil' Miss busts out laughin. She laughs so hard she gets red in the face. Ms. T. has to get her a glass a water. As she swigs it down, Ms. T. surprises us both by repeatin what I said for herself.

"Once you go Wop you never wanna stop..."

Her chuckle starts deep down in her throat, then explodes into a outright cackle.

"Ain't never heard that one." she says once she's got her breath back.

"Queen's full of things most people've never heard." Lil' Miss Thang adds.

"Hey, now!" I holler out, pinchin her arm playful like.

"I'm sure she is." Ms. T. teases back. "I'm sure she is."

We put our dishes in her dishwasher, thank her for the cake an head for the door.

"Mother?" We hear a voice call from the livin room.

"In here Bev." Ms. T. answers so loud the cat she's holdin jumps outta her arms an takes off down the hallway.

The kitchen door cracks open an first thang we see is some big ass, blonde, teased haired woman. Mmm, looks more like lemon cotton candy comin through the door. Then we see the pale, made up face that goes with it. So much blush on those cheeks looks like she's on her way to be one a them clowns that entertains the kids at the hospital.

Soon as she lays eyes on me, she goes a paler shade a white. Wouldn't a known how it'd be possible, but she does it. Look like some kinna albino.

"Didn't know you had company, Mother." she says all cold an icy as snow.

"These are my neighbors. This is Charlotte Grace and this is Ms. Queen. They helped me get one a my packages in." Ms. T. goes about introducin us.

Poor thang cain't read the room an see her daughter don't care who we are. Thinks she already knows. Only thang she cares about is that we're inconveniently takin up space in her momma's kitchen.

"I'd have been glad to help. Did you forget I was coming?" she gripes keeping her eyes on me the whole time.

I don't take my eyes off her either. We goin toe to toe. Ain't backin down for nobody. It's on her whether or not we gonna go peacable or we gonna be like Ms. T.'s cats an scratch it out on the back porch.

"No, I didn't forget, Beverly." Ms. T. says softly.

If I reached in the dishwasher an got that cake knife Ms. T. used to slice our cake with, wouldn't be fit to cut the tension in this room. Lil' Miss Thang looks over at me. She puts her hands in her pockets like she does when she's tryin to stick it out when she's smack dab in the middle a somewhere she don't wanna be. Seen her doin it every time she crosses the street from my house back to hers.

"We were jus headin on." I tell Bev tryin to put her mind at ease.

I move forward. She lunges to the side like I'm a tiger that jus escaped the zoo an ate up her momma an now I'm comin for her. I don't pay it no mind. Openin the door, I let Lil' Miss duck out ahead a me to the front.

"Good luck tomorrow." Ms. T. calls to Lil' Miss. "You're gonna do just fine. Now you let me know how it turns out."

"I will." Lil' Miss calls back.

"Thanks again for that cake, Ms. T. Mmm, gonna have to have some a that again soon." I tell her pattin my belly.

Beverly all but pushes her momma further back inside. If she has anythang to do with it, I won't see another slice a that cake the rest a my natural born days.

As we walk out in the yard, I can tell by the way she's got those eyebrows scrunched together that Lil' Miss is carryin the weight a somethin on her slumped shoulders.

"*You worried bout tomorrow?*" *I ask.*

She nods. I stop in my tracks, not even carin if I'm late to work. I put my hands on her shoulders, turn her towards me.

"*You ain't got a thang to worry about, chil'.*"

Tears well up in her eyes.

"*But I'm not as pretty as the other girls.*" *she sniffles.*

I shake her real gentle like.

"*Now, you hush that talk. I ain't gonna listen to it, an you shouldn't neither. My momma always said 'Pretty is as pretty does' an in my book that makes you one beautiful girl.*"

"*I'm fatter than them and I don't have a good talent and ...*" *she tries to argue.*

"*Hey!*" *I say real loud.* " *You're kind, sweet as pie, an helpful. Oh, an don't forget funny as hell. Plus, you got a smile that can make any bad day turn good an I know you ain't tryin to be arguin with my momma, are you?*"

She wipes the tears off her cheeks, shakes her head.

"*Good. Cause we were this close to havin a scuffle right here in this yard an I sure didn't want to.*" *I tell her all serious.* "*Not with these nails chil'.*"

I hold up my hands showin all my mangled, oily nails. She laughs. Fore I know what's hit me, I do somethin that comes so natural. I hug her. I let her head rest on my chest then I suddenly realize we're out in a front yard in this here white-bred neck a the woods. I don't pull away too soon, though. I jus pat her back then ease away. Wish I could hold her long as she needs. Wish we whatin shackled by the chains a who we are an who we ain't.

"You knock em dead Lil' Miss Thang. Go out there an strut your stuff like you done won it already." I dole out advice as I walk backwards to my house.

She stands watchin me as I go. If she don't look jus like Rodrigo did out by that dumpster fore we finally broke down an brought his ass home.

"Remember, you got nothin to lose. You don't win, hell, you'll still leave with everythang you come in with." I remind.

The sound of a car turnin onto the street causes us both to look up. Damn if it ain't her momma speedin our way. I hustle into the house, but I'd bet money she saw me. Partin my front curtain jus enough to see out, I watch as she gets out, stomps over to Lil' Miss Thang then looks over my way. I shut that curtain up fast, but could be the damage is done. Sure hope Lil' Miss ain't gonna have to quit comin over an takin Rodrigo out. More than that, I hope she ain't gonna have to quit comin to see me.

I do a quickie manicure, make my hands presentable then I scoot on over to the diner. Try to keep my mind on my tables an whose ordered what. Halfway through the night, Lisa's askin if I'm alright. She complains I'm in a zone. I tell her I'm fine, an I kinna am. My mind's jus back in that yard is all.

Back tellin Lil' Miss all the ideas I got about how to tackle somethin you're scared of. Standin there holdin her to me, feelin somethin I didn't think I could feel. Something no surgeon can help you feel no matter how much you pay him...all of a sudden, I felt more maternal than I ever thought possible.

The Girl

The morning of the pageant, Daddy followed mother's car onto the freeway with me in the passenger's seat. They'd taken two cars as he was set to leave for Nashville to interview a witness as soon as it was over. I could tell by his deep sighs as he gripped the wheel that he would be broaching a topic he'd been assigned. I was sure Mother had agreed to let me ride with him for that very reason. It was so rare that I got to spend much time alone with Daddy that I didn't care what the reason was.

"How's school?" he started off.

"Fine."

This was one of his typical *fatherly* questions. It was as if he'd memorized a list of them from old late night T.V. shows he liked to watch; Ward Clever serving as his role model. I didn't mind as I knew it was all he had to go on.

His own father had been a stoic character. He'd made a far better court judge than he had a parent. Daddy never said as much, but the fact remained that even though my grandparents lived a half hour away we only visited them at Christmas and Easter. The lack of involvement in between spoke for itself.

"How's math going?" he continued.

"Fine." I answered.

"Think you might need that tutor again this year?"

"No, sir."

"Well if you do, just let us know. Math's a hard subject. Never was my strong suit."

I nodded. The year before, I'd struggled terribly with Geometry. When

I brought home my first D, mother had immediately obtained the services of Mr. Rush, a high school teacher who tutored for money on the side. Reveling in the extra male attention, I had been disappointed at my quick progress under his tutelage. I half contemplated faking failure, but couldn't live with costing my parents undue fees. We rode a bit further before Daddy got down to brass tax.

"Your mother mentioned she saw you out in the yard talking to that man." he accused.

"What man?" I asked out of genuine confusion.

"That one who moved in over at the Lawson's place."

I readily recognized his tone as part of his courtroom persona. He reserved it for anything to do with mother and her allegations which he always dealt with as quickly as possible so they didn't pile up. Besides, the longer things dragged on, the more dramatic these situations usually became.

"You mean Queen?" I played dumb.

"You know who I mean. The one she's told you not to talk to." he barked.

At times like those, I found myself wishing my rights were equal to that of a common criminal, the right to an attorney. It seemed unfair that any bum who got arrested was given more advantages than I was.

"She was just helping me carry a box in for Ms. Terrell." I defended.

He looked down at me likely speculating whether or not this seemed plausible. Up to that point, I'd been trustworthy. I'd never been caught in any lies bigger than whether or not I'd eaten some of his cookies, and even those sorts of small indiscretions had been few and far between.

"Hmmm. Yes, well, that was nice of you, but I'd prefer you listen to your mother. If Ms. Terrell really needs help, you can tell her I will be glad to see to it when I get home." he calmly offered his alternative.

"Yes sir." I sheepishly replied.

He turned on the radio to his favorite news station. As we listened to how the War on Terror was going, I secretly wished I could fill him in on my own news. I wished I could tell him all about Queen. About how he was a *she* as far as I could tell, and how nice she was. Then I'd tell him all about how most people at school thought of Donnie and me as a couple now and how it was Queen who'd given me the confidence to talk to him in the first place.

"I can't believe we don't have this all wrapped up by now!" he fumed following the announcer's statement that the insurgence was still gaining ground in Kabul.

Watching his left hand stear the car while his right hand anxiously pulled at his slacks from time to time, I wondered how my Daddy came across in the courtroom. If he was cool and collected or more like Rodrigo when he got all hyped up waiting for our walk. It snuck up on me, as it tended to do every now and then, that there I was in the presence of a man whose abilities dictated people's fate. Whether they went to jail, whether they went free.

Whether they lived or died.

"Daddy?"

"Hmmm?"

"Daddy, I was wondering how you do it." I started.

"What?"

"How you decide all those hard things, like who's guilty or not, and what's going to happen to them." I asked.

He turned the radio down, and stared straight ahead as if the lines on the road would curve into letters that would form the answer he should give.

"The jury helps the judge decide that. It's not really up to me."

"But you help them don't you? You convince them." I pressed.

A car whizzed passed us.

"God damn! Look at that! Now if I did that, I bet good money every patrolman in this county would be right behind us lights blaring!" he raged.

Believing our conversation to be over, I turned my attention to the fevered speech of the reporter on the news.

"You have to do what you can live with." Daddy flatly said so long after the question was asked that I'd almost forgotten what I'd wanted to know in the first place.

"Oh." Was all I could utter.

It seemed sufficient enough. A simple mantra by which to live. Though as I digested it, I found myself curious as to exactly how that philosophy worked. What if what you could live with was not what someone else could live with? He turned the radio up again. I laid my head against the seat to get a bit of a nap before the hellish events that awaited.

I was awakened by heat from the sun beaming through my window followed by the sound of Daddy's door slamming. I looked out at a herd of giggling, happy, fellow contestants bustling into the building. Some already had their makeup on, and their hair done. My hairdo was to be a simple bun, a decision mother came to due to the roundness of my face. We hadn't bothered to do it before we arrived. The second we parked, mother hurried over to our car.

"Where've you been? I thought you two were right behind me." she scolded.

"We stopped for gas. Didn't take five minutes." Daddy protested.

"Well, come on. We've got catching up to do." she groaned grabbing my hand, leading me up the walkway.

"Good luck everybody!" Ms. Saunders excitedly shouted as she emerged from her car.

Her smug look of pre-emptive victory was enough to turn anyone's stomach. My mother only smiled and waved.

"She thinks it's in the bag. Well we'll show her!" Mother hissed in my ear.

I would not have dared to burst her bubble. It would provide a soft cushion for her to fall on when they announced the winner. I turned and looked mournfully back at Daddy. My sad eyes crying out that there was still time. He could still put a stop to it. We could drive off to Nashville stopping at the IHOP on the way to have hot fudge sundaes, but he only winked.

"Knock em dead." he encouraged followed up with a half smile.

He'd never said that before. It didn't sound like him at all, though I wasn't sure what else would have been more appropriate. I returned a smile, all the while wondering what show he'd watched the night before that had given him such a line.

The dressing room was abuzz with mothers hurrying here and there. There was a sort of unspoken language that we weren't privy to holding the secrets of who could borrow this and trade that. Curling irons were swapped. Sewing kits were handed off. Mother had remembered everything she'd needed. She'd rightfully predicted that, after what became referred to as *the Hello Kitty Catastrophe*, we'd be placed on their invisible social blacklist.

I sat looking in the mirror as she brushed my hair. Her rough strokes were worlds away from the gentle way Queen had brushed it. In Queen's bathroom I'd been pampered, treated as a person of note. Sitting there in front of mother, I knew I was nothing more than a show pony, and worse than that, I was one that hadn't measured up to the price that had been paid for me.

With a bun so tight it pulled my eyebrows up higher on my forehead, I resembled one of those alien women on Star Trek. Lietenant Charlotte Grace at your service, Captain. My mother didn't notice and went scavenging through our bag for lipgloss.

"Now, I know I remembered to pack it. I..."

Looking down at the pocket of my jeans, I remembered I had the lipstick Queen had given me. Knowing I'd have to wait until I was out of mother's clutches to apply it, I assured her I could go without the gloss.

"Here, at least put some Vaseline on. It'll give you just enough shine." she demanded pulling it out of her purse and dabbing it on my lips before I could agree.

"Ten minutes!" A mother yelled wielding her clipboard as if readying to lead us into the beauty battle to top all battles.

Mother jerked me up, rushing me over to the changing area. The moment of truth had arrived. I hadn't tried the dress on for a couple weeks. So sure was she that her strict diet coupled with her appeals to Daddy as well as Ms. Terrell had done the trick, she hadn't pressured me about actually putting it on til that moment.

From out of the garment bag rose my poofy purple nemesis. She unzipped it, holding it out to me.

"Come on." she prodded.

I took off my jeans and carefully slipped my t-shirt up over my head so as not to destroy my hair. Deep down, something in me knew it would not go well. Not only had there been a couple after school ventures to the corner store with Donnie, but just the day before there'd been the binging on the cake that Ms. Terrell had lavished Queen and I with. I stood there knowing this, all the while praying for a miracle. I told God if he came through it would be right up there with multiplying the loaves and the fishes, and his whole water into wine bit. I vowed to swear off all sugar if only he'd do me one favor.

It went up over my hips and I felt a glimmer of relief, yet as I listened to my mother struggle with the zipper in back, I knew there was to be no miracle. I consoled myself by thinking about the drumstick cone I'd have as soon as Donnie and I could steal one. The sound that followed mother's grunting was a sound that would go on to cause me undue trepedation forever after. It was the odd, especially given the situation, yet unmistakeable sound of tape, duct tape to be exact, being peeled from its roll then torn off. I faced my mother in disbelief as she took the dress down to my waist.

"Suck it in!" she commanded.

I complied, holding back my tears as she mummified my mid section and what little bit of a chest I had. When she finished, she whirled me around then zipped up the dress without a hitch. It felt as if a boa constrictor had wrapped itself around my ribs.

"It hurts." I breathily complained.

"You've left me no choice." mother insisted.

She flung open the dressing room curtain. I slipped on my patent leather shoes hoping they'd turn into a pair of Queen's heels right before my eyes. Looking down at them, I had no choice but to admit to myself that the day had rendered me no favors. With all the discomfort of a tightly bound Geisha, I wobbled over to take my place in line.

"Nice dress." Amy commented.

"Thanks." I managed.

"Glad to see all of you could fit in there." she quipped.

With a flip of her hair, she turned to wait for her name to be called. Danita Witherspoon went down the line begrudgingly complimenting us all. She may have been the only one who was more unhappy than I was. I thought of suggesting to her that we make a great escape through the back, but then my name was called. All I could think about was how I'd left the lipstick in the back pocket of my jeans.

The bright lights seemed much brighter than they had during practice. There were at least a couple hundred people all taking pictures of their little darlings. I squinted to see if I could spot Daddy, finally finding him in the third row. He was easy to spot as he didn't have a camera out. I don't think we'd even brought one. We were not a family who was into nostalgic details of that sort.

I tried to walk, smile and wave all at the same time. The room felt as though it was spinning. It took all that was in me to remain upright. As I took in as much air as possible through short quick breaths, I couldn't help but look at him there and think of the conversation we'd had earlier.

"*You have to do what you can live with.*" he'd said. It seemed so apropos. Putting my hands on my hips, I tried to take a deeper breath, attempted to steady myself. It was all to no avail. I teetered, flailed my arms then went right off the stage onto the floor. A disastrous fall much worse than Amy's a couple weeks earlier. Kharma at its best.

Lying there, I looked up at the people yelling over me, lights becoming less like the plastic bulbs they actually were and more and more like tiny illuminated fairies floating overhead. I pondered the question of when was what I *could* live with going to be something I actually *wanted* to live with. On that note, I passed out.

The Cop

He saw her turn the neon *open* light off before he exited his patrol car. Not ten minutes earlier, he'd seen Queen pull out, likely headed back to *their* house. The house where Lisa had grown up had been *theirs* for only a short time yet.

He'd stood in the alley across the street ensuring that only Lisa remained before he'd returned to his vehicle and pulled it around parking in front of the diner. Undoubtedly, if she'd caught sight of him, she'd have asked Queen or Mary to stay. He couldn't risk that. He wanted to get her by herself, all to himself.

Rain drenched him from head to toe on his way from the car to the door. The very weather itself refusing to serve as a compliant accomplice or ally. This did not dissuade him, however. The world at large had been against him since he could remember.

"We're closed." her voice rang out from somewhere in the back.

He sat up to the counter. A new cake plate accosted him. It was a bright, pink porcelain, and more than that, it was clear sign to him that *the Queen* was making *itself* right at home. Lifting it, he used a knife that lay conveniently next to it to slice a piece then lop it off onto a napkin.

This cake plate reminded him of the hermit crab his father had let him purchase on the one trip they took to the beach the summer before he started junior high. Once he brought it home, he became fascinated. He read all there was to read about the species. Nomadic creatures that would find empty shells, leaving their old ones behind. They'd embedded their bodies into the new ones, to afford themselves space to grow. They did so without any thought or credence to the former tenant.

As he twirled on his stool, he easily picked out the other evidences of Queen's *embedding*. There were the chairs that had been reupholstered with black faux- leather fabric, black and white checkerboard flooring. An Elvis clock that shook his hips with each new hour had found a home over the bathroom door. A large framed poster of Marilyn Monroe hung by the cash register.

It was clear they were going for a classic 50's feel. He quickly categorized it all as outlandishly overdone, biting off a hunk of his cake and chewing it slowly. Oh, how he longed for the plain days of Old Man Lawson. This longing was one of the few he could put a name on; a longing for what was and would never be again. It was a yearning like that of a man much his senior, another clear indication to him that he was indeed a man out of season.

In the corner, a poster of a black woman singing snagged his attention. Her dress was pink, and the only part of the photo that was not black and white. He did not readily recognize her. Getting down off the stool, he walked over and read the label underneath: *Anna Mae Bullock*.

"Sorry Carter. I'm just closin up." Lisa matter-of-factly informed him.

She purposely stood near the door, keys in hand, to let him know she was more than ready to lock it.

"Who's this?" he queried.

Ignoring a person's cues was one of in many of a wide array of tricks he'd acquired to demonstrate dominance. A not so subtle way of letting people know he came and went when he pleased. That he did what he wanted when he wanted.

"Tina Turner before she was Tina Turner." Lisa obliged him.

He sauntered back to his stool to finish his half-eaten slice of cake.

"I thought Tina Turner was her real name." he replied coolly.

"Most people do." Lisa said. "She was Anna Mae Bollock until Ike came along."

She remained by the door, fumbling nervously with her keys. Seeing his blatant reluctance, she went around to the register and began retrieving the day's take from the drawer.

"Quiet out there tonight?" she attempted small talk.

He nodded taking another bite.

"Hope that still tastes alright. Been there since early this morning. I was just about to throw it out." she babbled.

"Awe, thas too bad. Not a thang wrong with it." he lamented.

As she organized the cash in the bank drop bag, she glanced out at the rain coating the front windows in unusually large torrents.

"God! It's really comin down!" she exclaimed.

He nodded, licking icing off his index finger, keeping his eyes fixed on her. She bustled around behind the counter, wiping things down, rambling about the storm, then her chihuahua and how he hated to get his feet wet.

All nervous banter. All feeble attempts at staving off whatever it was he'd come to say or do. Her erratic behavior took him back to hot days when he'd amused himself by using his father's reading glasses to burn bugs on pavement. He himself was not altogether clear on his objective. Possibly this was to be a simple gathering of information, or possibly a chance to make her squirm, possibly both.

When she had done all she could think to do, Lisa tucked the deposit bag under her arm then turned to him once more.

"Well, I gotta get on and run this by the bank." she prompted with a pensive smile.

He popped the last bite of his cake into his mouth, and stood up.

"No problem." he said. "What do I owe you?"

She shook her head.

"Nah, don't worry about it. It would've gone to waste if you hadn't come along anyhow. Go on an take the rest. Shame to waste it." she offered uncovering the remains of the cake, digging a box of tin foil out from under the counter.

Laying out the wrap, she hastily plunked the entire half of the cake onto it, and wrapped it up. Stepping out from behind the counter, she handed it to him. A meager peace offering, in his opinion, considering the years of unspoken wrongs that had passed between them, but it would suffice for the night.

"It'll keep for another day or two, longer if you freeze it." she persuaded.

Reaching out to accept it, he made sure to graze her hand with his fingers.

"Mighty kind of you." he plastically noted with a snarky sarcasm.

Her face reddened as she stepped back, then darted around him. With long strides, she reached the door in no time, throwing it open.

"You stay dry now." she dismissed.

"I'll try." he answered giving her a grin, and tipping his hat.

He heard her turn the lock behind him as soon as his feet stepped outside. Leaning forward, he tried hard to keep the cake dry as he made his way to the car. He gingerly placed his parting gift on the passenger seat next to him as if it was a person.

As he started it up, all he could think about was that it was in the same seat where the girl had sat. He wondered why she still emerged at such inopportune times. Why she could not remain in the cell she'd been allotted in the Alcatraz he called a brain.

His hand did not move to put the gearshift in reverse. He instead sat studying Lisa as she systematically lowered each and every set of blinds. When she got to last one, she happened to see him still sitting there. Upon seeing him, a momentary expression of unmistakable fear hijacked her face. She regrouped, replacing it with a strained smile followed by a robotic wave right before letting the final blinds fall.

Only when the entire place went black did he finally put the car in reverse then back out. The rain pelted his windshield with a violent frenzy he'd seldom witnessed. He drove slowly, feeling no anxiety in a situation that would otherwise immobilize anyone else causing them to pull over and try to wait it out. This was how it was for him: anxious when others weren't, calm in the face of formidable foes.

He logged the night as somewhat successful. He'd accomplished at least two things: showing Lisa he did not play by other's rules, and stealing an undesired touch. Though he'd wanted to pry a bit more, say a few more phrases that would have caused her mental distress, he resigned himself to be moderately satisfied with his handiwork.

The car rocked with the sheer force of the wind. He thought of coasting to a stop beside Mr. Donaldson's pasture, but he wanted to get home. He was intent on eating the rest of the cake, before spending the remainder of the night pleasuring himself on his couch to his own customized visions of Lisa. The imagination could go far on just the grazing of a hand.

Up ahead, a white blur moved alongside the road. He leaned forward, craning his neck, squinting to make out what it was, yet little else was visible in the pitch dark. Slowing to a stop, he rolled down his passenger window enough to see more clearly, the reason it had looked like only a white flash, a spooky apparition. It all too quickly became delightfully clear.

"Get in." he shouted over the elements.

The stranded individual froze, debating the wisdom of accepting his offer, looking down the road to see if anyone else was coming, staring at him momentarily assessing his demeanor. His was the only car, however and Carter made sure not to grin, yet also took care so as not to make an expression that could pass for a frown. This created the illusion of his being somewhat non-threatening.

It looked back at him, biting *its* lower lip, first stepping back from the car, shaking *its* head. Then the rain railed harder. The wind picked up speed as if coercing *it*, causing *it* to again step forward. *It* reached out and opened his passenger door.

He slid the mass of cake over out of *its* way so *it* could situate *its* long black legs in such a way that *its* knees wouldn't hit the dash. Hugging the door, *its* manicured hands pulled at *its* tight white tank top, though it did little to help the fact that *its* breasts remained a taut eyeful under the wet cotton.

"Whew! I sure appreciate it. Damn car! I tell you what, an my phone's needin charged to boot. I cain't never remember to charge that thang. Done walked a country mile out here for the storm picked up sent me doublin back. Like a drowned rat, mmm hmm. Lord knows I don't know another soul who woulda even tried it in these." *It* babbled as *it* pointed down at *its* candy –apple- red high heels.

Easing slowly back out onto the road, Carter considered that perhaps he'd misread things. An opportunity such as this could sway any mans long held beliefs. That indeed the weather was not against him as he'd assumed. That for once in his life, the world was on his side. The wind continued to pummel the car, a confirmation of this epiphany.

"Mmmm! Now, we had us some storms in Florida. Sure did. Nothin like this here though. This here ain't no storm. This here is what my momma woulda called *the wrath a God*." the passenger stated.

Carter kept his eyes on the road, his hands on the wheel, and his head on the plethora of possibilities that were unfolding. It seemed to him that God wasn't the only one who had reason to rage. No, he was of the mindset that there were other forces; ones expelled from God's own good graces. These too would have ample reason to rail against this world. Turning off the main road, he was well aware that he'd long been more than willing to be the very vessel with which they could choose to do so.

"This a shortcut?" his passenger naively questioned.

Cater only gripped the wheel more tightly, not satisfying *it* with a response.

The Tranny

From where I'm standin in the driveway, I see Lisa's shadow pacin back an forth in front a the livin room winda. I reach one a my shakey hands down my leg an take off the only heel I got left on. Hell, the other one must still be back in his car. Couldn't get out fast enough. Whatin worryin about no shoe.

I raise my arm, throw it off in the woods back behind the house. Nearly hit the neighbor's garage. The ones who don't dare speak to us. They do more than don't speak. They go outta their way to run in their house so they don't even have to lay eyes on us. Them an the rest a this shitty subdivision.

Rain's gone down to a drizzle. My legs don't listen. I keep tellin em to walk up to the door an go in. Walk right up there, push that door open an spill my guts. Tell Lisa all about what happened, then call the sheriff. He'd have to believe me. Cain't be the first thang that fucker's done. Ain't no way!

Fore I can talk my feet into obeyin, Lil' Man peeks his head out the curtains. He goes to barkin his fool head off. Lisa looks out to see what's got him goin. She sees me for herself an flings open the door.

"What're you doin?" she hollers.

I'm froze up. My mouth ain't listenin to me tellin it to talk.

She runs out, Lil' Man trailin her. First off, her steps are angry an fast, but as she gets closer, they slow down.

"Where've you been?" she needs to know.

Lil' Man jumps against my legs. My hands don't connect to my brain sayin pick him up. Lisa scoops him up instead, tries to calm him. Both of em gettin soaked to the bone.

"I made the bank drop an saw the car on the side a the road. I got home an there wasn't any sign of you. Like to scared me to death!" she fusses.

"It broke down again." I finally mumble.

"Why didn't you call?" she's demandin.

I reach out an stroke Lil' Man on the head. He licks my hand knowin somethin's off. I jus about go to pieces.

"Couldn't get a signal. Took a shortcut down by Benson's. Had to take a dirt road so I could walk barefoot. Wouldn't a made it in my heels in this rain no way."

She looks down at my bare feet.

"Where are your shoes?" she asks

I bite my lip, try to think fast.

"Left em in the car. No sense in sacrificin a perfectly good pair a Jimmys." I weave my tale.

The look on her face tells me she's mullin over my story, tryin to swalla it, but it ain't goin down. Gotta hand it to her. She can spot bullshit a mile off, but she don't call me on it.

"Come inside." She coaxes, reachin to me.

I look down at her tiny pale hand. Takes my hand extra time to register me tellin it to go on an take it. Feels like there's a million miles between our two hands. Like the wedge thas between me an the rest a the world's done gone an fixed itself between me an her now too. Like this one night, this one fucked up situation's gone an done it. I finally reach for it anyway.

We walk up to the porch, an go on in. Ain't no sense in trackin up the carpet. I wait on the tile by the front door while she gets some towels. Lil' Man sniffs my muddy feet. He don't like what he's pickin up. I hope I ain't branded with that bastard's scent.

The livin room's dark enough Lisa cain't get a good look at me. I put a hand on her shoulder to balance so I can wipe my feet. I follow her down the hall. The sound a bath water runnin reminds me a the rain beatin against his car *windas.*

Soon as I get in that bright bathroom an stand still for a second, we both get us a eye full. My arms an my legs jus chalk full a scrapes, got a cut across a swolled up cheek from the punch I took. I'm dirtier than I ever been, mud smeared on my clothes an arms.

"What the hell?" Lisa whispers.

In the time it took for me to get from outside to inside, I done gone an lost my nerve. Any fight I even thought a havin, I'm over it. I jus wanna get in that tub an wash it all away.

"I...I tripped. Went right off over in the ditch, hit my head against some rocks. Like to thought I'd never climb out. Thank the good Lord nobody saw me. Looked like a turtle tryin to get up off his back." I tell her tryin real hard to sell it.

She stares at me. She's about to open her mouth an give me what for. I look so pitiful she stops herself. I blink back tears. Real gentle, she helps me get undressed an lower myself down in the tub. I lay back, close my eyes an feel her run a wash cloth over my filthy skin.

Starin at the ugly flowered wallpaper, I see where it's peelin back in every corner a the room. We're plannin on strippin it all off first chance we get. I think to myself that he knew this is what I'd do. He knew I'd jus go on home, an not say word one.

How is it wolves can spot a wounded sheep from a long ways off? It's like once you been bit, you never quit bleedin. All of em, all the sharp teethed devils from every corner a the country's gonna get a whiff an keep trackin you every God damned day a your life.

"Hon, you're just so torn up." Lisa whimpers, dipin the washcloth in the water, sprinklin it over one a the worst scrapes on my thigh.

"It was a big ol' ditch." I hear myself say takin the cloth from her, pattin her hand.

She gets up an ducks out to get my clothes. Those tears are pressin on my eyes, jus threatenin to break out. I cain't let em. Gonna have to wait. I know if they start, I cain't stop em for nothin.

When she comes back, she's totin my favorite sleepshirt - the one I got when we saw Tina in concert at the Madison Square Garden. I let her wrap a towel around me as I step out of the tub. She dries me off real gentle, like when we brought Lil' Man home an washed him up. She's real cautious like she was with him, like she don't know my temperament, an whether or not I'm prone to snap.

"Thank you baby." I tell her. "I'll be out in a minute."

I put my shirt on over my head. It feels like nails goin down chalkboard skin. Lisa's arms surprise me from behind an hug me to her. I keep pattin her hands.

"You sure you're gonna be alright?"

"Ain't no thang. You know me, I'll be fine." I answer cause I know thas what she needs to hear.

Her arms slip away slow. She's registerin that this is all she's gonna get. That this is how it's gonna go down. That the first lie to ever pass between me an her was jus born. My stomach is sick at the thought a how we done our best to never see this day, to never have anythang dark pollutin what we've made.

I close the door behind her, look myself in the mirror. Starin at Tina there faded on my chest, up there singin her heart out, I feel closer to her than I ever have. Me an her been through the wringer more times than we can count.

Then jus as fast, I feel far from her. Farther from her than I ever thought possible. There she is free an singin; here I am all scuffed up, playin the victim again. I wonder how she got out from under Ike's thumb? How did she get the *courage? Had to do it all on her own, this I know for a fact.*

Ain't no way Lisa can be my Wonder Woman all the time. She cain't be everywhere at once. No, I got to do it for myself. Thought I could. Thought I was ready, but then he started in. An there I was goin all the way back to that bedroom. Layin on that floor, smellin that chicken, feelin my cousin on me, an not sayin one word. Not one word! It was like I was that kid again, settin quiet as a church mouse in his backseat watchin it happen. Lil' Jermaine sellin Queen out.

Lookin down at my shirt, I know it ain't right for the two nights to meet this a way. The night we bought this shirt an I heard my idol, saw her for the first time up there on that stage. The other night havin a skeleton resurrected up from the grave that I been doin my best to bury him in. I take my shirt in my two tore up hands an rip Tina right in two. I don't deserve to wear her! I ain't no Proud Mary! I ain't no Queen! After everythang, I'm still jus a weak motherfuckin lil' boy!

Here I am, naked, starin in this mirror. For the first time in a long time, I don't know where to go, what to do or who to be. Don't feel like I'm who I see in front of me. Sure as hell don't want to be the person I left behind.

I imagine that bastard back at his house. I think a him takin off his uniform, starin hisself down in the mirror. Gave him a few scratches an bruises he's gonna have to deal with, but I bet he's still proud, real proud. I know he is cause thas how wolves are. Ate up with so much pride, ain't a scrap of it left for the rest of us.

The Girl

It took Daddy a good week to speak to mother after the whole pageant fiasco. Needless to say, he had not been privy to the duct tape plan. After he lifted me up off the floor and took me to the back to rest, Amy Saunders was crowned princess. I remembered thinking if I'd have worn Queen's lipstick it wouldn't have happened like it did. It would've given me good luck, like a rabbit's foot in my pocket. In no way would I have placed, but I would've at least stayed upright.

The whole ride home from Atlanta, Daddy had gone on and on about how carried away Melanie could get. How she wasn't like this when he met her, and he didn't know what had gotten a hold of her. He went on to label her *outright obsessive*. This jarred me, going down in the books as the first time he'd used her first name in a harsh way and demeaned her in front of me. It was also the first time he'd openly taken my side.

I didn't know exactly what obsessive meant, but I knew it wasn't good. It certainly served to ease the pain of the embarrassing incident. To have him acknowledge that mother was not just going off the deep end. But that she had likely been there for years swimming the backstroke, made the whole thing worth going through.

I didn't talk to anyone at school about the ordeal. There was no need. Only one of my fellow competitors in the pageant, Jill Marks, even went to my school, but she was two years my senior so we seldom, if ever, saw each other. It amazed me that I'd gone through such a catastrophically horrible weekend only to return to classes that Monday with everything picking up where I'd left off, business as usual.

Donnie didn't care about things like pageants. I don't think he even remembered that it was why I couldn't hang out with him on Saturday. His list of cares seemed to fall into simple categories of wearing pants with good pockets so they could be filled with things that didn't belong to him, coming off as the toughest one in front of his friends and, when it was just he and I, being a good kisser.

He regularly reminded me that I was his favorite girlfriend so far. I would've liked to have achieved that status due to my good looks, but he told me it had been awarded to me primarily because I didn't nag him about his bad habits like the smoking, or the stealing. However I came by the title, I eagerly approved. It meant that we accepted each other for who we were and who we weren't, moreover who we tried to pretend we were yet who we'd never be.

That afternoon, Queen nearly fell out in the floor right there in front of Tina Turner when I told her about what happened. At first, I was upset that she'd laugh about it, but then she pointed out that you had to learn to laugh at yourself or you'd be miserable most of your life. I went on to point out that she wasn't laughing at herself, but at me.

"True dat. True dat. I'm sorry. I owe you one a my times then, an whew, I got a lot. Chil' this one night when I hosted drag queen bingo in Tallahassee, wouldn't you know my dress caught on the wheel? When I spun that thang, it flipped my dress up an there it was. My cheetah thong greetin everybody. Right there for all to see." she shared.

I giggled at the thought of this, and then I broke into a full out belly laugh imagining my mother's face if she discovered that I'd heard such a tale. Queen laughed so hard, and slapped her leg just remembering it. Rodrigo hopped down from my lap and ran down the hall to take cover. Queen stood up, demonstrating how she'd spun the wheel and showing me the look she'd had on her face when she realized she was *giving the world a free show* as she called it.

When our laughter died down, she saw by the look on my face that I hadn't just come to laugh. I was clearly waiting for her to give me a bit of her sage advice.

"Miss Thang, when situations like that happen, you got to take stock. Thas all. I know it feels like your whole lil' life's done gone up in flames, but you got to sit down an write you a list, memorize it, recite it out loud while you walk Lil' Man. You got to remind yourself a all the thangs you still got thas in good order."

I nodded, but my furrowed brow exposed the fact that I needed some help in actually executing it all. She plopped down beside me using her big black fingers on one hand to keep count.

"First thang on that list should be, you got a momma an a daddy who love you."

I opened my mouth to protest, but she shook her head.

"Now, I didn't say they know *how* to love you, or that it's the kinda a love you need, but they *do* love you, only way they know how an that counts for somethin."

Closing my mouth, I resigned myself to listen.

"Second thang, you got friends. You got me an Lil' Man an Ms. T, an you got you a boyfriend too, what's his name again?"

"Donnie."

"Yeah, you got you a Donnie, an he whatin even there when you fell out in front a all them people. The third, maybe the most important, thang is that you're a smart cookie."

Again I opened my mouth to offer evidence to the contrary.

"Ah! Don't you dare! Don't you remember? Ain't no sense protestin. It's a losin game, chil', a losin game."

Likely having heard his name dropped all the way from where he was resting in the back, Rodrigo ran out and jumped up in my lap.

"Number four is, you're a do gooder. You always helpin me an Ms. T an I bet you help your momma too."

"Not as much as I should." I confessed.

"Sounds like you at least try. From the way you talk lately, she needs more help than you qualified to give anyway, mmm hmmm. Sure does. Number five, well five an six, you rich an you white. Them right there are two thangs that give you a leg up in this here life. More than you'll ever know."

She went on about how all those things had nothing to do with any old pageant, and stood firm as reasons that it hadn't amounted to anything. By the time I was ready to go, she had me convinced.

"Take stock. Thas what you do, chil'. Take stock." she reminded me as I walked out the back door.

I stopped on the porch, and turned back. With Rodrigo wriggling in her arms between us, I hugged her tight.

"How do you know so much?" I asked.

She let Lil' Man back inside the house so she didn't drop him.

"Whew, chil'. Now I cain't tell you that."

"Why?" I pressured her.

Patting my head with one of her huge, manicured hands she replied, "Cause I didn't come by it no easy way. Sure didn't. An if I told you, it'd turn your hair jus as white as you are. Then your momma'd have my hide for sure."

"You better get on inside. Weatherman says there's a doozy comin an I got to get to work." she warned looking up at the black clouds in the distance.

I all but skipped home replaying all the things she'd counted out for me. There was no question she was right about mother and daddy, the friends and the being white and rich. The rest of it, the *do-gooder and the smart* one part, I didn't think I agreed with just yet.

Until that day, I'd never thought about being white as something to take stock of. I'd taken it for granted like having food in my cupboards, or clothes in my closet. I wondered how being black had made Queen's life harder. I wondered if it would be worse, to be white and a fake woman or black and a fake woman. I realized the longer I knew her, the more I thought of her as a just a woman. There was nothing fake about her.

There were so many things I had not pondered in my little life there in Murfeesboro. I supposed they were the very things that made mother and Daddy purposefully choose to live there to keep from ever crossing my mind.

Strange how they found me anyway.

For some reason that whole year, all the things they'd tried to keep out, things like the diverse nature of sexuality itself, racism, my own womanhood, and my very independence, all joined forces to come pounding on our door like a battering ram. Looking back, I see that nothing was spared. Nothing was left unscathed, not even their seemingly perfect union.

The Cop

When he'd reported for duty the day after their *opportune interlude* and there'd been no repercussions, no talking to by the sheriff, he'd proceeded with his usual tasks. They'd been in the diner a few times since that night, and he'd pretended not to be watching for *it* to emerge from the back or pop in the front door to take *its* place at the regiser. Tom was the first to comment on *its* absence.

"Wonder what Lisa'd have to say if I ask her where the dyke is." Tom muttered under his breath.

Carter shrugged. He'd taken one look at *it*, that night out back playing basketball with the trash bags and known *it* would never be one to cause any real trouble. He'd surmised that *it* being what *it* was, was trouble enough to bear. Somehow Carter had this gift, a knack for knowing who'd be tight lipped. Too embarrassed by the very nature of the deed to ever speak a word of it. He could pick out those who loathed themselves so much, they'd even take some, if not all, of the blame.

Lisa was up front. It seemed to him that the look on her face, as she rang people out, was one of worry, one of trepidation. An emotion with which Carter was most familiar, well versed in identifying it as it was one he readily called forth eversince he could remember. However, it was not directed at him this time. He was invisible to her. He was immediately compelled to change this somehow, some way.

"I don't think they're called dykes if they were born a man." he corected Tom.

This was one of the times that his partner's ignorance disgusted him. Tom drank the last of his coffee, wiped his mouth with his sleeve.

"You a queer expert now are you?" Tom laughed.

He did not dignify this with a reply, only picked his ticket up from the table, moved out from the booth, and walked over to the register. Lisa took his ticket without looking up.

"That'll be $6.45" she muttered.

Reaching into his pocket, he pulled out a ten-dollar bill sliding it across the counter. She reached for it. He made sure their hands touched again by moving his forward at just the right second. Her knee jerk reaction was to not to draw it back until she looked up, registering then who it belonged to. She quickly pulled her hand out of reach without so much as even a fakey smile. He noted however, that she did not exactly frown either.

"How's it goin Carter?" she asked out of polite necessity.

"Fine. And yourself?" he took his turn.

"Alright." she answered.

Moving in beside him, Tom plunked his ticket down on the counter. She finished Carter's transaction, handed him his change.

"Where's that flashy friend a yours?" Tom blurted.

Lisa turned her gaze towards him, searched his face, tried to think of a good reason he'd be asking this. They had never been anything but abrasive to Queen when they came in. It was clear to Carter that Tom's sudden, and odd interest alone was cause for suspicion. As he often had to in social situations where his partner was concerned, Carter took the reins.

"Bet you're glad to be outta that hot box of a grill." Carter gibed with an uncharacteristic wink.

She bit her lip, slowly nodding. He saw that he was too late. They'd been added to her list of suspects. The one that was getting longer by the hour. The one she'd been adding to in her head since the night her *friend* came home looking like *it* did. They walked out like it was any other day, and it was to him. He felt certain that his gut was right. That *the Queen* would not talk, and even if *it* did, nothing could be proven this many days after the incident.

He dropped Tom off at the station after work. They'd foregone their usual Monday night football games since he'd finagled Lara's lawyer into giving him joint custody. The two of them still had their work lunches though, and that would have to suffice what with the baby around more and more.

For the first few weeks afterwards, they'd tried to continue with their ritual, yet the baby always cried. Tom would have to jump up and hold him, or prepare bottles. It was no use.

On the last Monday that they'd made their futile attempt, he'd been asked to hold the child while Tom took a call. The baby didn't cry that time, only sat chewing on the nipple of its bottle looking at him warily then glancing back down the hall as if biding the seconds until his daddy reappeared. Not wanting to lose his chance, he leaned in to deliver a secret he felt this miniature version of Tom should be privy to.

"We were fine before you." Carter whispered.

The baby stared back. If he hadn't known better, he thought he saw the boy's mouth curve into a tiny grin of satisfaction. Though he'd never be sure as Tom stalked back into the living room and scooped him off his lap. Since that night, he'd made excuses anytime he was asked to come over. It didn't take long before the invitations ceased.

A few of the locals waved as he turned his cruiser onto the street he'd come to know well. A street that, until Lisa's return, he hadn't visited since high school, but that he now found himself frequenting. As he sat across from their house, he looked for any signs that *it* might have up and left town. He hoped he'd been successful in driving *it* from the place he himself had called home most of his adolescent and now adult life.

The curtains were drawn, but *its* car still sat in the driveway. This didn't have to mean anything. *It* could've had Lisa drop *it* off at the airport or the bus station. Reaching under his seat, he pulled out a large Ziploc bag. Its contents were one tube of lipstick and one candy-apple-red stiletto.

Running his hands along the top of the plastic, he debated which one to keep, which one would come in most handy if his adversary had foolishly chosen to remain. He opened the glove compartment removing one of the rubber gloves they kept for bagging evidence and slipped it on. Shoe in gloved hand, he opened his door, looked both ways, performing a quick surveillance of the neighborhood. Seeing no one, he darted across to their porch, and rang the bell.

Once back inside the safe confines of his car, he sat up, and waited. No one came, and just as he was about to open the door rush back and confiscate it once more when, the door opened a crack. A chihuahua came strutting out, inspected the item, then the door opened wider. *It* leaned out in *its* plush bathrobe, leaning down, picking up the *gift* that had been delivered.

Queen looked up, spotting the onlooker who tipped his uniform hat as he slowly rolled by. Carter made certain that he didn't take his eyes off *it* until *it* commanded *its* dog to get back inside, and slammed the door. Having no reason to hide the sheer enjoyment this brought him, Carter laughed out loud.

The plastic bag containing the tube of lipstick sat on the passenger seat. The reason he'd chosen to keep it and not the shoe, he did not yet know, but it somehow seemed more important. It was one of his inexplicable notions. He'd learned to heed these as they often guided his rudderless ship to the next shore.

Opening the glove box, he placed the bag back inside and snapped the rubber glove from his hand. He tossed it out the window. From where he surveyed it in his rearview mirror, he saw it whisked into the air, coming to land on the side of the road. There it lay - bright blue latex against the dirt. It struck him as looking very out of place.

The Tranny

Changin your name don't change you. There was a time I thought it could. Thought if I gave myself a name that had some kinna power, nobody could touch me. Layin in our bed, I listen for Lisa to lock the front door an head on to the restaurant. Tol' her I'll go tomorrow. I been sayin that for a whole week.

She ain't one to nag or dig, but I know I cain't keep this up. It's drivin her plumb crazy an leavin em shorthanded at work. I don't want to stay here. I don't, but I cain't describe it. It's like somebody's got their hands around my throat every time I step out that door.

Was about to pull myself up by the straps a my purple slingbacks an get on down there when I opened up the door an saw his ass settin outside. Had the gaul to bring the shoe I left behind too. I came right in an buried that thang at the bottom a the trash.

I was wrong about him. He's one a the million thangs I been wrong about. Like thinkin if I'm nice enough, people won't mind what's goin on under my hood. Like if I keep a knock out figure an wear my make up like a movie star, people won't be none the wiser that I whatin born with what's under there now. That Manny was gonna be the love a my life. That me an Lisa's love is enough to conquer all. That movin here was gonna be a new start.

Lil' Miss Thang's gonna be comin by later on. I been keepin real quiet an she thinks I'm at work, jus goes on lettin Lil' Man out for his walk like she *always does. I don't want her to see me like this. She thinks I hang the moon. Want to keep it that a way cause she might be the only one who does anymore.*

Slingin my legs over the side a the bed, I pat the blanket next to me showin Rodrigo I want him to jump up. He just looks at me then turns right around an trots down the hallway. You know you bad off when your own dog cain't stand your ass. Mmmm hmmm. I put on my robe an follow him.

I set down at the kitchen table, look at another cake Lisa's made me. She's been makin all my favorites tryin to make me snap out of it. Hadn't wanted to touch a single one of em. Throwed half of em out back in the trash can, acted like I ate em while she was gone. Our life's becomin a whole mess a actin. An it ain't the kind nobody's linin up to give me any Oscar for neither.

Not wantin to eat, not gettin outta this house, or seein Lil' Miss Thang, those alone hadn't been that worrisome. I've had spells like this before. When momma died, I stayed hold up in our apartment nearly a month. Lisa thought it might help so she sent for Jarvis. She hadn't ever met him. She was jus pure outta other options in her mind. He whatin on our couch five minutes when she realized callin him was a big mistake, like pourin gasoline on a forest fire. Mmmm hmmm. She hadn't never called him again. Knows better. Knows he's worlds away from bein a solution. Knows he's a problem all his own.

This time's worse. Only way I know it, is cause even lookin up at Tina up there on my wall don't bring me a bit a comfort. Makes me feel worse. She ain't never had that effect. Always been a source a strength I drew from, but not this time. Now all I see when I look at her is a source a shame. Somebody who wouldn't never be handlin thangs the way I am right now.

Takin a cup a tea back to the bedroom, I put it on the night table an open up my bottom dresser drawer. Momma's night gown. I slip it on an lay down. Rubbin my hands on the silky sleeves, I feel like I'm right there next to her, layin beside her, listenin to her tell me one a her stories about growin up back in her day. Those tales sure made me glad I was born when I was.

A lot a her talk was about how tough thangs were. I figure you a live in a hard time like that, it makes an impression. She liked to tell us how when it turned winter they had to put on all their clothes an tiptoe to the outhouse in the dead a night jus to "make water". An then there was how they had to pile rugs on their beds to keep warm when the fire went out. She didn't never rub it in how much easier we had it, but when she talked about it, you'd feel that way all on your own.

Rodrigo jumps up on my stomach. For the first time in days, I laugh. Cuddlin him to me, I curl up in a ball, hold him close. Don't take long for my laughin turns to cryin. He don't squirm to get down. He lays here tryin to be what I need.

When I was bout four or five we had this woman who lived down the street. Momma'd do some cleanin for her to make ends meat. She had herself a little lap dog with a jeweled collar. Barked its fool head off any time we got near it. That lady spoiled him, gave him steak on china plates. Momma'd tell us how the lady combed him, put him on his own fancy pilla. She'd laugh an say, "I wish I was somebody's little dog."

Wonder if Rodrigo remembers life before me an Lisa,? Havin to scrounge for food, gettin under dumpsters when it rained, fendin off other dogs. With how tiny he is, mighta seen his fair share a scrapes with cats too. Maybe he don't remember. Maybe dogs don't work like us. Maybe they move to a new place, get them a new name an they got theyselves a clean slate.

Don't know why I cain't be that way. Be glad I am who I am an that Lisa took me out from under a dumpster too. Til that night there in his car, I was comin out on the other side. It was like I was crossin the street to the greener grass, but he done revved his engine an run me clean over fore I could get there.

Cain't let him win! I tell myself this a hundred times a day, but then I go in the bathroom, or take a shower, see my cuts still healin up an know he already has. How you gonna keep fightin when you down for the count an the other guy's already got the trophy in his hand doin his victory walk round the ring?

I pull the sheet up over me an Lil' Man, make us a tent. Don't know what I'm gonna do. Don't have to right now. I'm gonna give it one more day. Thas all I need…one more day…

The Girl

There were few constants in my life in those days. Since the pageant debacle, hardly a day went by when mother and Daddy weren't fighting about something. I'd lived long enough to know it wasn't my fault, that the incident had only awakened, exposed in plain sight, a plethora of problems they'd managed to keep swept under the rug.

"We're just going through growing pains." Daddy assured me one evening after yet another one of their loud shouting matches they'd become comfortable with having. "This kind of thing happens when you've known each other as long as we have."

He'd thought this would serve to console me. Little did he know that this was the worst thing he could've said. He had no way to know about how Mary Hough in my gym class had sat in front of her locker for all of to see, bawling her eyes out. When we finally persuaded her to tell us what was wrong, she'd wailed on about how her parents were getting a divorce. Among the many things she spouted was something her mother told her: "when you've known each other as long as we have..."

The thought of my parents going their separate ways didn't disturb me in the ways it should have. There were nights after mother went on one of her tirades over my weight, that I had indeed prayed for it to happen. The only thing about it that caused me anxiety was the question of whether or not Daddy would keep me or if mother would instead have custody the majority of the time. His schedule alone would be the deciding factor. Remembering this, I would then do a three sixty and pray my little heart out that they'd remain together.

"My parents fight all the time." Donnie told me on one of our walks home from school.

"What do they fight about?" I asked.

"You name it. Don't really matter. T.J. says it's just how they talk.

Says they don't know any other way to be. Says we should worry when they quit fighting."

I watched him as he picked up rocks and launched them at his usual entourage who were riding their bikes up ahead. He pelted the smallest one, Gary, right on the arm causing him to hightail it back our way, hop off his bike and attempt to tackle Donnie to the ground.

They tumbled down the embankment while I stood at the top shaking my head. When we first started hanging out, this kind of rough housing unnerved me, but by then I came to understand this was how they played. That like many things about Donnie's world, what was customarily thought of as *bad* was, in fact, *good*.

"I gotta go!" I shouted down.

"Where?" Donnie yelled up.

"To walk Rodrigo."

Gary untangled himself from the hold Donnie had him in. Wiping pieces of grass from his mouth, he glared up at me.

"You sure spend a lot a time over at that faggots." Gary accused.

Putting my hands on my hips, readying to properly school him on politically correct terms and whatnot.

"Queen is not a faggot. She's *trans* and there's a big difference. I looked it up on my Daddy's laptop." I fired back.

Donnie hopped up brushing off his pants, extending a hand to Gary.

They climbed the hill. The other boys, who by now had also pedaled back, came to a stop beside us.

"You ever see anything worth *seein* over there?" Gary pried.

I looked at Donnie. He looked at the ground. From their lunch table banter, I gathered that I was the only one whose thievery stopped at the corner store. There were snippets of conversation about electronics swiped from people's cars, items snatched from backyards that had no outdoor dogs to be leery of.

At times, I was aware that in their limited little universe it was likely they didn't know who my father was, and I certainly wasn't going to tell them. Every cute girl who sashayed by our lunch table reminded me of the fact that my status hung by a thin thread as it was.

"Yeah, anything you think they wouldn't miss?" Another boy I'd heard them call Vance interjected.

This was the first time he'd spoken to me directly. Though I steered clear of him most of the time, in some weird way I felt honored that he finally acknowledged me. He was the loose cannon in their makeshift gang. One of the times he'd gone off, had sent him to juvey. From what Donnie told me, that's why we hadn't seen Vance for the last year.

Standing by the side of the road, I looked across at the woods I daily cut through to get to Queen's. Something in me already knew that no matter what I said, it wouldn't satisfy them. They wouldn't believe me. They would have to look for themselves, but I knew I had to do my best to put out the embers of their curiosity.

"Nah, she's got nothin but clothes an shoes, just a lot of junk." I said with an air of *big and badness* I felt certain would help me maintain my place for at least one more day.

"That ain't true. That little rat dog would sell for a hundred bucks easy at the flea market. Maybe we can nab him an you can just tell him it got away from you an run off while you was walkin it?" Gary suggested.

Whirling around, I gave Donnie a look that I felt clearly communicated I was in need of bailing out. He only picked up another handful of rocks chucking a few at a mailbox. I was on my own. In that second I was not as in love as much as I was in a state of fear. Not fearful that he wouldn't love me, but gripped with a fear that if he didn't, no one would. That I'd go back to the being lumped in with the dregs of junior high, eating alone, no one paying any attention to me. The thought of falling off the social ladder I'd worked so hard to scale was unthinkable.

"Nah, he's too old. Nobody's gonna pay for an old dog. People want puppies." I stated.

A couple of the *natives* shifted restlessy on their bikes. Vance took a cigarette and a lighter out of his back pocket. He cut his eyes at me as he lit it. I hadn't fooled him. To this day, I'd tell you that in the moment I did it as much to save Rodrigo as I did to save Queen. I'd come to love that little dog as my own. No matter the reason, what followed was one of the most idiotic things that's ever come out of my mouth.

"Now if you want the good stuff, that lady across from Queen's, Ms. Terrell, now she's loaded. Always ordering jewelry and all kinds of stuff from the home shopping channel." I blurted.

"Oh yeah? Like what?" Donnie suddenly entered the discussion.

"I'm not sure. All I know is she usually has to sign for the boxes. Has to be some good shit if they don't just leave it on her porch." I embellished, having thrown in a curse word for effect. As I said it, I pictured my mother simultaneously standing in the supermarket having the first of many in a long line of inevitable heart attacks.

I slunk off through the woods as they headed to Donnie's. I hoped I had scattered enough crumbs to throw them off the scent for the time being. I'd at the very least managed to divert them from rummaging through Queen's house, and most of all I'd bought myself some time. They wouldn't do anything about Ms. Terrell's in the immediate future. I would figure out something. If I got lucky they'd find someone else's place to pillage all on their own and I'd be off the hook.

Standing at the bottom of Queen's steps, I thought about how I loved seeing that door; that back door Lisa'd painted a bright turquoise with flowers in bright pots littering the small porch in front of it. It struck me that this was a constant. In the temperamental world in which I lived, this one thing I could count on. Opening the door, Lil' Man running to me, Queen's kindness to me when she happened to be home and our walks. This put me at ease in a way nothing had before.

When I opened Queen's back door that day however, things weren't right. Rodrigo was nowhere to be seen. There were no lights on. An unsettling silence filled the air. Queen always left E T.V. on for Lil' Man. She said it was so he could tell her all the celebrity gossip when she got home from work. She also said that dog loved him some Britney Spears.

I briefly considered that she'd taken him to the vet, or since it was Friday, maybe they'd all finally gone on one of those weekend trips she and Lisa were always planning, but never got around to. I was about to shut the door and head home, but then I heard my name. I stopped, listened, and heard it softly whispered a second time.

Stepping further inside, I craned my neck to see Lisa sitting at the kitchen table. Since she was usually at work when Queen and I passed the time, our paths had only ever crossed a handful of times. She'd always been polite and pleasant though. She motioned for me to sit across from her.

"How's it going?" she asked in a hushed tone.

"Okay." I mouthed.

Lifting the lid off the cake plate in front of me, she lopped off a slice of the carrot cake. I couldn't believe there was any left. Carrot cake was Queen's favorite. Lil' Man wasn't around either...that's when I got the idea that all hell had broken loose. Tears welled up in my eyes as it crossed my overly dramatic mind that Queen had gotten hurt or worse died!

"Hey, hey, what's wrong now?" Lisa asked.

"Where's Queen? Where's Lil' Man?" I blurted.

She leaned forward, putting her hands on the table, then clasping them together as if she was about to pray. She lowered her head.

"She's in there asleep and he's right beside her." Lisa reassured.

I breathed a sigh of relief.

"Queen's always going on and on about *Charlotte Grace this and Charlotte Grace that*. She sure likes you. I know you an me haven't talked much before with me working so much and all, but I have a favor to ask." she went on.

She looked up. Our eyes met. I felt the enormity of whatever it was that was coming. No adult had ever really asked anything of me, not anything noteworthy.

"Sure." I told her, sitting up tall.

I could tell this made her feel better. She eased back against her chair, took a bite of her cake.

"Queen ever tell you how we met?"

I shook my head no.

"Yeah, well she whatin Queen back then." she confessed.

"Who was she?" I boldly inquired, mouthful of my own cake, scooting up in my seat.

"Jermaine. She was Jermaine Braxton. Came to work everyday in these sorry ass jeans and *gangsta* T's. Given it his dead level best to be all *man*." she laughed, dabbing a finger in a clump of icing on her plate.

I took another bite. An unfamiliar feeling washed over me - a feeling of importance, of being essential in some way. The way you feel when someone tells you something you know they've never told anyone else.

"Didn't turn into Queen overnight. Naw, Queen was a long time comin. Started for I ever knew him, though. Still remember the day he told me. Sat me down by him on the beach down there in Tallahassee. Florida beaches are something. You ever been?"

My lips glued together with cream chees frosting, I only managed to shake my head no.

"She sat me down, well, *he* sat me down an he told me all about who he wanted to be. I can tell you, it whatin easy. It whatin a thang anybody ever plans on, but I respected him. Respected that he knew what he wanted in this world an that was more than I could say for myself. It didn't change that I loved him, loved everything about him. By then we'd been through our fair share of mess together an we understoond each other. You know? Really understood each other. We saw each other for who we were and we didn't run away from it. We ran towards each other."

I stared back at her as I licked the last bit of icing from my fork. She smiled recognizing a girl my age couldn't fully ascertain the mess she was describing.

"I just loved how he got up every mornin even though life had dealt him a bad hand more times than he could count an still tried to see the beauty of things. Even saw the beauty in me when there wasn't much to see. Most people woulda cashed in their chips if they'd a lived half of his life, but not him."

Her smile fell into a lip-biting grimace. She put a hand up to her head, rubbed her temples.

"The thing is...do you think you might talk to her? She's real outta sorts, I cain't get her to tell me why an I...I've tried everything I know to try. This isn't like her. She can usually see her way clear after a while, an she loves you. Thinks the world of you. Always goin on and on about you. Loves you to pieces. Thought maybe if you talk to her, she'll snap out of it." Lisa pleaded.

The only thing I knew to do was nod. As she cleared the dishes, put the lid back on the cake plate. She informed me she had to get back to the diner. The front door shut. All I could do was sit there. It was just me with the task ahead staring me down.

My mind raced with what I would say. I ran through all the go-to-things I'd heard people say to make someone feel better. Things like *there's a light at the end of every tunnel, when the going gets tough the tough get going.*

Oh, and there was the one that Daddy always said *be the change you want to see*, but none of those seemed to fit.

Part of me wanted to bolt. The part of me that hated doing anything that resembled something difficult or stressful wanted to run for the door, but I knew if I chickened out I'd lay in bed that night, maybe every night after, tossing and turning. Mostly, I knew that Queen wouldn't run. When I told her about Donnie and about the pageant, she stepped up to the plate. She'd told me about taking the time to list things out, about taking stock.

I sat for what seemed like forever trying to think of something wonderful or inspiring and coming up blank. Just when I thought I'd have to give up, I lifted my head, and there she was on that Vegas stage, Tina hanging there above the T.V. and I knew. I knew exactly what I had to say.

The Cop

He stood in the hallway watching as the water flowed from under the bathroom door. His father had naively dropped him off without ensuring that his mother was home. Most people would have said that was negligent. He was only six. They would have said he should have been walked up to the door, but it was his father's weekend off. So eager was he for time away, that the usual concerns had not occurred to him.

His new girlfriend was to accompany him on a trip they'd planned to the beach. When he'd hinted that he wished they'd let him come along rather than visit his mother, his father hadn't batted an eye while, informing him there was no chance. His visits with his mother had become increasingly dull, if not borderline sad. She had not done well with living on her own. Even her friends, who still came by now and again, only did so out of pity.

The water crept closer to his feet. This wasn't like her. In spite of it all, she had maintained a degree of tidiness. It was one of the few qualities left over from her married days, and he knew she would never want to see her hardwood floors ruined.

Removing his shoes, and socks, he inched down the hallway and came to stand outside the bathroom door.

"Mother?" he called out, gently tapping on the door.

No answer. He did not open it. Partly out of respect, but partly out of wanting to delay discovering what he felt certain would greet him on the other side. His steps made it sound as if he was in a marshy swamp as he hurriedly sloshed back down the hallway to the kitchen. By his estimation, he'd concluded that he'd have a small window of time before the water overtook the house entirely.

Taking hold of the stool that sat under the telephone, he scooted it into the pantry, teetered carefully on it, using it to take the chocolate syrup down from the top shelf. The blessed stuff that she only doled out every now and then if he was good. Opening the fridge, he took out the carton of milk and poured himself a glass. He made sure to leave enough room for the sugary goodness to be added.

Retrieving a spoon out from the drawer, he stirred the syrup. He watched it swirl and churn the white liquid into a dark, tantalizing brown. His mouth salivated at the sight. It was so dark and thick that if someone had come in they would have mistaken it for the oil he'd seen his dad put in the car.

Sitting up to the kitchen table, he looked out the window, stopping to observe the mailman as he placed their mail in the box - only one letter, likely an ad or other junk. No one wrote to her. She was not important. Even at his age, he recognized this. Her relationship with his father had been the last thing that had given her any real value.

One more glass followed, then another, and before he knew it, he'd drank the last drop of milk. There was still some syrup, however. All that mattered then was how he would go about obtaining more of that vital ingredient. By that point, the water had crept out onto the living room floor, and even the rug in the entry way was sopping wet.

His damp shoes squished and squeaked as he stalked out of the front door over to the neighbors. They were his best chance. They had a baby - a baby meant milk. It didn't take more than two knocks before the woman opened the door to him.

"Carter, how are you?" she asked smiling down, baby on her hip.

"Fine, ma'am. I was wondering if you could spare some milk? We're all out." He politely requested like a little businessman, with manners he'd seen his father use whenever necessary.

She looked past him, searching the sidewalk for the adult that must surely not be too far behind.

"Where's your mom, hon?"

He didn't answer, only batted his eyes, hoping she wouldn't dwell on this, but would go ahead and deliver what he'd come for.

"Wait here." she instructed.

Ducking inside, she quickly re-emerged. Milk carton in hand, she insisted on walking him home, baby and all. He reluctantly complied as it was his only means of getting what he craved. The baby cried the whole way. He wished she'd left it at home.

As he opened his door for her, water trickled under their feet and out onto the porch. He paid it no mind, sloshing forward, and going inside. He picked his glass up off the table. Walking over to her, he held it out, yet she was too distracted by the state of things to readily comply.

"Denise? Denise?" she loudly called down the empty, water coated hall.

He raised the glass higher. She hurriedly opened the milk then poured some in hopes of appeasing and distracting him. This pleased him.

He pranced back into the kitchen to prepare yet a fourth glass of his blessed chocolate concoction. Needing to know the cause of the catastrophe, the neighbor inched further towards the door at the end of the hall, the only door that was closed.

As he squeezed the syrup, there was the sound of knocking. The baby continued to squall. He stirred the milk watching it turn the coveted murky hue. There was the sound of a door opening, and the baby squalling louder. He lifted the glass to his lips, closed his eyes so as to enjoy it more fully, and shut out their racket. Lastly, there was the sound of the woman shrieking.

"Denise! Oh God! Denise!"

He set his glass down on the table. With his small hand, he wiped the milky mustache from his upper lip. He needed a refill. He turned, setting out to petition the woman yet again. Maybe she'd let him pour it this time.

The Tranny

Anna Mae Bullock wouldn't a got up off the floor an left Ike. No, she stayed there for years bein his dog, but Tina, now Tina was a different story. Thas what Lil' Miss Thang reminded me of yesterday when she busted in my bedroom. There I was, Rodrigo curled up with me, wallowin in my misery. She threw open that door, like to took it off its hinges, mmm hmmm.

She stood there hands on her hips, jerked my blanket off an gave me the scoldin I needed. Later that night, I tol' Lisa that for a white girl, that girl sure went black on my ass. Had to try real hard not to laugh while it was happenin. Not on account of it bein funny, but on account a I hadn't never seen her get so worked up. Her gettin all fired up mighta blowed me outta that room on it's own.

Lil' Man took one look at her an knew she meant business too. He ran off an got under the couch. Wished I coulda fit under there with him. She went off about how she whatin sure what was ailin me, but whatever it was, I was still alive so stayin in bed whatin no way to live. Raved an ranted bout how there I'd been tellin her to take stock a couple weeks ago, an now there I was coverin up my head. Lord, if she didn't go an throw in the word "hypocrite" somewhere along the line. She must go to a damn good school.

Halfway through, jus when I thought she was give out from all that fussin, she walked over an fumbled through my CD box on the dresser, found one I've *played for her several times, put it in the player an skipped to that song. The one Queen a Rock song she somehow thought would seal the deal: Something Beautiful Remains. Lil' Miss Thang sat on the edge of the bed an we listened to Tina sing out, "And you wonder sometimes how we carry on when you've lost the love you knew, but it's alright, it's alright. To your own heart be true. Tears will leave no stains. Time will ease the pain. For every life that fades, something beautiful remains."*

I scooted up beside her. Rested my head on her shoulder, put my arms around her. She reached over an patted my cheek with one hand an then my hand with her other. Lookin at her hand on mine, I knew there's no way in hell she coulda known. No way she could known this was the very same song Lisa played for me when momma died. Played it to break the spell a agony that had taken hold of me.

Tears came crashin down my face. I squeezed her hand. In that second, seein her pale lil' hand under my dark chocolate one, I knew God hadn't forgotten me. All this time I thought I was on his shitlist an that he'd a been happy to see me crushed under his feet, but here he was. Here he was settin right here beside me in the body a Miss Charlotte Grace Danby. An I knew, if he could see fit to shine through her, jus maybe he had some shinin left to do through me.

Lisa grins ear to ear watchin me get dressed this mornin. I know I scared her. Specially when I didn't have one bite a her carrot cake. The ol' Baptist side a her probly checked out the winda to make sure the sky whatin fallin an Armagedon hadn't started.

I put on my makeup as I listen to her fill me in on what's been goin on at the restaurant. Talkin bout how some people's takin to the new look an some people got some new complaint every time they come in, but it don't stop em from comin in. Lisa says she figures it's her lot in life to give the complainers something to do, an how we all got to do what we can for our fellow man.

I comb out my wig, an watch her rub Lil' Man's belly. He's my boy, but when she does that, he's all hers. He don't like neither of us near as much as he loves him some Charlotte Grace. I'm grateful he's got a friend an all, but somedays I got to admit I'm jealous all the same.

Lisa an Lil' Miss Thang are cut from the same cloth. Both of em good at comfortin an lightin a fire under my ass when I need it. Strikes me that the women I've loved most in my life are that a way. Momma sure nough was. Strong as hell that woman.

Fore I had my reassignment, I had to go see one a them head doctors. A surgeon, if he's worth his salt, wants to make sure you ain't jus wantin snipped an clipped cause you had a fucked up childhood, an I ain't one to argue it came in to play for me, but it sure whatin my only reason.

We got to talkin bout the influential people in my life. He listened to me tell him about my grandmother, my momma, a couple a my best girl friends in high school, then Lisa an thas when he asked me if I had any men who I could recall had a good effect on me. I sat there an wasted damn near ten dollars a his time an mine tryin to think a one, but I couldn't. Even though he signed my paperwork, he wrote on his notes that he couldn't be sure if I wanted the surgery due to, how did he put it… "a lack a positive experiences with my own gender". First time I read that, I was pissed. The more I thought on it though, the more I couldn't help but agree… Knew he was probly onto somethin, but it whatin no reason not to see it through.

Lisa stretches out, puts one foot on the floor an then the other, asks me if Lil' Miss Thang's comin by for Lil' Man today. I nod. Then it hits me full force. Lil' Miss Thang…another woman to add to that list. Another Wonder Woman who's saved my day.

.

Cain't help it I keep addin to that side a the list. Ain't no man ever stepped up. God knows that cop bastard's on the same side as my cousin, Manny, an Jarvis. Ain't a man I know who hadn't been a villain I've had to fight. Fixin my wig on my head, thought crosses my mind that Jermaine's been the main one I done had to take up arms against. Some days I ain't convinced I won that battle yet. Gettin up, Lisa slips her arms around my shoulders, she rests her head on one side. We look at us there in the mirror.

"You know I love you." she reminds me.

"Right back at you, honey."

She smiles, then gets that serious look she gets when she's got words to deliver that you may or may not be ready to hear. Lord only knows what's comin.

"If you ever wanna tell me what happened, you know you can, but it won't change a thing between us if you decide you don't ever want to utter a word about it to me or another livin soul."

Holdin me tighter, she kisses my neck.

"Only person you have to tell is you. Gotta admit it, face it head on so you can move on." she whispers in my ear.

She releases me, I pat her arm fore she heads out. I call to her that I'm right behind her. My arms shake. I blink back tears. Cain't mess my mascara. Ain't got time to do it over, an ain't wantin to waste one more drop a water on him.

"It's done, but you still here." I tell myself out loud. *"Cain't go back. Cain't undo it, but you the beautiful thang that remains. Mmmm hmmm. You, Queen Mae Braxton. You the beautiful thang that remains."*

The Girl

A junior high cafeteria is not just a place to eat. What I ate was the last thing I thought about when I walked in there every day around noon. Mother presumed I'd been losing weight due to her watchful eye, and Weight Watchers dinners. Little did she know that the sole culprit was the change in my lunch seat.

In sixth grade, I had nebulously matriculated to the back tables. I had not been banished there unwillingly like some who committed such faux pas as kissing the boy with the most acne, wearing dental headgear or joining educationally stimulating afterschool clubs. It had happened to me simply by my lack of association with anyone who sat at the other tables.

On that particular day, I became acutely aware of my upward trajectory through the ranks. From the spiteful looks given by the girls who passed by, I could tell they too were well aware that luck had been my ally. In their books, I had done nothing to deserve to be sitting with Donnie and his disciples. I had, in fact, bypassed all the things they toiled over on a regular basis - the small amounts of food they allowed themselves, hours of primping, the purchase of new clothes every chance they got, shaving legs that barely needed shaving, cutesy waving, and the swooning they'd lavished on him since grade school.

As I picked at my lunch however, I found that I was not fully glorying in this as I should have been. After the boy's inquiries about who'd be a better candidate for their next heist, I did not feel as much a part of Donnie's group. I was becoming aware that I was a prop, an inconsequential inroad in to the neighborhood adjacent theirs. The one through the woods that they'd only peered at from behind the trees. The wall of forestry that separated them, left them drooling at the thought of what they could only guess lay inside our huge homes just ripe for the taking.

"You gonna eat those?" Gary asked as he reached and took a handful of fries from my plate.

"Man, get your own!" Donnie chastised, swatting at his hand. "You already broke again?"

"Naw! It's just if she ain't gonna eat em, ain't no reason for em to go to waste." Gary lashed back.

Lila snuck up behind him, playfully squeezing his shoulders.

"Hey yall." she greeted them, sucker dangling from the side of her mouth.

She looked at me quickly making sure I knew she was aware of my threatening presence. This served to establish the alpha female vibe, and let me know that I was not yet to have the honor of her actually speaking to me. Leaning down, the tops of her rapidly growing breasts were exposed to everyone, myself included. I blushed and turned away. The rest of the table didn't even look twice. Donnie continued eating his burger, paying her no attention whatsoever.

From what I could gather about Lila, she was old news to most. She'd shown everyone at that table everything she owned, and no one had come back for seconds. No one but Gary. He'd been hooked from the get go. He dug down in the pocket of his dirty jeans.

"Got you somethin."

He pulled out a silver necklace with a heart charm attached to it. As he held it up, and I recognized it as being one of the signature Tiffany necklaces that had become so popular. You couldn't get them anywhere near our town, maybe in Atlanta, but not necessarily. I was familiar with them only because

Daddy had brought Mother one from New York City when he'd flown there to track down a witness.

It seemed a waste to bestow such a gift on the likes of Lila. She wouldn't have known the difference between it and Walmart jewelry. I pictured her laid out on her bed in her trailer with paneled walls, crudely hung boy band posters, gabbing about it on the phone to all her friends.

"Gary!" she squealed. "It's so perty!"

Without even bothering to look over her shoulder to make sure there were no teachers watching, she edged in beside him on the bench and kissed him full out on the mouth. She arched her back, giving her breasts a life of their own, then turned so he could fasten it on her faux spray-tan lotioned neck.

"How's it look?" she surprisingly asked me of all people, holding the charm out away from her skin.

"Nice." I said smiling ever so sweetly.

The first bell rang as a warning alerting us to get ready to leave for class. A large herd of girls meandered by heading for the bathroom. They had to have ample time to reapply their Cover Girl or Mabelline, whatever had been on sale at the drugstore. Lila kissed Gary's cheek then ran off to take her place in the group to show it off. The giggles and congratulatory shrieks she received echoed throughout the room.

Gary waved as she disappeared out the door then leaned in towards

Donnie motioning for him to do the same.

"I'm tapped out. That's the last at the stash from over there in Harmony Ridge. We ready for that one she was telling about?" he questioned under his breath, being sure to point slightly at me when he said *she*.

They hadn't forgotten. They had continued to talk about it after I'd gone, being sure to add it to their future plans. I had affectively steered them away from one friend's house only to shoot them, like poorly guided missiles, headlong into the house of another. The second bell rang staving off Donnie's answer. We all stood, cleared our trays, and took our places among the masses milling towards the exit.

"Ready when you are." Gary bellowed out on his way to woodshop. I followed Donnie out to our lockers. He'd procured one next to mine a few weeks prior. The only thing I'd been told about why the frail boy who had been using it before had given it to him was *he'd wanted to*. There'd been no arguing this point. I'm sure the boy had only to take one look at Donnie, backed by his crew, and had run in the opposite direction.

My hands slowly turned the dial on my combination lock. It came easily to me. Touching the steel, I remembered how I'd cried on the first day fearing I wouldn't be able to get it to work and I'd be late to class. The stress of it had been too much.

Standing there that day, however, Donnie by my side, I thought about how I'd give anything to return back to that time when opening my locker, or keeping mother off my back were the biggest problems I could fathom. You couldn't have told me that first day of seventh grade, as I cried over those numbers, that only a few short months later, I'd be toiling over whether or not to be an accomplice to a crime. I looked at Donnie next to me casually taking out his book, putting a pencil behind his ear. I knew he wasn't worth all this. More than that, I knew there was nothing I could do about it. Everything had been set in motion.

"You okay?" Donnie asked, running his hand down my arm.

I nodded.

"See ya." he dismissed me before darting off to Geometry.

I watched as he ran as fast as he could to the end of the hall. Mr. Phillips yelling at him about walking, even reaching out trying to snag his shirt. Donnie only increased his pace, rounded the corner leaving Mr. Phillips at the door of his room shaking his head. Even he knew it was no use. Everyone, the adults included, had accepted that Donnie lived by one singular rule: there were no rules.

Wandering into English, I found a seat in the back where I could look out the window. At the beginning of the year, I'd sat up front. I'd enjoyed giving Ms. Harper the right answers, but by then, I'd resigned myself to being a half-hearted participant. I was Donnie's girlfriend. This was a priviledge I'd come to realize had been afforded to me if not flat out expected of me.

If I got a B- or a C mother wouldn't be too upset since it rarely happened, and Daddy rarely looked at my report card. There was the once when I'd gotten an F in math. He was alerted immediately, and that's when I'd had to go to the tutor. I worked hard, and caught up. Eversince, he'd remained affably unaware of my progress.

There had been the occasional pondering on my part about whether or not I should get another F just for more attention. When it came down to it though, I really didn't want to have to carve out time for a tutor again. I had more important concerns, and Daddy would be far too busy to do more than yell about it for a few minutes before handing the matter off to mother. She certainly didn't need anything else to obsess about.

Ms. Harper interrupted my anxiety-riddled musings, by reading to us from the Diary of Anne Frank. She asked what we knew about World War II. Few of us knew much. One boy commented that he'd watched *Saving Private Ryan* with his dad so he knew the Germans were the enemy. From the look on Ms. Harper's face, I knew she was dismayed that most, if any, of our awareness came from telvision or movies.

She tried not to make us feel too sub par because of our ignorance. She went on to explain that Anne Frank was a Jewish girl who had lived in a small, hidden apartment with her family, and other Jews for nearly two years so they wouldn't be killed by the Nazis. Using her dry erase markers, Ms. Harper drew a diagram of their living space. It looked like it was smaller than the second floor of my house. This didn't serve to evoke gratitude as much as it served to embarrass me.

I was ashamed that there I was in a nice home, with what anyone would call a nice family, yet I'd gotten myself into the jam I was in. From the sound of her well thought out entries, Anne Frank would never have stolen from people. She wouldn't have ever given Donnie a second glance. She was too busy wondering if she'd live or die, and helping other people keep their minds off their own impending death.

As Ms. Harper read more of the diary, the words could only be classified as beautiful epiphanies about people's character, love, and the atrocities of war. Anne's love interest, Peter, seemed like a boy any girl would love - helpful, kind to his family, romantic. He was the type of boy I should've loved, but I knew a boy like that wouldn't have been interested in me. A girl all in black who sat at the rough and tough table, belonging to no after school clubs of any kind, sneaking food from any place she could.

Anne and I were the same age, but that's where our similarities stopped. I sat in that desk knowing if a war broke out the very next day, I wouldn't be able to write what she wrote. My silly journaling wouldn't be worthy of being immortalized, read to every seventh grader forevermore. Mine would consist of whining about food, complaining about mother driving me nutty, and how many chores had been heaped on me since we'd been in hiding.

I could tell by the impassioned way she read Anne's words that Ms. Harper hoped the diary would inspire us. She went on and on about how *prolific* Anne was. I wished it had inspired me, but it only depressed me. It made me think long and hard for the first time in a while about what kind of girl I was. My saving grace was when the bell rang, so I could scurry out into the hall.

The rest of the afternoon passed without incident. At the sound of the last bell, I loaded up my backpack, and filed outside among the dozens of other pre-pubescent hopefuls. I spotted Donnie and Gary and the rest of their gang in the distance, by the bus stop at the far end of the sidewalk. I stopped, looked in the other direction, and considered going that way.

"Charlotte!" Donnie beckoned.

I hung my head. The short window of opportunity was gone. My feet trudged one in front of the other, just as they'd done down the pageant runway. My stomach lurched as I accepted my place - a stand in, a tool needed so others could fulfill their seedy desires. I accepted that it was no different than my role in my parent's world, the world at large in fact. This sickened me all the more.

"Ready?" Donnie asked extending his hand.

Not everyone can be Anne Frank. Hardly anybody gets to be prolific. I thought to myself, tightening the strap on my backpack.

"Yeah." I mumbled, slipping my hand into his.

The Cop

A tight, bright pink dress was the first thing he saw through the window. It was his first inkling of failure. That his usual tactics of intimidation, ones that in previous standoffs had usually rendered an easy victory, in this case had had little to no effect. A deep-seated agitation boiled in the cauldron he called a heart.

"We gonna sit here all day or we goin in?" Tom demanded unaware of the gauntlet that had been thrown down, the standoff going on between the man beside him and the very universe itself.

Tom opened his car door not caring to wait for a reply. His life was largely ruled by his stomach and other caveman-like needs. He disappeared inside leaving Carter at the mercy of his anxieties. A few of the regular patrons exited before he made his decision.

Stepping inside, he scanned the room for *it*, but *it* was not at the register. Perhaps the garment had belonged to someone else? Perhaps Lisa had dressed up for once? Tom motioned for Carter to join him at their usual table.

As he scooted into the booth, he breathed a sigh of ease. A relief that a sense of order had been restored. The shoe had done its job. It had reminded *it* of their night in the car, while also single handedly spelling out that if *it* chose to stay, there was more where that came from.

"How you boys doin?" Mrs. Wainwright asked, unsteadily leaning on her cane as she approached the table.

"Fine, ma'am, and you?" Tom replied.

They went on to chatter about this and that. The two of them had investigated a burglary at her house over in Harmony Ridge the month before. Little of what was taken had been recovered. Carter had tracked down one diamond tennis bracelet at a local pawn shop, but the surveillance cameras showed it'd been brought in by a kid. They suspected he'd been given a few bucks to fence it for the real thief.

He listened as Tom explained this to Mrs. Wainwright. He told her the kid had worn a hoodie so as not to be identified and the shop owner had been fined for not following procedures like asking for I.D. or creating a paperwork trail of some kind. Tom explained the case was not closed and they were still hopeful they'd recover more of her jewelry like the Tiffanys necklace she'd been calling the precinct about every spare minute of her day.

"These things can take months." he told her.

"A shame these kids nowadays." she lamented shaking her head. "My own grandson turned fifteen last week. My son called me a few days ago and told me he had to find a new school for him cause he was selling marijuana, never would tell his daddy where he got it. Shame. Just a shame."

"Sure is." Tom echoed.

"Pray every Sunday the Lord will up and come. Yall keep up the good work til he does now you hear?" she admonished, as she patted Carter's shoulder.

He tipped his hat to her, and took a sip of his coffee. They both nodded a goodbye as she made her way to the register. A couple of customers were waiting ahead of her. Everyone who worked there was always Johnny on the Spot, but strangely there was no one to take the money.

The menu felt slick against his hand. Sliding his index finger down the list of words, he thought that on that day, he'd make a change. He wouldn't have his same-old-same-old. A victory such as the one he was celebrating was deserving of a dessert, or maybe a greasy basket of fries.

"Hang on yall!" A voice belted out from the back. "I'm comin!"

The clicking of high heels, the slight swish of thigh against pantyhosed thigh as *it* hustled down the aisle towards the register were the only clues needed. Carter dropped the menu on the table. The victory had been short-lived.

"I got you. I got you. I swear it's been busier than a bee hive in spring up in here." Queen went on.

Carter did his best to stare at the table, to keep his focus, his composure. Taking a salt shaker in his hand, he poured enough out in front of him to form a mound. He used his butter knife to divide it, then multiplied it into two, then three grainy white hills. This served to give his hands something to do. A technique he'd devised to keep them from doing the unspeakable things he regularly envisioned.

"Least we had us a break." Tom muttered.

"Hmm?" Carter grunted.

"From that bubble-assed faggot." Tom whispered, smiling all the while at Mr. Donaldson across the room. Who'd become the self-proclaimed head of one of the neighborhood watch groups that had sprung up in recent months.

The register drawer opened, then shut, then opened again. The last waiting customer taken care of, the phone rang, and Queen answered it.

"Lawson's" *It* sang out in that cheery way *it* had of saying everything.

Carter gripped his knife more firmly as he watched *it* write down a take-out order with a purple pen topped with a glittery shoe. This was how *they* were. Making everything sickeningly sweet, everything girly and queer. He wondered if *they* had secret manuals *they* read on how to do so, or if it came naturally to *them*.

Either way, it was more than enough to prod, to incite, his own loosely tethered beast. The savagely, rabid one that devoured more and more of him by the day. That left no love, no real want of anything. That only yearned for the quenching of its vengeful and putrid longings.

From Queen's chipper words and comfortable movements, Carter sensed that his presence had gone unnoticed. This was unacceptable. He blew the salt off his table, plunked down the cutlery, and proudly lifted his head.

"We're ready to order." he announced loud enough for all to hear.

Phone still to *its* ear, Queen turned and looked up at him. *Its* face froze and *its* eyes filled with terror. Carter smiled and nodded. The purple shoed pen fell from *its* large hands to the floor. Flustered, and caught off guard, Queen ducked down behind the counter to retrieve it. It wouldn't have surprised Carter if *it* had stayed there, but *it* surprisingly popped up finishing the phone call then hanging up.

Its fake fingernailed hands were shaking as *it* pulled *its* dress down, straightening *its* apron. *Its* chest rose and fell. *It* was taking a deep breath, mustering courage. Carter chuckled to himself.

It was a noble effort, but he doubted that courage was one of those things that came to you merely because you willed it. In his opinion it was not one of those things you could acquire over time. You either had it or you didn't. He, himself, had never encountered a lack of it. Though many other traces of humanity eluded him, courage had always been readily accessible.

"Be right there." Queen finally replied, *its* voice quivering.

Like a wolf detecting the faint scent of blood, Tom sensed Queen's hesitancy and chimed in.

"How long we gonna set here? They don't call it lunch *hour* for nothin." he barked.

A loud clang of pans erupted from the back, and just as Queen made it around the counter, Lisa preempted *it*, striding out, coming to stand next to their table.

"I got it." Queen nervously reassured her.

Lisa put her hand up, signaling for *it* to be quiet, to remain where *it* was. It was this motion that gave Carter the answer to a question he'd mulled over since the two rode into town. He'd heard it said that there always had to be a man in any relationship. It had been up in the air as to which one of them was which in theirs, but now he knew.

For reasons he couldn't put a finger on, this heightened his angst, snapping one of the few ropes that still managed to keep his beast in line. He looked quizzically up at Lisa as she lorded over them, arms crossed.

"Ya'll been to that new K.F.C. down by the overpass?" Lisa asked, her face deadpan, void of expression.

Tom looked across the table, searching his partners face for cues, for how exactly they were going to address the matter at hand.

"We're not much for chicken." Carter responded smiling sweetly.

"Gives me heartburn." Tom seconded, smiling as well.

Proud Mary emitted from the juke box that had been installed last week. The other customers chewed silently, bystanders, witnesses if needs be. Uncrossing her arms, Lisa leaned down putting both of her hands on the table, gritting her teeth; a pit bull growling as it came down off its porch, to confront unwanted visitors.

"I'm sure you'll like it if you give it another try." she stated with a sound resolve.

Carter took note that everyone remained in their seats. No one came to their defense. This was how the timid chose sides. Not by any outright action, but by looking the other way. By this permissive act, he came to understand that perhaps he and Tom were more tolerated than liked.

Seeing Lisa next to *it*, staking her claim, laying out for them how it was going to be, took him back. It took him all the way back to that day by the slide, and he hated this. He despised the fact that she still, after all the years between the past and the present, possessed such power. More than that, he hated it that she knew she did.

What he hated most of all was that he himself had never come close to having that kind of effect on anyone. People cowed to him out of fear, and never respect. He knew there was a distinct difference.

Hands clenched, he slid out of the booth. Forcing an unwanted touch was to be his only recourse so he purposely bumped into her in the process. He reached over to the small cup on the table that held toothpicks, positioning one between his lips.

"You know, come to think of it, I am fond of their mashed potatoes."

Carter glibly remarked.

Looking straight at Queen, he didn't let it end there.

"And since you mention it, I have a cravin for some gravy too, and some a that dark meat. Mmmm Mmmm. Nothing like dark meat."

Tom cut his eyes at Lisa as he too scooted out of the booth. He, however, made sure not to brush against her, leaving more peaceably than his counterpart. The other patrons cautiously resumed their conversations as the two walked towards the exit. Lisa cut in front of them, throwing open the door. Never knowing when to leave well enough alone, Tom leaned in to deliver a parting comment.

"Your daddy always liked cops comin round. You know he didn't never have a single break in all the years he was open. What with us havin such a slew a burglaries round here lately, it'd be a shame to be left all *exposed*."

Her eyes never waivered from his. Lisa was unphased.

"Awe, don't worry yourself about us. I'm here at all hours, an you wouldn't believe the gun collection daddy left me. He used to call me his own little Annie Oakley. Been itchin for a chance to break out his .22 . Always have loved takin that out to the range." she informed them as they stepped out. "Ya'll enjoy that chicken, now."

Not sure how to take this, Tom followed Carter out to their cruiser. They got in, and sat staring at the diner windows. Never had they been treated in such a manner. Not in all their years of law enforcement had their badge meant so little. Tom later remarked that he had only raised a fist to a handful of women, but it had unnerved him how much he'd wanted to rare back and hit Lisa full out in her mouth. The restraint he'd used was only due to how he knew it would come back to bite them, what with all the witnesses present.

As Carter put the car in reverse and headed towards the highway, he made up his mind, after they'd talked about it, he was indeed in the mood for some dark meat. That he'd have a huge plate of the greasy chicken with cole slaw and mashed potatoes on the side. It wouldn't be because she'd told them to. K.F.C. was the logical choice seeing that they were likely not as busy this time of day and there were few other establishments in Murfeesboro where you could get a quick lunch.

His foot pressed the gas. His hands turned the wheel. He stopped when a light was red, accelerated when it turned green. He went through the motions secretly thrilled all the while. His beast feasting on the sustenance that had, unbeknownst to anyone but himself, been laid before it. His skin felt too tight to contain the joy threatening to bubble over. The sheer elation he felt that the war was not over. No, on the contrary, it was only the beginning...

The Tranny

Got home last Saturday to find a package on the front porch. Tore it open an there was the same concert t-shirt I tore up, ripped to pieces that night - that night everything went to hell in a handbasket. Lisa musta saw it in the trash an found me another one on online. I slipped it on an waited for her to get home to thank her proper.

Soon as she came in the door, I took her in my arms an kissed her hard. We tied Lil' man out the back an went straight to the bedroom. When I first told Lisa I whatin wantin to be Jermaine no more, I worried she'd have to go cause she whatin into women. We never did even have no real words about that part a thangs it, jus gradually found ways around it. When it comes to pleasin a woman, those specialty catalogs bout to make men damn near obsolete.

Every now an then when we in the thick a thangs I look up an see her eyes closed. I don't ask her if she'll open em. I know she's fuckin Jermaine an not me. Made peace a long time ago that she loves me an thas as good as I'm gonna get. It's too much to hope somebody'll want me too.

Went to one a these meetups one time for people who been reassigned or are still transitionin. Only went once. Thas all I needed. Lisa'd offered to come, show support, but I didn't know how the others would take to her. Plus, I tried not to drag her into all my drama, still try not to. She chose me, not the whole trans world.

Shoulda known when it was at the conference room a the Tallahassee Howard Johnsons it whatin gonna be nothin to write home about. Place still had wallpaper on every wall. Mmm, ain't nobody wanna lay their eyes on that tacky shit. To top it off, there was stained carpet an foldin chairs.

They had finger foods out on a table they'd wrapped with purple cellophane stead of a tablecloth. Somebody'd put out pigs in a blanket on a serving plate. I wondered if that was intentional or they were jus that ignorant. A cheap disco ball was plugged in next to some lava lamps on a wood stage. Whole thang was like one a them proms they have for the mentally challenged at some rinky-dink community center.

Found out real quick the type a men who'd want me as Queen an only Queen. Men who wouldn't close their eyes while you're makin love, but would damn sure make you wanna close yours, mmm hmmm. From what I could tell that night, they tend to be old, an some of em still married. Most of em never had the balls to accept theirselves til their kids got grown or their wives died. Got so cozy pent up in their closet, they hung curtains, put out a rug an turned it into a home.

An some a the "gals" was only halfway to bein true blue certifiable, still usin socks as fake tattas. Several of em waddled like they hadn't gotten the hang of using athletic wraps, tape or whatever their tools of choice were. Painful to watch, honey. Mmm, painful. Found a wad a maskin tape on the floor a the bathroom. Felt bad they didn't have nobody to tell em usin that'll give you a hell of a heat rash, not to mention it's about as close to gettin a Brazilian as you can get without darkenin the door of a spa. Wheweeee!

An Lord they didn't know a thang about representin. There was this one, couldn't a been younger than fifty if she was a day, showed up with bobby socks an paten leather shoes like she was a little girl goin off to the third grade. I try not to judge, but you can get in any grocery store line an thumb through a magazine for five minutes an you'll see grown women don't wear that kinna thang. That whatin about wantin to be a woman. That was about a whole lotta other mess we whatin there to take up with her that night. Some straight up Freud worthy shit.

Above my pay grade honey.

I made nice with everybody, even the haters who were pissed off I was struttin my stuff in a jumpsuit they wouldn't ever be able to even get a leg into. Danced a couple dances with an old bald fella cause I felt sorry for him. Strobe light blinded me every time we twirled. He liked steadyin me with his hand on the small a my back. Thought he was startin out on some kinna romance. Come ten o'clock I bolted for the lobby.

Was nearly home free, done with all of em when a pink fingernailed hand slipped in partin the elevator doors, stoppin them from closin. A tall skinny Miss Thang I'd seen puttin out some more piggies at the snack table got in with me. She was the only other one in that room I felt even came close to passin for a tried an true lady. Sure didn't seem like her kinna crew either. She stood as far away from me as she could, jus eye ballin me.

"Dr. Johanssen?" she finally asked real snobby.

I nodded.

She looked me up an down one more time.

"Not his best work, but decent." she said flippin her hair back behind her shoulder, makin sure to show me it whatin a wig but "all naturale".

It was lucky for her that the elevator opened when it did. My fists were clenched an ready. Didn't know if I could keep em in check. Decent? Who was she talkin to? I knew full well, I was a hell of a lot more than "decent".

As I watched her strut her implanted ass across the parkin lot a that cheap hotel, I knew then, I whatin cut out for the kinna cruelty that seemed to come with turnin from one thang into another. That it was a whole different ballgame I hadn't come prepared to play. I'd had fantasies of all of us bein one big ol' girl's club, helpin each other out, but I saw it clear that night. I'd jus jumped outta one pen into another where dogs was still tryin to eat dogs.

When I got home, Lisa'd waited up so she could hear all about it. I'll never forget what she said. She tol' me welcome to the club, an went on about how I could consider myself a bonafide woman. That the whole catty craziness I'd experienced was what bein a woman was all about. She tol' me women ain't for each other as a general rule. Said havin your claws ready for the other women who'll tear you up whenever they get the chance is all part of it.

At first I felt honored, like I'd experienced some rite a passage or somethin, but the longer I thought on that, the longer I wished somebody woulda told me about it all fore I had my operation. Wished that was somethin they'd a gone over in therapy. Didn't know I signed up for that. As it was, life was already full a people to contend with what with bein a black man an all. There I was thinkin when I finally got to be myself, let Queen out to play, I'd be joinin a group who'd give me some acceptance. The whole damn time, nobody told me they whatin exactly takin new member applications, an the ones who were already in backstabbed each other every chance they got.

Settin up against the headboard, I watch Lisa sleep. She's got my Tina shirt on now, an thas how it goes. Gifts between lovers ain't never for jus one of you. It was good timin. Felt ready to see that shirt again seein as it's been a couple months since all that business. Might even wear it to work. Make me feel real good to walk around in it. Walk right by that table where that wolf an his partner used to set fore Lisa told them where they could go.

I run my hand through her hair bein careful not to wake her. Girl works her ass off. Needs her sleep. Sure enough envy her that pretty black hair. Got it from her Puerto Rican momma. Only thang about Lisa thas even got the hint a bein ethnic. Other than that she's white as a sheet. Her daddy's side had those strong genes.

When her daddy died, I asked her if she wanted to try to find her momma over in the Caribbean. She didn't even want to talk about it. All she ever says is her momma made her choice a long time ago. Returned to her family over there when Lisa was barely walkin. Says she don't blame her, jus wished she'd a taken her along.

When people look at Lisa an me they cain't see how we got together. Cain't see all the ties that bind us - the quilt a loss an bein outta place that we've woven together. They cain't know that a little half Puerto Rican girl raised in Georgia without a momma an only her whitebread daddy to see after her feels every bit as misplaced in this world as a little black boy in Florida who liked wearin his momma's nighties an didn't have no daddy around to tell him not to.

As I stare out the winda, a car pulls in across the street, Mr. Danby. He sets there for a few seconds fore he gets out an walks up to his house. Got that sad walk, like he's a dead man walkin down the hall on the way to be electrocuted stead of a husband wantin to see his wife or a daddy itchin to see his kid.

I watch as he unlocks the door an steps inside. I think a how Lil' Miss Thang worships him. How she wishes he'd love her for her, for bein the Ozzy Osbourne dressin, chunky, but funny, sweet girl she is. I'm real proud a myself that I hadn't told her the secret. That plain simple fact that we all got to find out *for ourselves, an usually got to go the hard way about it. I could, but she wouldn't believe me jus yet anyhow. Naw, I hadn't dared spill the beans to her that you spend most a your life tryin to forgive everybody you know cause only you can really love you for you.*

The Girl

When things with Donnie started to unravel, I should have been prepared that everything else would follow suit. I'd gotten lazy. I'd quit worrying so much about who saw me going to Queen's or if I was home on time so mother wouldn't miss me. I'd been worried about only myself and wallowing in the mire of the misery of my own making.

The afternoon everything finally went south, Donnie hadn't walked me to Queen's. He'd had plans with Gary. I refrained from wanting further details. They had put Ms. Terrell's on the backburner until a more opportune time presented itself. I had been commissioned to listen out for any hints of possible vacations or watch for which days she went to the store or to church and note how long she spent there. In Daddy's world they called this *casing a joint*.

As I dug in my backpack for the key to Queen's, I heard Lil' Man on the other side of the door barking.

"Hold on buddy." I sweetly called to him.

Even after dumping the contents of the bag on the porch, I came up empty. I hurried over to my house, praying it had fallen out in my room that morning when I'd packed up my homework. So monopolized was I with finding it, I neglected to see mother's car already in the driveway.

Leaving the front door wide open, I rushed up the stairs to scour my room. The longer I went without recovering it, the more I began to sweat. All of a sudden I heard the worst possible thing I could have imagined hearing at that moment.

"Charlotte Grace!" mother's voice rang out from downstairs.

I shot up under my desk, nearly splitting my head open on the drawer above me. There was a reason I could not find it. It was not lost...she had taken it.

My feet felt like they did the first time Daddy took me to Mill's Pond to learn to swim - heavy and slow, trying to move through the squishy mud lining the bottom. I held onto the railing as I inched down the steps. I knew I was to answer for far more than I'd ever wanted to.

"Come in here." she commanded as I peered in at her from the dining room doorway.

I slumped down into the chair usually reserved for Daddy, hoping that

I would glean some of its power simply by osmosis. The key was nowhere in sight. It crossed my mind that the pow wow was to be about something else entirely, and not going to be as catastrophically wretched as I anticipated.

Before I could get too relaxed, she brought her right hand up onto the table then opened it. There was the pink and gold high heeled key chain with Queen's key attached. My heart sank. My stomach gurgled. I wished I'd have known that the day before was the last time I'd walk Lil' Man. I'd have hugged him, given him extra treats, then I would've laid on that velvet couch and bawled my eyes out.

"Sometimes I just don't know…" she started in, putting her other hand up to her head. "You're just like your father! You think the buck stops with you, that you don't have to listen to anyone!"

"I've just been walking her dog." I lied.

"Walking her dog? She's not supposed to even know your name! How is it you're letting yourself in her house and walking her dog? I mean *his* dog. You know what I mean!" Mother yelled, taking it over the top in her signature, melodramatic fashion.

I didn't answer, only stared at her while breathing in and out looking at her lips as they told me all about how she'd warned me not to be going over there and that no good would come from associating with people like *him*. I wondered how she'd found out. The key alone had not been incriminating enough, and how had she known to search my bag for it? Had she seen me or had someone told her?

When I was younger, I tried to look like I was sorry, like I was really penitent, but I couldn't remember how to do that anymore so I sat there. I just tried to look alert while mentally being out on the walk I had intended to take with Lil' Man.

"You're always attracted to trouble. No matter what your father and I say or what we do, you find it. Just like with that Lee girl. What was her name? You and she were thick as thieves. The one who talked you in to running off from the class on that field trip." Mother agitatedly reminisced.

"Chrissy." I mumbled.

"Yes, Chrissy Lee. Good Lord, even that name spelled white trash, but you had to do whatever she did and be right there with her in the principal's office for your father and I to have to go down and pick you up. Do you know how embarrassing that was, young lady?"

"It was third grade." I shot back.

The minute I reminded her of this, I knew it was the wrong thing to say. Not that there was ever a right thing to say when my mother was in full swing. I should've learned from Daddy's example waiting it out was the only route to take if you had any hope of coming out with little more than one or two emotional wounds.

"That is beside the point! I am trying to show you that this is a pattern!"

This rabbit trailed into how she and Daddy wanted only the best for me. I loved how she spoke for him when he wasn't home. She knew that what he thought held more weight with me, but what she didn't know is that I never believed for one second she knew anything about him or what he wanted.

"I'll just give her the key back and tell her I can't do it anymore." I offered.

Putting her hand back over the key, she looked at me with a resolve customarily reserved for matters regarding what went into my mouth and how much of it there'd been. It seemed that whatever possessed her, she felt somehow that she was battling with the wiles of a twisted world and contending for my very soul.

"No, you won't be seeing *him* again. Your father will take care of this. He'll make sure it's returned."

"But I ..."

Slamming her fist on the table, she grimaced. I knew she'd surprised even herself, and I took some measure of satisfaction in the fact that it must have hurt. One leg moved and then the other as I gradually rose from the chair, and slunk towards the stairs.

"I hate to see what's going to become of you if you keep this up." she called, her final rebuttal.

Taking each step methodically one by one, I lashed back with exactly what I wanted to say. To this day, I'm not sure where I found the nerve, but just that once it came easily.

"Nobody said you have to watch!"

The huffy sound she made when she felt she'd undergone a personal assault was the last thing I heard before shutting my door. Outside my window dusk came and went as I tried to work on a biology project that was due in the coming week. I couldn't keep my mind on it, though. Digging in the side pocket of my backpack, I recovered the lipstick I'd been given. At least mother hadn't found it. Holding it in my hand, it brought me some relief - the lone piece of Queen that was still within my reach.

My thoughts kept drifiting to Lil' Man. I imagined him waiting by the door so patiently for me or maybe he went back to Queen's pillow where he loved to *piddle* as she called it, a last resort after having been left too long. When Queen came home to find it, she'd wonder what had happened since I had always been nothing but reliable. She wouldn't be able to come over to check on me. That much she knew for sure. I was certain of that.

My comforter pulled up around me, I lay on my bed and folded into the smallest ball I could manage. I cried myself to sleep, as I had done many nights before. Cried over how much I'd miss Queen and Lil' Man. Cried over how things were going with Donnie. Cried over the disgusting reality, that at the end of the day, I was who I was.

At some point in the night I rolled over. There was Daddy, on the edge of my bed. The hallway light revealing a fixed expression, a look of pure, despondent frustration.

"Daddy?" I sleepily muttered.

"Your mother itn't gonna let either one of us get a lick of sleep til we talk this over." he whispered holding Queen's key out in his hand.

There in his palm, the pink heel looked so foreign. Touching that same hand that filed through papers day after day. Papers that decided people's fate. The same hand that went up now and again in the courtroom to object, to have something rendered inadmissible.

"Why, baby? Why didn't you just listen?" he implored.

I scooted up, propped against the headboard, and rolled around a few stories that might work, but looking into his pained and tired eyes, I decided on the truth.

"She's my friend, Daddy. She's really nice and her dog just loves me. His name's Rodrigo, but we call him Lil' Man and I like havin a job. She pays me every Friday and -"

"You took money from *him*?" he erupted, abruptly rising up.

"For walking the dog."

He crossed the room, turned and crossed back again. Stooping down, he snatched me up by the shoulders, roughly shaking me.

"You don't know where that money comes from! You know what it'd look like if it got out, you bein my daughter takin money from that...that *guy*? Jesus Christ, Charlotte Grace! God damn it!" he railed.

Getting a hold of himself, he released his grip, giving me time to scramble back towards the headboard. I sniffled fighting back tears. He'd never laid a hand on me before. We both knew this was not only about the key in his hand, or the money exchanged. We were both aware that this incident had been the icing on the cake - a misshapen, bitter cake that had been being mixed, then baked layer by layer, year after year.

He walked to the door. To this day, I can still picture how small he looked with the light illuminating him from the hallway. So small and fragile. His hand quivered as he touched the doorknob, the other hand still tightly closed around the key.

"You're not to go over there again. You hear me?"

I stared out the window.

"Charlotte Grace? Do you hear me?"

"Yes sir." I regretfully relented.

My door was halfway shut when my sniffling caused him to pause and lean back in. He looked across the hall at the closed door, then back at me.

"Remember Don Hines at work? Well, he was just telling me the other day I should bring you over to swim in their pool. His daughter Marney's your age. She came to your birthday party that one year. She's a real nice gal. Seems I recall you liked her. You remember?"

I stared at him blankly.

"We'll pick a Saturday. We'll all head over there. Your mother'll bring cupcakes. Alright?"

Wanting to duck down in my covers, and not give him the satisfaction of an answer however, I fell prey to his look. That one that melted me every time. The look that told you whatever he'd done, it hadn't been the real him who did it. The look that revealed the honest to goodness, true Daddy. The nice, witty and sweet one. The one he was before the weight of the world had been thrust upon him. The one he'd been long before I ever disrupted his world.

"Alright, Daddy." I conceded.

The room went dark. I heard him cross the hall and go into their bedroom. My mother's muffled voice came next. She was undoubtedly giving him the third degree. That was her way - never wanting to do the dirty work, but always wanting the play-by-play afterwards.

I played out the future pool play date in my head as I tried to fall back to sleep. Seeing myself in the hideous orange and pink polka dotted swimsuit mother had bought. When I'd complained about the colors, she'd informed me there were very few choices for a girl of my size and it was either that or one with a big sail boat on the front of it. She'd added that I should be grateful she hadn't chosen the boat.

I thought of how Marney would look in whatever her mother had purchased. She was skinny. That much I remembered about her. Her mother probably bought her a bikini. I'd never owned one of those. Daddy'd be there to witness us disrobe before we swam - a pink polka dotted Orca next to a bikini clad mermaid. An afternoon like that would provide ample opportunity for humiliation.

It was odd that he'd bring up Mr. Hines and Marney when he'd never spoken much about them. As I rolled over, and looked at the wall, I recognized that the suggested outing was his consolation prize, meant to serve as a replacement for Queen and Rodrigo.

That's how mother and Daddy thought. If we didn't go to Disney World like they'd promised due to Daddy's interfering work schedule, we went to play Putt Putt. If we didn't get to shop for a new school outfit at the big mall in Atlanta because mother had overbooked herself and one of the pageant ladies needed her, we'd run in the local K-mart and grab the first thing off the rack. One thing was as good as the other where I was concerned. There was no hierarchy. No acknowledgement that one didn't measure up. And this was how relationships were to them also.

When I'd had to quit hanging around with Chrissy, mother had taken me to visit *the* Sarah Levine, daughter of *the* Heather Levine, who'd won the pageant the year mother was passed over. We in no way hit it off. I, in fact, had quickly infuriated Sarah with my disinterest in Barbies. On the way home Mother jabbered on about how I could never say my having so few friends was for her lack of trying.

This is what Daddy had done that night. In his mind, Marney was just as good as Queen, and our arranged friendship wouldn't be nearly as complicated. Though, as I lay there sniffling, I couldn't help but grin at the thought that Queen would win against Marney hands down in a bikini contest.

My eyes grew heavy and my final musings of the day couldn't help but turn back to the question of how exactly my mother had found me out. I knew I hadn't been as careful for a while, but with me walking in Donnie's neighborhood, there'd been little room for error. She wouldn't have been caught dead on his street.

It seemed a mystery to me. Right up there with how Donnie could've taken an interest in me at all, how it was that Anne Frank could write the way she did at her age, how it was that I was not adopted but the actual biological offspring of my parents, and how it was Queen had ever let Lisa talk her into living in our town in first place.

The Cop

When his father sent him the plane ticket, he'd wanted to throw it away. He had no desire to go to California. He relented when Tom told him it would do him good. It had been a month after they'd graduated from the academy, and they'd been newly hired on at the Murfeesboro police department. He figured if he was going to take a trip, it was the best time to do so as it would take a couple weeks for their paperwork to clear so they could begin work.

"Hell, you the only fucker I know who'd think about turnin down a trip to the West Coast. Lara's always sayin you got a screw loose. Here I am the first one linin up to say she's wrong, but I tell you what, you turn that down, she might just be right." Tom had scoffed.

So on a Friday, Carter found himself sitting on a plane headed for L.A. It was not so much out of wanting to see his father, whom he hadn't seen in over four years, but more out of wanting to prove Lara wrong. As he situated himself in the seat by the window, he could not take his mind off the fact that this was his first time on a plane. He had fully intended to die without ever adding the experience to the list of things he'd done.

He decided not to focus on that, but to concentrate on the festering anger towards his father for even requiring it of him. Resting his head against the back of his seat, he rehearsed the fact that this was why he avoided relationships with people altogether. Relationships meant that things would inevitably be required. Things others would want you to do that you had no desire to do. There were never enough excuses. Somehow, you'd end up complying or you'd have to disregard them altogether. Nine times out of ten, he chose the latter.

"Ah, beat me to the punch." A voice interrupted his rote contemplation.

"Scuse me?" Carter replied.

"The window seat. You're gonna enjoy the trip a whole lot more than me or the man on the aisle. If it's gonna be a man. Maybe we'll get lucky and it'll be a tiny little old lady, or better yet, it'll be empty." A stranger who was now standing at the end of his aisle speculated aloud while hoisting a duffel bag into the overhead compartment.

From the look of him, he was very sophisticated. Carter surmised that he was a businessman or salesman of some sort. Possibly he wouldn't be too boring. Maybe he'd have a bit of interesting conversation to offer, take their minds off being way up in the air in a machine Carter had so little knowledge as to the inner workings of.

"Business or pleasure?" the stranger questioned.

"Family." Carter answered.

"Oooh, neither huh?"

This struck him as amusing and Carter surprised himself by chuckling. A rare occurrence, especially in the type of anxiety riddled situation he found himself in.

"You?" he asked the guy, trying to play it cool.

"Business."

Carter nodded. The plane began to fill up. Soon they were ready for take off. The seat on the aisle was indeed empty. The guy commented that he'd move over so they'd have more room to breathe. As he did so, Carter caught a glimpse of the gold watch half masked by the sleeve of the man's suit jacket. The face of it was framed with diamonds, very fancy. In and of itself it meant nothing. Only later, after what transpired, would he look back on it as significant, as one of the many clues he'd missed.

"This your first time?" the stranger continued their exchange.

"Is it that obvious?" Carter laughed nervously, his face reddening.

"No biggie. Everybody has to pop their cherry." the guy quipped.

The plane gradually rose. Carter maintained a death grip on the arms of his seat.

"You know what I do?" The guy nearly shouted over the noise of the take-off. He paid no mind to the flight attendant readying for her speech about emergency exits and oxygen masks.

Carter only shook his head, knuckles turning white.

"I make lists."

"Lists?" Carter blurted.

"Yeah, like favorite foods, cars, movies, anything that gets me thinking about something else." The guy advised.

Unable to ascertain this, Carter turned his head to the side, looked out the window, then doubled over to catch his breath without vomiting.

"Lets do action movies. I'll start us off." The guy proposed. "*Con Air*."

Carter couldn't talk. He could barely breathe. He was convinced they were going to bite the big one. That it was indeed the end, and he most assuredly was not ready.

"Ahhh...given the situation, maybe that wasn't the best choice. How about *Speed*?" The guy submitted, patting his back.

The touch awakened Carter, and he shot up on the seat.

"Come on, just give it a try." the guy persisted.

"*Romancing the Stone.*" Carter whispered barely loud enough to be heard.

The guy laughed.

"*Okay.* Not at all what I thought you'd say, and not quite sure that's an action movie, but we'll go with it."

"My mother loved that one." Carter remarked, loosening his grip on the arms of his seat ever so slightly.

"I hear ya. Not knocking it. To each his own. My turn. *Fast and Furious.*" The guy submitted.

And this was how things went for the next few minutes. It did take his mind off what was happening. Off the fact that he, a human not meant to ever alight into the air, was then floating above everything in a massive contraption. After naming movie after movie, the guy reminded him that they were then well on their way, and he'd managed to keep his breakfast down, and still remain conscious.

"You're right!" Carter exclaimed.

"See, what did I tell you? Lists. Works like a charm." the guy gloated.

They swapped information about their jobs, their home towns, all the customary fellow passenger banter. It was the first time he could remember being so at ease with someone, besides possibly Tom. He couldn't pinpoint it. What was it that made the guy so easy to talk to? He wondered if perhaps some of the usual social pressure was gone due to the fact that they wouldn't see each other again.

"And you don't like her?" The guy inquired after Carter shared about his father's new wife.

"She's young enough to be my sister." Carter grumbled.

"Man, that's a tough break." the guy agreed.

"Met her at this coffee joint he went to on his way to work. Didn't date two months fore she moved in. Bullied him into movin out to L.A. soon as he retired. He coulda gone wherever he wanted, but she wants to be an actress. Majored in theatre at Georgia State. I told him those artsy, drama chicks ain't good for nothing but a wild fuck. He wouldn't listen." Carter babbled on.

"Had your fair share of *theatre pussy* have you?" the guy joked.

"Just once." Carter admitted with a smirk. "Picked her up at a bar. Most drama girls don't go for law dogs. They like their pot too much."

The guy shook his head, laughing at backwardness of Carter's offhanded comments.

"Any day now, he's gonna tell me they're havin a baby. Girl that young, she'll want one. Then I'll have some half brother or sister standing around dad's casket crying alongside me. After that his lawyer'll be tellin me how he willed them nearly everything he had."

Carter took a turn listening as the guy then described his own family, and how they didn't see much of each other. A tale of how he'd even spent that past Christmas on his own since they hadn't wanted him to bring his current partner with him for the holiday. This did seem overly egregious to Carter. He thought any parent should be pleased to have their son's business partner join them for a meal.

At one point the guy got on a roll about how his mother had never respected his choices. He said that she was so oblivious she couldn't see that her very attitude was part of why he'd chosen his lifestyle in the first place.

"Yeah, my dad's always going on about why I don't have a regular girl. Says he might like to have some grandkids while he can still see them. I always tell him what do I care about having a regular piece of ass waiting at home? Damn sure hasn't done him a bit of good. Hell, me and him walked out on my mom for I was old enough to tie my shoes." Carter disclosed.

He hadn't met a better listener. The guy offered his opinion quite sparingly, in between asking insightful questions. Every now and then, slight turbulance interrupted their in-flight therapy session, jarring them into lighter conversation. The guy made jokes about one of the flight attendants who spoke with a lisp, and Carter mimicked her to a *T*. When she asked them if they'd like *drinkssss* they snickered in unison, and smiled as she rolled her eyes at them.

"You must get out and see the sights while you're there." The guy encouraged when Carter confessed he was planning to hold up at his father's house in the Hills and wait out the visit.

"What would you recommend?" Carter queried.

"You simply have to go to the Walk of Fame, oh and Hollywood Boulevard of course." the guy replied.

As the guy sipped his Rum and Coke, Carter took notice of his chiseled cheekbones, his flawless skin. He found himself envying his good looks, more than that, he found himself dwelling on them. Closing his eyes, he leaned back to try to sleep, and take his mind off the strange yearnings that were catching him off guard. The guy took the hint, and pulled out a magazine, perusing through it.

The severity of the turbulance jolted him awake. Carter again gripped the arms of his seat, and looked over to run through a list with the guy, but saw that he was gone. Despite the lisp-plagued flight attendant's frantic warnings, he unfastened his seat belt, making his way unsteadily down the aisle to the lavatory. For unidentifiable reasons, he raised his hand and knocked loudly on the door.

There was the sound of flushing then the guy cracked open the door. Their eyes met. Carter's face went white. The flight attendant yelled at him again, but then became preoccupied with an older man on the verge of a panic attack. The guy grabbed Carter's arm, yanking him inside.

The plane jerked this way then that. The two of them tightly packed like ill-fitted sardines inside the closet sized bathroom, looking at each other in the mirror. The guy was the first to make a move. He put an arm around Carter, pulling him closer, before kissing his cheek.

Carter immediately felt himself go hard. He turned to face the guy. His hands slid along the front of the guy's pants and felt that he too was equally excited by their interlude. Their mouths met, and they might have progressed further, but the guy couldn't keep quiet.

"I knew it." the guy whispered. "The minute I saw you. I knew."

And just as quickly as he'd gone hard, Carter felt himself go limp. Those words infuriated him. *How had he known? What was it he'd known?* Carter wondered when he himself certainly hadn't been privy to any such information.

Freeing an arm from their entangled embrace, Carter reared back, delivering a blow to the guy's mouth. It caused the guy to squeal like a woman, his back flopping up against the mirror. He cowered, awaiting whatever else Carter was ready to dole out. They stared at each other.

As Carter opened the door, he was met with the flustered face of the lisp-ridden flight attendant. She caught sight of the guy straightening his suit coat behind him.

"Sir, are you alright?" she demanded of the assumed victim as

Carter pushed past her out into the aisle.

Glaring at the guy from over the attendant's shoulder, Carter administered a threatening look that plainly laid out for him what he was to say.

"I'm fine." the guy hurriedly confirmed.

Again Carter found his seat by the window. He continued to look out at the white clouds as the guy removed his bag from the overhead compartment with one hand, and held a bag of ice he'd been given up to his lip with the other. He heard the guy promise the flight attendant that he was just fine as he planted himself in a seat in the rear. She wasn't convinced and deposited herself at the end of Carter's aisle hands on her hips. Carter only handed her his empty drink cup without saying a word.

When they landed, his father was waiting for him in a designated area. Security had certainly tightened up after 9/11. No one could be waiting for passengers outside the gate anymore. He shook his father's hand, and expressed delight that he'd come to pick him up on his own. As the two rode the escalator to retrieve his luggage, he spotted the guy pulling his own fancy suitcase off the conveyor belt.

Letting his father move in ahead of him, Carter made a point to not let the guy get away without his having a final confrontation. He saw him hastily dart out to hail a cab. He menacingly strode in his direction. The guy attempted to gather his bag, and make a quick escape, yet it was too heavy for him to gain any real ground.

"You don't know shit." Carter hoarsely delivered through gritted teeth.

The guy winced. A single tear trickled down from his right eye coming to rest on his swollen lip. Carter's mouth formed into a smirk, but he finally let him pass. Defiantly he watched the guy get into a cab. Having recovered his son's bag, his father came to stand beside him.

"Who was that?" he wanted to know.

Carter reached for the handle of his bag, resuming control of it, he put an arm around his father's shoulders in a manly sideways hug.

"I'm starved." Carter declared. "How bout you?"

The Tranny

I look up from the register an there's Mr. Danby, handin me a twenty like it's any other day. Like he didn't write a letter. Like there ain't a thang in the world gone wrong, an I reckon it hadn't in his neck a the woods. I make his change, wish him a good one jus like I do everybody else as he walks out with his lawyer buddies.

The minute I opened the mailbox, saw the typed address on the front real formal, I knew who it was from. Well not exactly "who", but I knew what it was about. Lil' Miss Thang had always been like clockwork. Hadn't missed a day since I give her the key. Knew the minute I saw where Lil' Man did his business on my pilla couple weeks back that the jig was up. Wouldn't be seein hide nor hair a that girl anymore.

Lisa was hot when she saw it. Said she didn't care if he was the D.A. a the county, she had a mind to walk over there an give him what for, demand our key back. I told her it wouldn't change a thang. Men like that, you'd jus be provin their point. Key didn't make no difference. Whatin no body gonna use it no more anyhow. Her momma probly threw it out.

Wipin the counter, I watch him out front, jaw jackin with all those other suits from the courthouse. Don't take livin in a place long at all an you learn quick who's the kings an who's the peasants, the lil' folks. The royalty's the ones with more money than God. Most of em ain't done near as much as the rest of us to get their crowns neither. Nothing cept be born to the right people at the right time. Cops got a place right up there too, but they're jus soldiers doin the biddin a men like Charlotte Grace's Daddy.

I know my place. Always been a peasant. Me an Lisa got that in common. I think she had more choice in the matter. I didn't do nothin to get where I am but be born to the wrong person at the wrong time. Good as momma was, she whatin never gonna raise anythang but blue collar boys. Jarvis spends his life fightin it. I spend mine acceptin it, an lookin my best while I'm doin it. Lord knows I ain't thrilled about it no way, but cain't see tryin to swim up that stream. I got enough grain to go against.

As Mr. Danby an his homeboys take to headin down the sidewalk off back to their castle, I know I cain't be bitter. Kings is always gonna protect their own from us peasants. Thas how they keep their throne, pass it on down. They keep theirs squeaky clean, free from a bad reputation. He's jus bein a good daddy.

"Wish I could tell him to go eat KFC too." Lisa smarts off as she comes out from the grill seein who's got my attention.

I laugh, cause I know she knows we cain't never do that. Not unless we wanna be the only ones eatin here. Thas how it goes. Ain't nobody got to keep the peace most a the time. It keeps itself on account a repercussions. Most people can add 2+2 an know they sure don't want to see 4. She's gonna make his food, an

I'm gonna serve it like we never got a letter. Thas what we gonna do.

Lisa an I been takin turns runnin home to let Lil' Man out. Ain't been too bad, nice to have a break when it's my turn, but we sure miss our girl. When I walk near her place, Lil' Man gets a whiff of her an barks like crazy. I have to pull him an tell him a bunch a stuff he's too smart to understand about how we cain't see her no more cause her Daddy don't want her bein with my kind an how I'm sorry he's got to be another creature on this earth thas got to suffer jus for takin up with me.

Tonight, I get back from lettin him out an I hope there won't be hardly nobody in the place since it's close to closin. Soon as I walk in, I see a few stragglers an sure nough Mr. Donaldson's settin up at the counter. Lisa rolls her eyes where only I can see. I'm bettin he's givin her an earful about his neighborhood watch. Comin alongside her, takin over the register again, I hear I was right on the money.

"They were tryin to make off with damn near all a McHenry's lawn equipment. Can you believe that? Right in broad daylight." he rants.

"What'd they want that for?" Lisa asked.

"Hock it probly. Hell, bet one of em's got a booth right out at the flea

market. People out there off 54 sellin T.V.'s, vacuums, lawn mowers every weekend. You name it they got it." he educates her.

I look at his empty plate, an know in less than two minutes flat, he's gonna ask for cake. He's regular as they come. Always orders a chicken salad sandwich then has to have himself a slice a whatever's on hand. Told us last week the doctor wants him to lay off sugar cause he's got the pre-diabetes, an Lord knows I feel bad givin him sweets, but it's his body. I figure it's better he get a slice a homemade stead a grabbin Ho Ho's from the corner store on the way home. Those right there'll single handedly get you a prescription for insulin. Mmm hmmm, they will.

"Queenie, could you cut me a piece a that pound cake?" he asks.

Ain't nobody else I'd let call me Queenie, but he don't do it outta disrespect. I get the distinct feelin he thinks he's got my name right. After correctin him once or twice I let it go. Nice enough fella. Can tell I ain't won him over quite yet, but he's comin round. I dish up the cake an pour him his usual glass a milk with a smile.

He's like a lot a the folks who come in. Tolerate me, even speak to me now an again. Feels thas enough. I'm right down there with Ms. Smith's down syndrome boy. The one she brings in for breakfast every Friday when he gets his day out away from the home where he lives with other folks like himself. We're the same cause nobody outright hates us. They jus wish we'd stay home so they didn't have to be slapped in the face with the fact that we exist.

Mr. Donaldson nods at me in thanks an goes on tellin Lisa how if he hadn't stopped those kids they'd a gotten away with the clothes off McHenry's line. Said the man wouldn't a had a lick a tools to help him do his yard maintenance business or a thang to wear when he went down to the station to report it. Lisa makes over him, agrees with him on how important the neighborhood patrols are then starts helpin me clean up behind the counter.

We try to act like we're still listenin, but we got a lot a sugars to refill an cream pitchers to wash. Every now an then we nod an smile over at him. All of a sudden we don't hear him no more. I look over an he's spilled his milk. God in heaven if he don't got his hands up around his throat!

"He's chokin!" Loretta yells.

She's settin at the other end a the counter an don't make no move to help, jus hops off her stool an watches. I dash around the counter an put my Heimlich maneuver to work. Learned it back in highschool in health class. We practiced on *dummies. Ain't had to do it on a real live person, but here goes nothin!*

The few customers left are froze up. They stand gawkin, eyes big as plates, as I put my arms around behind him. He don't fight me. Knows I'm his one hope a gettin relief. Grippin my hands together, takes a couple thrusts under his ribs an he hacks it out. Big ol' piece a pound cake right on the counter.

"Praise Jesus!" somebody hollers.

I pat Mr. Donaldson's back an he sets down leanin on the counter. His face regains its regular color. He looks up at me with pure gratitude. Lord have mercy if he ain't gonna up an cry.

"Seems to me Jesus cain't take the credit for this one, but Queenie here sure saved the day." he proclaims for all to hear.

Jumpin up off his stool he does somethin that shocks us all. He gets me in a bear hug, smackin my back like we're ol' army buddies.

"I'm in your debt. Ms. Queenie. Cain't tell you how thankful I am you was here!" he gushes.

I step back a ways, pat his hand an squeeze his shoulder.

"It ain't no thang Mr. Donaldson. Cain't have people dyin up in here. Specially not from eatin anythang Lisa's made." I laugh.

He hugs me one more time, then pulls out his wallet to pay his ticket. I tell him he's square with us tonight. He jokes that he should choke more often then jus about dances out the door. Once he's outside, through the winda I see him he grab hold a the first person walks by him on the sidewalk. He turns em so they look in at me. He fills their ear about what all went on. I nod at em an smile.

Everybody else wants to shake my hand on their way out. Loretta whispers in my ear how sorry she was that she whatin more help. I assure her I had it covered. All I could do not to tell her not to ever bring her yella bellied ass back through this door. Woulda gone an let that man choke right beside her. Lord have mercy!

My momma'd say thas white women for you. First sign a trouble they under the table. Wouldn't a called momma no racist, but she'd worked for her share a cowardly whites who barked loud about how awful their husbands were an how they had a good mind to tell them where they could go. But to hear momma tell it, the minute the man walked in the door, though they'd be spoonin out his supper sweet as pie. Mmmm hmmm. White women for you. All bark no bite.

Lisa cain't say enough about how proud of me she is. She gives me a big ol' kiss right fore we get in our cars so she can head to do the bank drop an I can head home. All the way to the house, I'm full up with admiration over it. Cain't recall another thang I've done that measures up to savin a man's life. Done plenty a good thangs for myself, but this was the biggest thang I done for somebody else.

I let Rodrigo outside an slip his leash on. He's prancin ahead like he's the one who done the Heimlich on Mr. Donaldson an I been the one settin home scratchin myself. He starts barkin real loud an I look up to see Lil' Miss Thang's house.

"Come on buddy. We been over this." I tell him pullin him down the street.

Fore we get too far, I look up at Lil' Miss Thang's winda. Her light's on. I bet she's doin homework. Sure wish I could tell her all about tonight. Side from Lisa she's the main person I'd want to tell it to. Didn't realize til she hadn't been comin round no more how much I enjoyed talkin to her an listenin to her. Girl could tell a story, Mmm hmmm. Looked forward to seein her more than anybody else since we been here.

We jus about to round the corner outta sight when I see her raise up an look out at us. Bet she heard Lil' Man barkin. My arm goes up to wave, but I stop short. She puts her hand on the winda. I raise my arm, an put my hand up, *then she must be settin back down to her desk cause she's gone. Feels like I been kicked in the gut.*

Feel a deep sadness cause this is how so many thangs go. Jus when I go gettin somethin good, all wonderful, an happy in my life then…boom! Somebody who cain't see further than what is or isn't between my legs goes an ruins it.

I wanna tell Lil' Miss Thang it's ok, that I understand. I guess I jus did. Sometimes we don't get to say any a the thangs we wanna say. Sometimes all we get is a look an the wave a our hand in the night.

The Girl

"Charlotte. Charlotte Grace, honey." Ms. Terrell summoned me, broom in hand, from where she stood on her porch.

"Yes, ma'am?" I called.

"You got a minute?"

I looked out at the empty street. Most Saturday mornings everyone slept in. I wanted to avoid mother and Daddy. The plan had been to get out early, hide out in the library, look at magazines, and cross my fingers that Donnie didn't find me. For a couple weeks, I'd done a good job of being *busy* or having too much homework to hang out with him.

There was no reason not to help Ms. Terrell. No reason except that I'd been avoiding her altogether so I wouldn't hear about anywhere she might be going or what she'd be doing. That way when Donnie finally caught up with me and asked me about her, I could honestly tell him I didn't have a clue. Somehow he could tell when I was lying. I concluded that it took a liar to know a liar.

As I stepped up on her porch, I saw that this time she'd ordered something that had arrived in several crates. She explained to me that once we brought them inside, we'd have to use her crow bar from the basement and detailed for me where it was so I could fetch it. The stairs got to her. She tried not to go down there more than about once every couple of days to do her laundry.

I turned on the basement light, taking the stairs two at a time, I was eager to get it over with. Grabbing the crowbar next to her rake, I rushed back upstairs. With the musty walls, and the dark corners, I pretended I was Anne Frank escaping from the concentration camp.

I'd never used a crow bar before. I felt a sense of accomplishment as I cracked open the wood. Ms. Terrell leaned over, pushed the straw aside then held up a large vase in the shape of a swan. Its neck stretched up, a gaping mouth served as the opening for the water and flowers. The gold coating on it blinded me. It was by far the tackiest thing I'd seen up to that point in time.

"Isn't it exquisite?" she exclaimed in a broken whisper as she ran her hands over it.

I just smiled, my well of lies suddenly dry.

"There's five of em. One for my sister and each a my children. All 14 karat gold plated. Each and every one." she boasted. "My legacy. Had to sign for em special delivery.

My face must've given away my confusion. She went on to tell me all about how she hadn't wanted any of them to fight over her belongings or money when she passed - an event she felt certain could happen any day. That when she'd seen these up for auction on the new computer her daughter'd bought her, she knew they were the way to solve it. They'd each get a swan, and that would be that.

"I also picked them cause I loved that story when I was a little girl." she added.

"I'm not sure I know that one." I commented.

"Surely you've heard of it? The one where the ugly duckling becomes a swan."

I nodded. Yes...our teacher had read it to us in kindergarten or the first grade, but I hadn't thought about it for a long time. However, I did remember that as I listened to her read it in her Mother Goose voice, I had registered with it. For several years afterwards, I had wondered if I too would one day find a place I belonged like that duckling had.

When I'd first met Donnie, it crossed my mind that at last it had happened, though standing there in front of Ms. Terrell, I realized there was no such thing. I'd remained ugly. There were no swans waiting to welcome me. It was only ever a story.

I helped her unload each vase and cart them to her storage room in the back. All of the rooms we passed seemed like closets. How she ever located anything was a mystery. We rolled the swans up in quilts, placing them under a bed.

Before I could make my excuses and head out, she invited me to sit for a few minutes and have some of her lemon pound cake. Since my own house continued to be a wasteland of healthy rations, I wouldn't have dreamed of turning down sugar. I sat right up to her bar, and watched, mouth watering, as she sliced off of hunk of yellow goodness. It was mine, all mine!

It was wonderfully rich! I savored every bite as if it would be my last, and knowing mother, it very well could've been. Ms. Terrell babbled as she usually did about how her arthritis was acting up, how she needed to get out more, and how she wished her children would come by more often. The cake lulled me into a sugar coma so that I only heard snippets.

"Glad we're finishing this off. Hate to think of wasting it. Marcia's coming to pick me up this weekend. She and her husband just bought a house out at Lake Ellis and we're all going out there. Won't be home til Sunday. Sure hope we'll have good weather. Have you heard if they're calling for rain?" She wanted to know.

I shook my head, then just as I reveled in my last bite, she moved on to a subject I'd never anticipated.

"I'm glad you aren't upset with me." she said, patting my hand.

I continued chewing and waited. At one time or another, most people make the mistake of talking too much. Daddy taught me that. "If you wait long enough, if you're patient, most people will hang themselves." he'd advised me more than once.

"Don't get me wrong now, she's a nice enough person. I just didn't feel a girl your age should be spending so much time over there. Awfully confusing. Couldn't help but keep thinking about how if it'd been my Bev or Sarah, I'd have wanted someone to tell me." Ms. Terrell digressed.

Looking across the counter at her withered face, her eyes that had always seemed so innocently kind, her pursed pink lipstick stained lips, I saw her for who she really was... a nosy old bitch. She had been the spy! She was how mother found out about Queen! This woman had taken away my only friend!

One time when Daddy had the news on at the house, I heard a reporter say that most car accidents happened closest to your residence because you get comfortable. You stop paying attention. As I looked at Ms. Terrell rinsing our plates, I decided that this principle also applied to most betrayals. They are committed by the ones closest to you, right under your nose. You get comfortable. You quit paying attention.

Playing it cool, I thanked her for the cake and asked if she'd like me to take the wood crates out to the road. She told me they were good for storage, and not to worry with it. Her phone rang. I let myself out waving to her, giving her a sweet smile as I closed the door.

Standing on her porch, looking across the street at Queen's, my heart pounded, and ached. It felt as if it'd been ripped in two. I wanted to run right over there and bang on her door until she let me in. I wanted to tell her whose fault it was and that it wasn't mine. That I had been careful. I wanted to make sure she knew I had nothing to do with whatever Daddy had said in that letter he'd slipped in her mailbox with her key.

My feet didn't cooperate. They kept me glued to the steps. I looked past Queen's towards the woods. Those woods I used to cut through with Lil' Man to get to Donnie's. That's when I knew.

Whether the part of me that concocted what I did had always been inside, waiting to come out, I can't say. For most of my life, I'd been a good girl, eager to please. Sure, like most children, on rare occasions, I'd been led astray by the need for friendship or by hunger pains in my stomach, but overall I'd been an up and up kind of gal.

My report card comments had mostly gone in my favor. All my teachers stated that I was quiet but helpful. They had also noted, however, that I was not working up to my full potential. Perhaps that was what gripped me that day on Ms. Terrell's porch, those words... *full potential.*

Going against every ounce of goodness that vied for my heart, mind and soul, I broke out of my stupor. Donnie did not have to find me. I knew where he could be found. I ran all the way to the corner store, and darted down the alley.

There he and his gangly horde were, right out back devouring Nutty Buddies as they threw bottles from the dumpster onto the train tracks. I stopped, and leaned over to catch my breath. I hadn't run that far since gym class the year before, and even then the coach commented he'd come close to calling the ambulance.

"What the hell's gotten into you?" Gary called being the first to spot me.

Donnie threw the bottle that was in his hand then ate the last bite of his ice cream before sauntering over.

"You alright?" he asked putting a hand on my shoulder.

I nodded, heaving in then out.

"Where you been?" he wanted to know, playfully nudging me with his elbow.

I didn't answer, but looked at the bottles smashed against the metal and gravel. It wasn't real to any of us that this could cause problems for the train that nightly ran along those tracks. Maybe it was real to them. It was likely what that ignoramus Gary hoped for, replaying the scenario, as he sat watching T.V. in the shack where he and his Grandpa took up space.

"Saturday." I finally managed.

"What?" Donnie tried to clarify.

"She'll be gone to her daughter's lake house all day Saturday." I announced.

He smiled, waving the others over. I only half listened as he relayed this piece of good news to his minions. Huddled there alongside Donnie, I thought that those grimy boys weren't exactly swans, but they'd indeed welcomed me. It occurred to me that you don't get to pick. That perhaps what you are picks you instead, and that when it does, good or bad, then and only then, are you on your way to working up to your *full potential*.

The Cop

It was by pure luck, happenstance at its best, that he was the first to respond. As he rolled up to the house, he wondered if his patrol car would be seen from across the street as the little dog was let out. If the very sight of it would make the fag's flat stomach churn. The possibility of this gave him a certain kind of thrill.

Since Lisa had sent he and Tom on their way, banishing them to lunch after lunch of greasy fried chicken, he'd seen very little of Queen. Only on the nights he'd chosen to cruise past the restaurant around closing, had he seen *it* through the window, wiping tables in *its* tight t-shirts. There'd been more acclaim for Queen since *it*'d apparently saved Mr. Donaldson from an untimely death. Feeling this proved an obstacle for hasty retribution, he'd laid low. This down time was his reprieve, his time to think, gather the right weapons from his stockpile, make the next best tactical move.

A paramedic walked towards him. He got out, meeting him halfway up the drive.

"Nothin like a body to kick off the week hey, Dade? Hated to bother you all with it. Just followin protocol." The paramedic filled him in.

"Let's see it, James." Carter reluctantly ordered.

A cell phone rang. James fished in his pocket, pulling it out and putting it up to his ear.

"Just arrived." he told the caller. "Yeah. Mmm hmm. I'll let keep you posted."

Motioning for Carter to follow him, they ventured up to the the porch. Turning, James held his hand up to his co-worker who was still seated in the passenger seat of the ambulance signaling to him that he could stay put.

"Fucking newbies." James snarled.

The door was ajar. The glass from the window pane above the knob broken. No doubt it'd been the only way for E.M.S. to gain access. The faint smell of mothballs and the dated house numbers nailed by the mailbox beside the door indicated it was likely the home of an elderly person. As they stepped inside, Carter tried to ascertain what room they were entering. A storage area? A living room?

"Another damn hoarder." James complained. "Family couldn't reach her by phone. For it'd even been 24 hours, sheriff called it in cause his wife an the old woman's daughter are friends. Said old as she was, there was probably gonna be more need for us than you."

They winded through the stacks of opened and unopened boxes and empty crates until they reached a door in the hallway next to the kitchen.

"Now right this second, there ain't no call to think it's foul play, but that ain't really my area a expertise." James admitted.

The light to the basement was already on. Carter stood at the top of the stairs. There she was sprawled out at the bottom, a geriatric baby doll, arms and legs contorted unnaturally. Cocking his head to the side, he surveyed her with a momentary curiosity much like he would a sun-baked worm on a sidewalk. He descended slowly, getting as close to her as possible without disrupting any would be evidence.

    Blood had trickled from her head, culminating into a neat little pool under her placid face. He wondered if things would've turned out differently if she'd only appropriated some of the money that'd been used on all her needless paraphernalia to carpet her basement and thus preemptively cushion her fall.

    It looked to him to be a clear-cut case of a person not being in reality in regards to their own decrepid state. She'd misjudged herself, thinking she could climb those stairs whenever she pleased. He theorized that the ending was the only thing that had made sense in a life that had otherwise become haphazard and pointless.

    Deeming it an accident, he climbed back up the steps pulling the door to behind him. James went outside to rouse his partner so they could bring the body up from the bowels of the basement by way of their stretcher. This left Carter unattended to maneuver through the hodgepodge of junk, though there seemed little to no reason to think the situation was anything but what it revealed itself to be upon first glance.

    With the family pictures on every wall, and cards from relatives placed on the mantles, some of the rooms reminded him of his own Grandmother's house. She'd been kind to him, his mother's mother. He'd never known his father's mother, and his father seldom spoke of her. Once in a while a comment would be made, however, that let Carter know that the buck had stopped with her, that his father's seeming disdain for women, had began and ended at her doorstep.

If Carter hadn't taken the time to browse, James would've proceeded with the usual process. The old woman's body would've been sent to Harmon's mortuary. Her children would've come to wail, carry on, and select a casket befitting their dearest mother. But he did take the time, more out of a temporary appeasement of his own boredom rather than out of a desire to produce good police work.

The last room he happened upon was a small one in the way back. A blanket lay in a heap in the middle of the floor. Lifting it, he saw four dazzling gold vases, each in the shape of a swan. A few other things were strewn about the room, not in keeping with the way the rest of the items in the house were purposefully stacked and organized. There was something about the scene that alerted him to the fact that someone had been pillaging.

Standing up, flipping the blanket back into place, he saw it. There under the window was something gold and shiny. Instinctively, he stooped again and reached for it, yet instantly drew back, remembering his rubber gloves that he'd seldom had opportunity to use.

He pulled one from his jacket pocket, sliding it over one of his hands. Crouching down, he eyed the item closely. It was a tube of lipstick. Studying it closer, he saw that it was identical to the one tucked safely in the Ziploc bag in the glove compartment of his car.

His hand trembled as he closed his latex covered fingers around it.

Turning it upside down, he closed his eyes, whispering a silent prayer to whatever evil might be bending its ear. Slowly he opened them again. His eyes took in the small fine print on the bottom of the tube: *Queen's Quintiscential Pink*.

The Tranny

I'm on the side of the road. Rain's barely comin down. I see his car from a long way off. It's a replay a that night, cept rain aint' pourin like it was then. It's him, an I know it, but I jus stand there while his car pulls up. His winda rolls down.

The whole time I'm screamin at myself in my head to run, but my body don't listen. I lean down to see it ain't that yellow bellie pig…it's my cousin. Plain as day there in the driver's seat, same clothes he had on that day a the reunion.

"Storm's comin, Jermaine. Better get in." he warns.

My hand reaches for the car door, but it itn't my hand. It's a small hand. A boy's hand with flashy, acrylic nails glued to the end a my fingers. Lookin down at my body, I see I'm Jermaine, but in Queen's clothes. My twelve year old bird chest under a tube top. Knobby knees I ain't growed into yet peekin out from under a miniskirt. Touchin my head, a wig shifts to one side. The smell a fried chicken comes on strong, bout to cause me to vomit. There's a loud clap a thunder in the distance. I wake up.

Rain's peltin against our bedroom winda. Lil' Man's snuggled up next to my head. He hates storms like nobody's business. Him an me both. Settin up against the headboard, I rub my eyes, scoop him up, hold him to my chest. Ain't had a dream like that in forever. The feel a his lil' heart beatin against mine calms me. This dog sure nough saves some poor therapist from havin to hear all my shit. Somebody should give him an honorary doctorate in psychology. Mmm hmmm. He's earned it.

"*Stormin again?*" *Lisa mumbles eyes still closed.*

"*Yeah. I got him. You go on an sleep. You the one goin in early.*" *I tell her.*

With Lil' Man wrapped in my robe like a chihuahua burrito, I walk down the hall an me an him camp out on the couch. Old movie'll help drown out that thunder. Might help me fall asleep again too. Turnin on the T.V. I flip through the channels. Wouldn't you know Dirty Dancin's on? Love me some Patrick Swayze. God got it right with that one.

Lil' Miss Thang wanted to see this. Said her momma'd walked in on her one night when she was jus startin to watch. Told her in no uncertain terms was she to ever lay eyes on anythang where people were wearin leotards an doin all that grindin. This cracked me up to hear it second hand from her at the time cause from the sound of it, it seemed like she'd a let her watch it if they'd a been doin all that gyratin with they jeans an t-shirts on. Outta respect, her bein her momma an all, I tried not to laugh too much in front a her.

Instead, I promised when I got a day off work an she had a break from school we'd have us a girl's afternoon. We'd get us some junk food an watch it together. It'd be our little secret. Tol' her, in my opinion, the dirtiest thang about it was the title. The six o'clock news got a whole hell of a lot worse on it but people don't mind cause thas violence. You throw sex in the mix, they all in a uproar. Crazy thang is ain't a one a those thangs worse in the eyes a God. Mmmm hmmm. That'll preach.

Glancin out the front winda, I see there ain't a light on at her place. Wonder how she's doin with her fella. Wonder if her momma's lettin up about her weight, or if her daddy's makin time for her. I imagine her there in her bed sleepin away a pitiful lil' gal who don't got a prayer in this world a seein Patrick Swayze or hearin him sing Hungry Eyes now. It's a damn shame. Fore I know it, Lisa's wakin me up, kissin my cheek for she heads for work.

"See you round 3:00." she reminds.

"You know it." I answer.

Once she's gone, I lay back down. Barely get situated an there's sirens goin off outside. They must be cuttin through to knab somebody. I pull the blanket over my head, hopin it'll pass. Lil' Man starts howlin over the noise.

There's a knock on the door. Lisa's probly realized she forgot to take that cake she baked. Girl would forget her head if it whatin screwed on.

"It ain't locked!" I yell out over the sirens not wantin to have to get up yet.

The knockin breaks into poundin. I jump up, grab Lil' Man, tuck him under my arm. Cain't get there fast enough. God knows! Whatever's goin on, all that cain't be necessary.

"I'm comin!" I shout.

Soon as I open the door, there he is, the hillbilly partner a that wolf. A feelin sinks deep in my gut. I shoulda seen this comin. That dream last night... momma woulda called it a prophecy, a warnin.

There's four cruisers out front! Don't think O.J. had any less show up when he killed that blonde girl an her boyfriend. Across the street, Ms. Terrell's daughter's standin on her mother's porch, an officer besider her. She's jackin her jaw a mile a minute, pointin an jus a shakin her head.

Saw E.M.S there real early in the mornin one day last week. Figured Ms. Terrell done took her a fall. Ol' people's always tumblin, breakin their hips or somethin. Way word travels round here, knew we'd hear tell of it soon enough. Whatin but later on that same night that a few folks at the restaurant were already talkin bout how there'd been a burglary. She'd fell down the steps, died right there all by her lonesome in her basement. Fore I know what's goin on, the partner's readin me my rights. Lil' Man's growlin at him for all he's worth.

"What's goin on? I don't..."

"Now, I'm not obligated to, but out a the goodness of a my heart, I'm gonna let you put that thang back in the house fore we go down to the station." he tells me noddin at Lil' Man.

"You ain't got no cause to be here!" I blurt. "Tell me what I done!"

Two a the cops ease away from their cars an start headin our way. One of em puts his hand on his gun. Only thang I can think about is all the movies I've ever seen where a black man gets shot jus for bein black. All the news reports I've ever heard about the very same thang. I remind myself I ain't nothing to them. Nothin but another nigger who's steppin outta line. Worse than that, I'm a tranny nigger. Worst kind. Mmm hmmm, you know thas right. The partner turns an holds up his hand. The others stop in their tracks, but shift uneasy — coyotes waitin to be turned loose on a rabbit.

"You can either put the dog away yourself, sir or one a these gentlemen's gonna take him to the pound." He informs me under his breath like he's doin me some favor he don't want them to know about.

I look him in the eyes an know it don't take a genious to see who sent him. Because a the company he keeps, I know he means business. Steppin back, I let Lil' Man down in the kitchen. He tries to run out at him, but I stamp my foot an send him scamperin.

He must sense how thangs is goin, cause any other day there'd be a fifty fifty chance he wouldn't listen to me. Most at the time he does whatever he sets his mind on, but this time he runs over an gets right on his cushion by the stove. As I shut the front door, an join them on the porch, my body feels more like a car I'm drivin stead a somethin I'm livin in . I feel myself bein turned around. Feel the cold steel a the handcuffs on my wrists. The gruff hands a the partner as he hurries me to the car then pushes me into the back seat.

I'm outside myself, my body separate from my mind. It's all more like somethin on the Lifetime channel, happenin to somebody else. Somethin unreal, too terrible to be true. All of a sudden, I'm way back to that day on the floor a my bedroom. Back to when Manny'd get to wailin on me. Back under that cop that night in that car. The passenger door slams. I lean against the seat, stare at the partition between us as he's radioin in that I been apprehended. Outta nowhere, there's bangin on the winda across from me. I look up to see Lil' Miss Thang beatin on that glass for all she's worth.

"Queen! What's goin on? What's happening? Queen!" she's demandin, tears streamin down her chubby cheeks.

Fore I can say a word, her daddy's pullin her away. Her momma's callin from their yard where she's planted herself, bein sure to keep her distance.

"Charlotte Grace! Stop this! Stop this right now!" she's shoutin at her.

The partner rolls down his winda, says somethin to Mr. Danby, but I cain't make it out. As he puts the car in gear, drives off, I can still see Lil' Miss Thang pullin against her daddy. Her mouth's still movin, an she gets close enough I can hear.

"What about Lil' Man?" she's shriekin for all she's worth.

Sure nough, true to her nature, she's thinkin about somebody sides herself. Turnin around, hands cuffed behind my back, all I can do is look at her, let her know I see her. I see she cares. She's still got my key, but I bet her momma'd rather let Lil' Man shrivel up an die there in my house fore she'd let her use it even one more time.

We pass the restaurant on the way. Full up with the usual folks. Won't be no time an somebody'll tell Lisa what's gone on. That or come 3:00 she'll call home an won't nobody pick up. She'll worry herself sick.

I keep my head down. The partner stops at the station, opens my door, an jerks me out. Didn't dawn on me til now, I'm still in my robe, the pink silky one a momma's. Wind blowin against my head, reminds me I didn't even have time to get my hair neither. Don't know which is worse. Bein arrested or leavin home for the first time in over five years with a bald head.

We get in the station an every cop in the place stops to see the show. First time in their ignorant redneck lives they seen who they think is a black man with breasts, a head shinier than a penny an in a pink robe to boot. I can already hear each an every one of em tellin their wives or their mommas, whoever the hell's waitin on em at home tonight jus what kinna freak they got in custody.

I see him from behind. I'd know those shoulders an that neck anywhere. There he is propped up at his desk, feet up like he's home watchin his T.V. As we get closer, I see he's got a wide grin on his face. He's eatin this up. Tears hadn't come til I laid eyes on him right now. Much as I fight em off, try to will em away, they come.

Same way I know the sun sets, an the moon's comin after it. Same way I can count on my life continuin to be a trial, I know for certain this is all his doin. Know full well that he set it in motion.

I don't want to give him the satisfaction a lookin at him, but I don't want to make him think I'm too scared to neither. As I walk beside his partner, I glare right at him. His grin gets wider. He lifts a hand up to his head, salutes me like he's a soldier.

I resign myself to bein a object. Come to terms with the fact that thas the only way to get through this. Let em treat me like a rag doll, like a thang an not a person cause thas how they see me.

Finger prints are taken. I get felt up by one of em who says he's makin sure I don't have nothin I ain't allowed to have then I change my clothes in front of a room of em. If they thought of me as a woman they'd have a female officer in here doin all of this. Wouldn't doubt they placed bets out in the hall on whether or not I got girl parts or boy parts, an now they want to see with they own eyes who's right. Inbred motherfuckers!

I set on a hard bench against the wall waitin to hear what it is I'm bein charged with. Two of em's havin a chuckle by a drink machine. That wolf, an another one followin behind him, take me down the hall, open the cell for me real polite like we on some kinna first date an he's holdin open the door to a fancy restaurant.

I walk through bein sure to stay as far away from him as I can. Got the feelin whatever he wants to haul off an do here, wouldn't be witnessed by nobody but me. He don't take his eyes off me as he shuts the door. I stare back til he's all the way gone. Settin down on a cot, I hug my legs up to my chest, wrap my arms tight around em.

Hadn't heard mention a my phone call. Soon as I hear the charges, I'll ask for it. I know it's gonna be to Lisa. I know it, but I don't want it to be. Don't know what in the hell they got on me, but I don't want her to know about it. Don't want her to know I was right an she was wrong.

Tol' her fore we ever decided to come down this way that this was how it was gonna go. Tol' her by how squirrely everybody acted towards me at her daddy's funeral that there whatin nothin could make this town ready for me. Tried like hell to make her understand it's dangerous when you throw people into thangs fore they're good an ready. Most dangerous thang in the world cause there's no tellin what lengths folks'll go to tryin to set thangs back the way they want em.

The Girl

I sat against the side of my bed, empty blanket in hand, I wracked my brain for what could have happened to it. When I had been given the job of concealing it, I'd put it the only place I knew to put anything: under my bed.

The obvious answer was that mother found it when she was cleaning. I wondered what I would tell her about where it came from?

I thought back to how Ms. Terrell had been so proud showing it off that day. How her bony fingers looked as she gingerly helped me wrap them in the quilts. I kept hearing her unsteady voice saying *legacy*. Because of what we'd done, one of her descendants wouldn't receive their due.

Putting all worries concerning the contraband on the backburner, I thought about how Queen being in custody was far more urgent than my mindless pursuits. I sat up to my desk, the best vantage point to watch for Lisa coming home to check on Lil' Man. When she finally did, Queen was not with her, and I knew that did not bode well. I knew then she hadn't made bail.

Two of the police cars returned not long after Lisa arrived home. Officers exited and stalked up to the door. They knocked loudly, and once she opened it, wielded a paper in her face. With no other option, she moved aside for them to enter. Mother only interrupted my vigil only once with one of her tedious chores to try to keep me from the window.

They officers didn't resurface for an hour or more, and when they did, one of them had something a little larger than a football wrapped in plastic, tucked under his arm. Lisa followed them cursing and yelling as she did.

They pulled away, leaving her there, hands on her hips, pacing back and forth. Suddenly, she looked my way. I ducked out of sight, the same as I'd done the first day I saw Queen. It felt so wrong to have progressed so far only to have arrived back in the same spot.

Not an hour after the police pulled away, the phone in Daddy's office rang. This wasn't an unusual occurrence, yet for some reason, I paid attention to it that day. The sound of it made me think of the countless times I'd heard it before, and how each of those times it had meant one more person was sitting somewhere crying, worried sick about their loved one who'd been arrested. It had never been just a phone ringing, but in reality, the sound of someone's future hanging by a thread.

Mother had eagerly retreated to her land of oblivion. Below me, she flitted around in the kitchen, preparing my favorite dinner. There was the clanging of the pots and pans as she fried meatballs, boiled noodles, chopped tomatoes, and diced onions. These methodical, menial tasks done to dull the frustration over what had unfolded on our street. The very street where she and Daddy had intentionally moved so they'd never have to witness such *lowly* atrocities.

Though her spaghetti sauce was nothing short of miraculous, it did not make up for my friend being arrested. It angered me that she assumed it would. I was no more than her dog to be easily distracted by whatever morsels she put in my bowl.

The aroma of garlic filled our house, yet my appetite was not piqued. All I could think about was Queen sitting in a cell. Sitting there without her hair, or her flashy clothes or makeup. Without any of the things that made her who she was. Knowing her the way that I did, I knew she rarely let anyone see her without her hair nevertheless a room full of men in uniform. The humiliation had to be unbearable.

Opening my desk drawer, I instinctively reached inside to retrieve the tube of lipstick she'd given me. It was as if holding it would make all that had transpired dissipate, but it wasn't there. That had been the last place I'd remembered putting it, but I dismissed this, assuming I'd left it in my locker at school. I instead ran through ways I could sneak her hair to her. Maybe I could pass it in through a window the way they did in those old westerns I'd watched with Daddy. The criminals in them created a diversion then snuck things through bars to their buddies.

"It's ready!" mother sang out from the dining room.

She was not going to let me skip the charade by any means. No peace would be allowed unless I indulged. This would make her feel better, and that is what we all existed for. No one was exempt from this burden - not Daddy, not me, or anyone that ever met her for that matter.

Inching down the stairs down to the dining room, I felt the way I imagined Anne Frank felt when the soldiers came for her and her family. Wanting with everything in me to run, flee into the night, but where would I go? Just like Anne, I was only a girl, and I was surrounded. She'd been surrounded by Nazis. I was surrounded by bigots. It struck me that the difference between our foes was only in the pronunciation of their names.

"We have plenty of sauce." mother gushed, spooning some onto a plate already teeming with pasta.

In our house, the only good thing about crisis was that it meant you'd be encouraged to *fall off the wagon*. Everyone would be sure to look the other way. They'd do more than that. They'd make a soft place for you to fall once you did - a soft place cushioned by carbs.

"It's real good, hon. Sauce tastes different." Daddy made over it while being sure to avoid my gaze.

"I put in some cloves I bought at the farmer's market. They really make it pop, don't you think?" she babbled.

Picking up my fork, I used it to swirl noodles in a pool of sauce. The compilation resembling a vat of grease more than nourishment. Normally, I'd have splattered my cheeks with the stuff as I lapped it up, but in light of the day's events, it was inedible. It was like everything else - once beloved and treasured, now a detestable, muddled mess.

The two of them yammered back and forth about frivolous drivel. It was the best they'd gotten along in weeks. It crossed my mind to suggest that we should live in a worse neighborhood since all it took for them to bury the hatchet that had sliced their relationship in two was an arrest at their doorstep.

In response to mother's begging, I ate a couple of bites, hoping, if I stuck it out, they'd eventually get around to talking about what was going with Queen. To my dismay, they maintained their conversational frivolity until the meal ended. They rose, picked up their plates, and I saw that they were going to be content to let it lie. They were going to leave me tormented by my visions of Queen rotting in jail. I was at my wits end. For the first time in my young life, I was going to insist on more than their usual substandard parenting.

"Daddy?" I said far more loudly than I'd intended.

"Hmmm?" he answered, briefly stopping on his way to the kitchen, turning only slightly.

"Why'd they take her?" I demanded.

Stretching to reach my plate, mother pulled it closer to her and began spooning even more sauce onto my cold noodles.

"You hardly ate a thing. Now it's gone dry." she rattled off in an attempted to divert me.

"Daddy!" I barked again, not be to rabbit trailed.

He sat back down in his chair, placing his plate back in front of him, then forking meatballs from a serving dish onto it.

"I know it might be hard to understand, Charlotte Grace, but some things have to be left to adults. I know you knew him but…"

"*Her!*" I corrected.

"What?" he snapped, bewildered by my backtalk.

"Queen is a *she*." I protested.

At this statement, my mother dropped the sauce ladle and burst into tears. She scurried into the kitchen. She might as well have had her fit right there with us since we could still hear her wailing through the door.

Daddy stuffed a meatball in his mouth, chewed it, shaking his head as he did. I glared at him, letting him know that they would not get off so easily. So many times, we'd cowed to the whims and needs of mother. I'd lazily permitted it because it only concerned me, but this had to do with my closest friend. This time, if he pushed it, I was fully prepared to hang on his ankles kicking and screaming until I got an answer.

He looked across the table and seemed to understand. His fork clanked down on his plate. He sighed, and rubbed his temples.

"Hell, if you're old enough to be sneaking over there, I guess you're old enough to know." he caved. "Ms. Terrell's fall wasn't an accident."

I gulped. Sweat beaded on my forehead.

"It wasn't?"

"No, it wasn't. From what they can tell, she was robbed. The burglar probably thought she wasn't home, and she surprised them when she came up from the basement. They must have tried to shut her down there, an that's what caused her to fall down the steps." he regurgitated the information as if reading me a police report.

My hands nervously ran over the legs of my pants. I wanted to wipe my forehead, but I didn't want to call undue attention to my instant anxiousness.

"That's awful!" I exclaimed. "But I don't understand. What's that have to do with Queen?"

Chunking off a piece of French bread from the basket in front of him, he dipped it in the sauce on his plate then stuffed it in his mouth. He wouldn't look at me. He only stared at the sauce. Mouth half full, he finally gave in.

"They found something of his at the scene." he disclosed.

I opened my mouth to correct him again about the whole *his* verses *her* thing, but seeing the way he was slumped in his chair, I refrained.

"Then they got the warrant, and found what'd been taken from Ms. Terrell's right there under his bed."

The words were audible. I understood them as English, but could not process them. How could that be? How could what had been under my bed, be discovered under hers and what in the world could've been found in Ms. Terrell's house that incriminated Queen in any way?

From behind the kitchen door came the sound of mother blowing her nose. The key...they hadn't returned the key...mother had kept it! She'd been the only one who could've taken that swan over there and hidden it! She was the only one who could ever convince herself that would be the right thing to do. I could just see her, shushing Lil' Man as she went, creeping down their hall, kneeling down, pushing it under Queen's bed.

Shell shocked, sick to my stomach, I stayed put. Daddy got up again. This time he left his plate for mother to see to. He slunk in the direction of the hallway to go to his office. As he passed, he patted my shoulder.

"Sometimes we see what we want to see, honey. We don't see people for who they really are." he cautioned, then kissed the top of my head.

All alone in our fancy dining room, I knew what he said was true for some, but it wasn't true about Queen. No, not her, though it was true about me. People saw me as the daughter of the D.A. and his Peach Princess wife. They saw me as a quiet, priviledged Southern girl who, what with all my black clothing and weight problem, was just going through a phase.

What they didn't see was that the wrong person had been arrested. What they could never have fathomed was the scheming, rancid sidekick I'd become. Leaning back, I stared up at the ceiling. All I could picture was that tragic image. The one that awaited me that night when Donnie and I had opened her basement door. That horrid mental polaroid of Ms. Terrell, pitiful, and bleeding, as she took her last breaths at the bottom of the steps.

The Cop

He saw her sitting on a bench with the fancy lawyer who'd swooped in from Atlanta. Everybody said he'd taken it on pro bono since he was making a name for himself with gay rights cases. There'd been tell of him helping two old flamers get their marriage license out in the Midwest. The first time he came, the sheriff had remarked that from the look of him, he was probably a *pretty boy* himself.

The lawyer was going over something very important, talking elaborately with his hands as Lisa sat next to him staring catatonically ahead. He hung back, peering at them from around the corner. At some point, she would have to leave. Biting his lip, he mulled over the options of how he could get the much needed acknowledgement he'd become slave to. Deciding on one, he ducked out a side door.

Once back at his desk, he made sure to be as inconspicuous as he could, watching as she walked out to her car. She shook the lawyer's hand before getting in and starting it up. He stood, opening his drawer recovering his own keys, but unaware of his plans, the sheriff strutted over.

"Lord knows I hate those freedom fightin, platform mother fuckers. They think it's on them to right every wrong in this God damn universe. Second time this week that fella's come all the way out here. Still hot doggin bout that *thang* needin a private cell. Went on an on about how they should a put *him* in the women's prison anyhow. Told him around here, they go by the birth certificate. I told him what I told him the last time. Talk to the warden. It's up to him. Ain't got no stake in what goes on at the prison. I got enough to keep up with on my end. Whether or not that fella's gonna be everybody's new *bed buddy* is on the warden's plate."

Carter nodded, trying to appear relaxed, as if he were listening, but he was revved up - a snake whose mouse was slipping further from reach with each passing moment. The sheriff set his sights on a fellow officer at the coffee pot, making his way over jabbering all the way about a time card discrepancy. This was Carter's out and he quickly took it.

Just as he was about to be home free, Tom emerged from the locker room. He'd been tied up that morning with the bi-monthly fitness test he'd been prescribed not long after his divorce. His gut had begun to bulge what with all of his frequent trips to Dunkin Donuts. When his mile running time became drastically deficient, he'd no other choice but to succumb to a more rigorous training regimen.

"Hey, thought we were headin to eat." Tom called.

"I'll uh...I'll meet you there. There's somethin I have to do." Carter retorted, keeping forward motion towards the door.

"Hell, it's already 11:30. You know how that place gets. We're gonna be..."

"I'm right behind you." Carter stated with a gruff finality.

"*Al-right.*" Tom consented shoulders slumped and pouting as he meandered down the hallway exposing him as the emotional five year old that he was.

There was time to be made up. The fact that he now was uncertain of her exact wherabouts frayed the edges of his already agitated mood. Possibly she went to the prison to take up the issue of the private cell with the warden? No, he decided she would've left that to the lawyer. She had gumption, he'd give her that, but that situation was above her pay grade. He felt sure she was smart enough to admit it.

Slowly, he turned down the street where their restaurant was located. Driving by at a turtle's pace, he saw a small sign taped on the door. *CLOSED* scrawled in marker across white typing paper. This didn't make him happy, but it certainly didn't make him sad. It was only logged as a clue to be used in determining her whereabouts.

As the minutes ticked by, he knew Tom would be increasingly frustrated, by his tardiness. He didn't care about that per se, but hated to have to come up with fabrications about why he'd been late. For some time, his powers of persuasion, ability to conjure illusions had been off, and he'd found the accessibility to his more cunning, calculated side was erratic at best.

It seemed he would have to give up, yet as he rounded the corner on his way to the Kentucky Fried Chicken there she was kicking one of her car tires, fuming at the machine as if it had deliberately conspired against her. He did not know why she would've come this way, and it was a more trafficked street than he'd hoped for. This wouldn't matter. It was in play now - the *collision* he'd skillfully constructed.

The car in park, he sat behind her for a few seconds to heighten the tension as only he could. She didn't see him right away, so enraptured in her fury. He went through what might evolve, panning through the scenarios like slides through a mental view master. He'd cherished his toy one as a child. It had been used to view glorious depictions of King Kong, clinging to the top of a skyscraper as he held a screaming girl in his grip.

At last Lisa looked over at him. It was a long look. Her lips tightened into a snarl. Though, he'd been meticulously careful to jab the nail in near the tire rim, out of sight, he thought for a moment that she knew. That she'd somehow seen his craftsmanship.

She turned her back to him, and commenced with digging through her purse. He knew he must act before she found her phone. Once she'd dialed, once someone answered on the other end, the window of opportunity would be slammed shut.

Shifting the gearshift into drive, easing up slowly beside her, he rolled the passenger window down, just as he'd done for *it* on that fateful, rainy night.

"Got a flat?" he asked politely as if she was a stranger, and in essence she was, as was everyone else he ever encountered.

She didn't dignify this with a response. Continuing to rifle through her purse, she succeeded in recovering her phone.

"I can give you a ride." he interjected with a tone he felt simulated a kind of sweetness that came naturally to most.

Phone up to her ear, she leaned against her car, and waited for an answer on the other end.

"Hi. This is Lisa Lawson. I'm stuck out here on Davis, bout a half mile from the K.F.C. No... that's alright. I have Triple A. I just wanted to let you know one of your officers is harassing me... yes...Officer Dade. That's right. I'm starin straight at him." she coolly delivered.

He sat still, not pulling away, not rolling up his window. They were back in grade school facing off, only the slide between them - her calling his bluff. This time, however, she was alerting other people about his oddities. Moving his hand up to his belt buckle, his fingers grazed his firearm, but stopped short of removing it from its holster.

She hung up then stared at him, phone still in her hand, a smoking gun all its own. Stepping closer, she leaned on his door. Her perfume wafted across the passenger seat polluting his sterility. Her smile caught him off guard.

"You'll get yours." she declared in a whisper. "People like you always do."

His foot hit the gas, nearly knocking her backwards in the process. Looking through his rearview, as the dust cleared, he saw her standing in the middle of the street one hand on her hips the other lifted, flipping him off. Upon second glance, he swore she was a girl again, taunting him from the top rung of the slide's ladder - his childhood nemesis.

His hands gripped the wheel whitening his knuckles. He could go back and clean her clock. It was still a viable option, and this appeased him. The simple fact that it was a possibility. They could bury her in the same woods where they'd buried the girl. Tom would be game, and it would not be hard to dismiss with his sheriff. When asked about her call, he'd say that he'd seen her on his way to lunch, and she'd not taken kindly to his offer to assist her, but as to what happened to her after that, he had no idea...

He was still entertaining the thought of it as he peeled into the KFC parking lot. A few patrons looked over their shoulders as he zoomed into a parking space. He took a deep breath in then expelled it. As he walked inside, he reminded himself he was Carter Dade, a distinguished Murfeesboro P.O., not that boy who'd been so flippantly labeled *strange* so long ago.

"What's goin on with that queer? You know, the one who killed that old woman right in her house?" A short, bald man quizzed them as he and Tom took their place in line.

"Come end of the week he'll be arraigned." Tom was all too happy to reply.

"Good. Hope they make an example a that Tranny. If they don't, fore you know it, they'll all be comin this way thinkin we're fine with it. Thinkin we're *tolerate* an all." The man griped in a manner that served only to illustrate the breadth of his stupidity.

As his order number was called, Carter made his way to pick up his tray, taking this in on the way, fully digesting it all. He couldn't remember a time when he'd felt so utterly successful, not even on the day he'd graduated the academy. Lisa might be right. There was that chance that kharma could be at work, but he wouldn't be robbed of glorying in what Queen had coming.

That he'd been the one to bring *it* up to speed on the charges, had been more than he could've asked for. The look on Queen's face when *it*'d seen the golden swan. *It*'d been quite the actor. If Carter hadn't been more familiar with *its* kind, he'd have thought for certain that *it*'d honestly never seen the contraband before that moment. But he was all too familiar. He knew *its* sort was famous for their deceitfulness.

The kicker had been the lipstick. As soon as Carter laid it down on the table in front of *it*, Queen accused him of planting it. Only when the Ziploc bag containing the other tube was brought forth from Carter's pocket had Queen's countenance dissentigrated from that of warrior to victim.

That one small token demonstrated that, though it was something Carter wished he could take credit for, it wasn't his doing. There'd been no excuse offered as to how the lipstick came to be in the old woman's home. Queen's crying had broken into a full out sobs there in the interrogation room. The demand for an attorney had followed.

Carter was set to testify that D.N.A. evidence had proved the lipstick was indeed Queen's, and that was the truth. He knew, however, that he'd have to lie about the other unidentifiable prints that had been on the tube. They could cast unwanted doubt. He'd also have to cover up the fact that those prints had matched an identical set that had also been lifted from the swan. No one would be the wiser. As demonstrated by the bald man alongside them in line, everyone was primed and ready to assign blame to the *queer*.

His chicken had less skin on it than usual. Knowing how much his partner loved the crispy coating, Tom peeled remnants from his own wings and plopped them onto a napkin, sliding them across the table. Carter questioned his partner at length in regards to Queen's state the day he'd arrested *it* at *its* residence. Since he'd been the first responder, and had been the one to uncover the evidence, the sheriff felt it best he, himself not go along for that part. He'd reluctantly agreed knowing that his sheer, unadulterated delight would be hard to mask.

Tom had done a fine job, yet much to Carter's chagrin, his friend was no storyteller. His rendering of the events had left much to be desired as did most of his conversation.

"He was hoppin mad, but he knew the deal. Hard not to laugh at the fucker standin there in his girlfriend's robe holdin his little dog. Craziest thang I seen lately, maybe ever." was the most Tom had offered.

A klutzy customer hurried past their table on the way out the door.

absentmindedly, missing the trashcan, sending what was left of their drink plummeting to the floor. Carter wiped his pant leg with a napkin. A young worker, a black girl, scurried out, mop in hand, to take care of the mess.

"Sorry bout that officer." she groveled, using a rag to towel off his shoe.

He nodded, smiled, and watched as her dark hands pick the pieces of ice up off the filthy tile. Her skin was every bit as dark as Queen's, and her face bore a remarkable resemblance also. As he took another bite of his mashed potatoes, the thought that *they all looked alike* raced through his mind. He wondered if from that day forth, anytime he saw a black person, he'd only see the *fag*, and if that was to be the case, then Lisa would be right. With this repetitious reminder, he would indeed *get his*.

The Tranny

Enough time on your hands an you'll start thinkin all the bad thas come your way is nobody's fault but your own. Here in this place I've had enough time to reason out that I've done enough wrong all by myself to send Jesus to the cross. After midnight, everybody's meds have taken hold an it's mostly quiet for a few hours. Thas when, like momma used to say, all the crows come home to roost.

I lay on my bunk starin at the ceilin, thinkin bout how she's probly turnin over in her grave with my bein here. If she was still livin, she wouldn't never be nothin but nice an kind. She'd be comin to visit askin em if she could bring me some a her collards an cornbread. She sit on the other side a that glass, talkin in to the phone, lookin right at me an wouldn't never outright say I was a disappointment.

She always could make it known with what she didn't say. How she wouldn't talk about seein me in that dress or noticin how I always seemed to be strikin out with women. If she'd a been alright with it, we coulda put it out on the table. Avoidin the subject itn't as bad as disagreein about it, but it's a far cry from givin your blessin. Cain't fault her. Thas how it is with most. People only love you enough to talk about the thangs that ain't uncomfortable. Rest of it gets swept under the rug, specially in the south. Everybody's rug's coverin up a cellar door, so you can sweep a whole hell of a lot under there fore it causes any lumps that'll make it hard to walk over.

My thoughts fall to Jarvis, an how I ain't been the brother he wanted. Lord knows with daddy dyin, we needed each other, an I didn't do it to spite him. He thinks I did, but thas only cause he needs there to be a reason. Somethin to explain why I'm me an he's him. Reckon most people do.

Lord knows I've wrecked any kinna normal life Lisa mighta had. She coulda been married an had her some kids by now. Grandkids mighta helped her reconcile with her daddy. That mighta been what she was hopin for when we met. I tell myself she knew what I was an she made her choice, but I know we're all out to change somebody. I knew who she thought I was, who she thought I might get back to bein an I jus let it keep on. It was really me who made the choice for us both.

The longer I lay here, the further back I go. Dredge up my cousin, conjurin up the idea that it all went down cause I sent him the wrong signals. Maybe that day he somehow thought I'd be into what he was into. When the family got together, me an him always did spend time by ourselves playin games or throwin the ball around. Maybe I gave him an open invite an I didn't even know it?

That fella down the way starts his screamin. Won't be long now til a guard'll come an beat him til he shuts up. Hope they beat the side they didn't get to last night. Fella won't be able to walk. Fool cain't sleep without a beatin. Shame…damn shame.

With his fit in the background, the thought a Lil' Miss Thang seeps in. Why couldn't I jus take Lil' Man from her that day - that day she brought him back. I coulda thanked her an jus shut the door, but I didn't. I started that ball rollin. I think it's cause I saw her. Saw somebody jus as lonely as me in this world, an I wanted to make sure our worlds kept collidin.

When that pig pulled out that lipstick, I knew no matter how it got there in Ms. T's house, it whatin her fault. It was mine. If we hadn't been friends, there wouldn't a been no lipstick. I see that now, an thas why I ain't about to ruin her life over it.

Lil' Miss Thang's got her whole life ahead of her. I figure if I'm anythang like my kin, I'm already about halfway through with mine, but she's got time to be somethin more than I could ever be. I can live with the thought a this more than I can live knowin that our bein acquainted added her to the list a people's lives I've smashed to pieces.

The door at the end a the hall buzzes open. I hear that fool takin his licks. He laughs his crazy head off. Does it every night, an all it does is make em beat his ass harder til he cain't make another sound. I hear the door a his cell shut. The door buzzes for the guards to leave. Finally the quiet comes again.

When my lawyer tol' me bout the other evidence, some tacky gold swan an then that pig showed it to me, didn't take a genious to know Lil' Miss Thang's momma had to have used my key she hung on to. Snuck right over an put it under my bed. She'd do anythang for her youngin an thas an admirable quality in a momma. My momma mighta done the same, but then again, she mighta made me own up to it, her bein the God fearin woman that she was. Lil' Miss Thang's momma don't fear nothin, cept maybe gettin old an ugly. I shoulda remembered those are the worst kinna people - people without any real fears. They'll jus as soon cut you as to look at you.

Only God knows why, but the screamer starts up again. He ain't never went two rounds in one night. Good-ness! They rush right back in an go to beatin him some more. Ain't gonna be like him, mmm mmm. I'm can take a hint. Hell, I'm takin all this as a sign myself. A sign that my bein locked up frees everybody else. Frees Lisa up to have her a normal life. Frees Lil' Miss Thang up to get on with hers. Whether it's wrong or right or the truth or a lie don't matter. I ain't fightin anymore. I'm all give out.

Me, out walkin around, bein Queen, don't seem to be somethin the world's gonna stand for. No matter what, I keep havin that fact slap me in the face. Naw, tomorrow mornin when I meet with my lawyer, I'm gonna tell him I know what my plea has to be. Tell him that this road I call livin's been leadin me here since the day I was conceived.

The Girl

In the days that followed Queen's arrest, I spent as much time away from home as possible. I felt increasingly helpless as her arraignment loomed closer and closer. I was trapped in a vat of lies not only because of who Daddy was but also because of what mother had chosen to do. So great was my mounting hatred for my mother, that I hardly trusted myself near the cutlery when she and I were in the same room.

How she could've resorted to planting that vase was not something I could begin understand. If I'd have outright accosted her about it, I'm sure she'd have said it was all for me, because she loved me. I knew better. I knew it was because she loved herself. Whether or not she was capable of truly loving anyone else remained a reoccuring question that marinated in the minds of all of those who lived in her world.

Before that, neither her morality or her honesty had never come into question. Though she'd never claimed to be particularly chaste, I suppose, as a child, you assign certain attributes to your parents for no other reason but that you came from them. I'd never spent much time thinking about who my mother *was*, only about who she *wasn't*. The events of that summer had brought my negligence to the forefront.

Daddy was consumed with the details of the case, and fielding questions from everyone and their brother who came out of the woodwork including reporters from an Atlanta T.V. station. Family dinners had ceased altogether. Mother immersed herself in volunteer duties for the P.T.A. It was my impression that, in her mind, this balanced the scale. Her good deeds a counterweight for her inexcusably evil acts.

There was no more *Donnie and me*. We passed in the halls without even exchanging a second glance. He likely assumed that distancing himself from me could only help matters. I could never be sure of his exact reasons for excommunicating me as we never spoke after that night - the night that we did what we did.

When I'd see him sitting near me in class, I wondered how he could do it. How he could come to school, roam the halls, maintain his place on his throne, his loyal imps still paying their daily respects. Had he killed someone before? Was it old hat to him? These were things I found myself wanting to know, and yet at the same time, praying never to find out.

He'd given his locker back to its previous owner so he and I could avoid any awkward intermissions during the day. Honestly, I had been relieved that he'd thought of it. The closest we came to anything that remotely resembled contact happened one afternoon. He and his gang rode their bikes past me on my way home, and he momentarily turned his head, and looked at me. I looked back at him. He turned away and rode on.

I didn't miss him. I missed who I'd thought he was, who all the girls thought he was. I missed how it felt to kiss that boy in the dark movie theatre. I did not miss the boy who'd let his friends pressure me about stealing. The boy who'd looked down at Ms. Terrell bleeding there in her basement, and ran the other way. In that second, when it all went down, he'd had no regard for me, Ms. Terrell or even Gary or his gang. He'd only thought of himself.

Most of all, I found that I missed the girl I'd been with him - a confident, proud girl, one who the other girls envied. A girl coming into her own. How quickly she'd disappeared. It hadn't taken long for all the girls in the cafeteria to go back to laughing, and whispering about me as I once again trekked to a table in the way back. It took even less time to see that Donnie's girlfriend, the Charlotte Grace I'd been when I was with him, had died right along with Ms. Terrell.

    I didn't see Lisa out walking Lil' Man until the day before Queen's arraignment. She tried her best to pull him back, but with all of his struggling, his collar snapped off sending him racing right to me. I did the only thing I could do. Leaning down, I scooped him up, and walked him back over to her.

    She reached out for him, keeping her eyes down. We did not speak. I watched her as she tenderly fastened his collar back on. He continued to writhe, trying to get to me. Tears rolled down Lisa's cheeks. I could tell they took her by surprise by the way her patience lapsed and she then jerked Lil' Man into obedience. Standing at the end of my driveway, I watched as they hurried off in to their house.

    That evening, mother concluded we'd had enough drudgery. She announced she'd ordered a pizza for the two of us as Daddy was inevitably working late. Never before that night had junk food been delivered to our house. To this day, I don't know where she even got the flyer for a pizza place. She dangled it in front of me as I worked on homework at my desk. The picture of the cheese-smothered bread coerced me into being a willing participant. I nodded my head agreeing to eat some if she ordered it.

    As I finished my work, all I could think about was how I was going to manage to sit next to her when all I really wanted to do was scream at her for using the key, and framing Queen. I wanted to shake her and demand what she now intended to do about it all. Lucky for her, there were no forks or knives needed. She couldn't have known what a good choice pizza truly was.

The doorbell rang then came the muffled sound of mother's voice as she talked with the deliveryman and paid him. It was followed by her more pronounced call upstairs for me to come and join her. Gathering my composure, I made my way down, lingering in the doorway outside the living room. I surveyed her airy contented mood. She hummed to herself, bopped around the coffee table laying out plates and napkins. There was even a can of Coke for the both of us.

I glanced outside the front window making sure there had not been an apocalypse or worse than that, an alien invasion. I entertained the idea that this person serving slices, might not be of any relation to me, but instead a general in an alien army sent here to take over our planet one hungry child at at time. She looked up, giving me one of her plastic smiles. Instantly this theory was dispelled. Only Melanie Danby in the flesh could smile like that.

"It'll get cold. Sit, sit, sit." she prompted.

Slowly, I made my way over and sat up to the coffee table directly across from her on a cushion on the floor. We'd never had dinner in the living room. As she lifted a piece of pizza to her lips, I was mesmerized. I was more than eager to see her actually bite, chew and then swallow the greasy goodness.

The fact that she had given up on my weight was possibly the only sliver of a silver lining in the patch of black clouds looming over our heads. She bit it! Her jaw worked overtime then the dough went down the hatch. I assessed that some turn to drugs or alcohol to assuage their guilty conscience. My mother had turned to food.

Her greasy lips yacked on and on about the woes of the P.T.A.'s homecoming dance. As she rambled, I continued eating, all the while compiling a list of reasons I would present to her as to why we had to come clean. Why we had to march into that courtroom the next day and confess.

None of them seemed adequate enough to persuade her, however. She wouldn't care that Queen had been good to me, that she hadn't hurt a soul, and in no way deserved a fate like the one that was to be handed to her in just a matter of hours. Mother wouldn't care that Queen had already experienced enough pain in her life to last two lifetimes. She would not care about any of this enough to admit fault of any kind.

A scrap of pepperoni dropped onto my lap. As I picked it up, it hit me. I would have to be the one. I would have to tell mother that I wanted to fess up to my part in it all. I would take sole blame for the swan. In her twisted mind, my mother had done what she did to save me, and our family. I would not let her bare the brunt of any punishment for my actions.

"Mother," I began.

"...and that Arnold Wilson, he wants to donate carnations to put on the tables. I hate carnations! Laura says we should be grateful because they're from his florist shop, and they're free, but I..."

"Mother!" I exclaimed.

"For goodness sakes, Charlotte Grace, I know we're eating on the floor, but it doesn't mean we have to act like dogs and lose all of our manners." she chided.

"I have to get to the courthouse! I have to tell." I asserted as sternly as I could.

She looked down at the pizza box, using her fingers to gather bits of sausage scattered across it.

"And what exactly will you say? Hmmm? With your Daddy standing right there about to prosecute him?" she sternly asked.

Before I could respond, the doorbell rang. We both looked up, searching each other's faces as neither of us was expecting any visitors. Mother slowly rose, and walked out into the foryer to answer it. Like any good D.A.'s daughter, I rehearsed my rebuttal so that I'd be ready to deliver it with poise and eloquence once she returned.

Hearing footsteps, I turned to see Lisa in the doorway standing next to mother. She looked so tired. The puffiness around her eyes an indicator that in the past couple of weeks she'd cried more than she had her entire life. I jumped up.

"Hey." I said out of not knowing what in the world else to say.

"I just came from talking to her lawyer." she muttered in a daze. "She's gonna plead guilty, Charlotte Grace. Guilty!"

The news hung heavy in the room, like already wet laundry sagging on a clothesline in a storm. Lisa scurted around our couch, reaching out, clutching both of my shoulders, she pulled me so close I could smell the coffee on her breath. My mother didn't protest or even move from her spot.

"You can't let her! You know you can't! The only reason she's doin it is to save your ass!" Lisa chastised.

All the emotions I'd pent up, kept safely corralled, came crashing through the gates. In the heat of the moment, I lost what little protective instincts I'd had where my mother was concerned and as for Daddy, he and I regularly sailed each other down the river for her comfort any way. The Danby motto was one of *every man for himself*. Our family was a family of sell-outs. In that moment, I followed suit.

"I didn't know she'd do it! I didn't know she'd hide it in your house!" I wailed raising my hand, pointing in mother's direction.

Mother's face went sheet white. Lisa and I stared at her as she clenched her fists and bit her lip to hold back tears.

"God in heaven, Charlotte Grace! You think I'd do such a thing?" she whimpered.

Releasing my shoulders, Lisa stood still unsure of what the next move should be. Mother darted out into the hall and I watched her feet ascended the stairs two at a time. I replayed her earlier comment... *"With your daddy standing right there about to prosecute her..."* I'd presumed she said this, so I wouldn't embarrass him, but I'd had it all wrong. She hadn't cared about how it would look. No...that wasn't it at all. She'd said it because my confession would also serve to incriminate him.

I'd already summed up how it would play out when mother was the one at fault, but what I was to do with the new revelation, I had no earthly idea. That my Daddy, a man of the law, a well- known, upstanding, community minded man would do something so contrary to what he supposedly stood for was beyond my comprehension. Unable to remain standing with the sheer weight of it, I leaned over, folding down onto the couch. Lisa slumped in next to me.

As I cried, she slipped a hand into mine, patting my arm with the other. I knew I wasn't just crying for Queen. I was grieving the loss of the Daddy I thought I knew. I wondered if there was room for him in that graveyard. The one where the Donnie I'd first loved and the girl I'd been before all this began lay decaying side by side.

The Cop

"You goin to the arraignment?" his partner wanted to know.

Carter nodded.

"Not me, man. I'm settin this one out. All the coverage it's been gettin. Crazy niggers takin up for him. Hell, most of em never laid eyes on him fore they saw his picture in the paper. Tomorrow's my day off anyhow." Tom explained.

"Understandable." Carter replied.

"I'll be over at the K.F.C round noon for lunch though." Tom reminded as he got in his truck.

Walking back inside to do his monthly night of overtime, Carter knew that his response had been disingenuous. He did not understand, not in any sense of the word. Once the local blacks had been made aware of the charges against Queen, they'd taken on his plight as a way to grind the longtime ax they'd had to grind with the Murfeesboro Police Department. All the potential hubbub that promised to erupt that next day was exactly why he *would* undoubtedly be attending.

In his opinion, it was all coming to a rather satisfactory head. Earlier that very morning, the department had held an emergency meeting to discuss their town's r*acial climate*, as the sheriff had put it. When they'd walked in, there was the captain standing next to the him at the front of the room. They'd rarely been graced with the captain's presence, due to him recently making the rounds with political candidates. When he was present, he was often hold up in his office returning phone calls.

He and the sheriff stood reading over a set of index cards. Word traveled around the room at lightning speed that the captain was taking the upper hand in this investigation. Their objective was to keep Rutherford County out of the national news. They also wanted to ensure the long, dark fingers of the N.A.A.C.P. didn't dip down into the already shitty pie this situation had become, serving to make it even shittier.

Carter had never heard the sheriff say words like *racial* or *climate*. It was evident that the captain had composed the speech. The sheriff's intellect was not a quality that had earned him his position. It was widely known that if it hadn't been for his uncle putting in a good word for him, he would've never risen up through the ranks at all.

As for his race relations, the sheriff could regularly be counted on to drop the *N* word in any conversation regarding any person of color who was unlucky enough to be dragged into their station. The sheriff was first in line to apprise the prisoners of the dire circumstance they now found themselves in. He never hesitated to remind them what happened to those who *forget their place*.

Having never mastered delegation, the captain couldn't hold back. He took up the mantle right at the tail end. He went on about how a friend of his had worked the L.A. riots and they in no way wanted to be the town that was known for anything resembling anything close to that kind of chaos. He made reference to how the coming days could usher in a *virtual*

Helter Skelter, the likes of which they'd not yet witnessed in those parts.

So intrigued by these words was Carter that he'd skipped lunch with Tom. He had instead used his time to go to the library. There he used the computer to look up this foreign term and discovered it referred to a race war. It as a term coined by a serial killer by the name of Charles Manson. Back in the late sixties, according to the articles online, Manson had been convinced such a battle was unavoidable. A *Helter Skelter*...

Carter memorized its definition. He sat in his cruiser continuing to read excerpts from copies of articles the librarian had so graciously printed out for him. He felt slighted by his high school history teacher who had lectured at length about John Wilkes Booth, Adolph Hitler, and Lee Harvey Oswald, yet had never introduced them to this iconic figure.

Manson... he'd poured over the coverage of the murders with a certain admiration. Though, he himself would never want to accumulate the kind of followers this fellow had, he found Manson's philosophies about life and death both innovative and fascinating. A kindred-ness was sparked. An overall feeling that if he and Manson were to have met, they'd have struck up a friendship. He was still thinking about his newly discovered idol later that evening as the headlights of his vehicle reflected off of Tom's truck where it sat in Lara's driveway.

His instincts told him there was no simple outcome to be derived from the scenario that would undoubtedly ensue. A neighbor had called in a complaint and there was the fact that his partner was not to be within a hundred feet of the premises. A restraining order against Tom was still in effect. Lara had taken it out on him after he pushed her down the stairs of his apartment one of the times she'd dropped off the baby for his bi-weekly visitation. Eversince then, a court liason had to be present whenever Tom even visited with his son. It was only the flirtatious relationship that Carter himself kept fueled with the Sheriff's homely niece who worked in dispatch that had afforded him the chance to be the one to respond.

He lingered on the stoop going through a list of things he might say, if so inclined. Things that could defuse the explosive episode he felt certain lay in wait behind the door. Things he'd heard on the cop shows. Things to say that he'd committed to memory in order to access when needed. Things he could not count on his own mind to naturally formulate. Things he felt a friend might try to say, though he recognized they were far from friends. He and Tom were more aptly to be categorized as accomplices.

As he walked up, from behind the door, the baby's squalls grew frantic. These were followed by Lara's shrill screams then a shot rang out, spurring him into action. Bounding up the steps, reaching down, unholstering his gun, then turning the knob, he found the door unlocked. As he burst in, he immediately saw Lara huddled on the floor. It was the same position she'd ended up in the last night he'd visited several months prior. Though this time, there was her baby bleeding out in her frail arms. His small eyes already turning as lightless and lifeless as those of an old fashioned, dimestore doll. Carter lowered his gun.

Lara looked pleadingly up at him, fully recognizing that she suddenly found herself in a horrifying alternate reality of sorts. One where he was her only hope. Tom lorded his stalky frame over her, a chilling expression on his face. His gun still drawn, he now pointed it at her forehead. His hands firm and steady.

"She said they're movin up to New York." Tom sneered, his gaze never veering from his mark. "I'd like to see her try to take him now."

"God! Oh God!" Lara repeated, rocking the limp boy.

Carter made sure to remain where he was. To his knowledge, his partner had never fired his weapon at a live target, not even in the line of duty. Sure, they'd done their fair share of shooting out at the range. There'd also been the rare occasion after a trip to the bar, when they'd ventured into the woods flagrantly shooting off their guns. Given this special set of circumstances, however, he intuitively sensed he couldn't vouch for Tom. It was one of the few times since he was a young child, that he felt utterly unprepared and uncomfortably subservient.

"She says she's already put a deposit on a place up there near her brother. Figures. Shit, me an him never did see eye to eye. Member that fuckin toast he made at our weddin? Member that? Motherfucker's always had it out for me." Tom continued.

"I shoulda listened to him too! He was right! You're fucked in the head!" Lara hissed, hugging the boy up closer to her chest with one arm, balling her free hand into a fist, raising it up at Tom.

Looking down at the child's face, she unclenched her fist, using her hand to instead close his little eyes, kissing his forehead as she did so. Gently, she placed him on the floor in front of her. Glaring up at Tom, she rose on her knees so that her forehead met the barrel of the gun full on.

Carter stared in disbelief. He couldn't believe her brazen idiocy. He wondered if perhapse she'd relapsed and was drunk. He questioned if this was her way out of an existence that had disentigrated into some nightmarish, desperate kind of half-life.

"You think movin up there'd a changed anythang? Hell, you'd a been back on the bottle just like you would be if you stayed here." Tom fumed.

Slowly, without speaking, she reached up, taking his hands in her own. Tom winced at the feel of them, bloody and cold on his skin.

"Do it you fucker! Do it!" she ordered.

This caused them all to freeze, a terror-induced paralysis setting in. If a neighbor would have peeked through the window at that precise moment, they might have thought someone simply pressed pause on a low budget crime drama. Only Lara's deep, guttural cries finally confronted them with the fact that they were indeed living beings - participants in the tragedy at hand. Carter restlessly shifted his weight to one side. Tom's hands began to quiver.

"I didn't want to have to drive to see him." Tom groaned.

Carter cleared his throat.

"I'll tell you where I don't want to drive." he rebuked. "I damn sure don't want to have to drive over to the U.S.P. in Atlanta to visit your ass on death row, Tom."

Upon hearing this, fully understanding Carter's meaning. Lara registered the stark fact that her foolish wish was seconds away from coming true. This seemed to change her mind. She then pleaded for her life, latching onto Tom's boots. For reasons known to only himself, Carter's mouth formed a smirk as he raised his own gun again.

It was clear to him that this was how he'd repay his debt. He would do what his partner could not then they'd finally be even. In a matter of a second, he aimed and fired. In the cracker box of a living room it sounded like a cannon going off. Lara immediately crumpled on top of her child like a threadbare tablecloth sliding neatly in folds from off of a table onto the ground.

Tom faced Carter before looking down at his own feet. Disappointment found him as he surveyed the fraction of the woman laying there. This person, who at one time, he'd once loved more than anything, yet had grown over a few short months to hate as much as he hated everything else.

Tom suddenly looked up, a rage infilling his face and with that look, that one look, Carter saw that he'd misjudged his cohort's needs. The first shot Tom fired did not take Carter down. It took a second shot for him to join Lara on the floor. All those years Tom had mistakenly been logged as a lackey, an underling in Carter's mind ...how very wrong he had been. In that moment, he acknowledged Tom for who he truly was. Not less in any way, but a more than worthy equal.

Crouching next to his victims, Tom made sure not to look them in the eyes. He turned his gaze in the direction of the hallway as if picturing a better day, a day only a year or so ago when he'd walked down that same hall bringing their baby out to see Lara. He lifted his gun, positioning the butt of it directly against his chest so that the barrel was directly under his chin. A final shot sounded. Tom's body slumped in the middle of the rug - the last corpse needed to complete the horrifyingly graphic quartet.

Streaks of moonlight wormed their way through thin curtains down onto Carter's face. He lay motionless, ruminating on a singular, incriminating idea. What if he would have staved off satisfying his own sadistic curiosity? What if he'd have gone to lunch that day as planned instead of going to the library? If he had done so, would he have been able to divert Tom's attention away from this whole saga? Could the evening have gone differently? Could it have all been avoided?

Managing to roll over onto his back, Carter closed his eyes, squelching such foolishness. He had no desire to waste his last thoughts on his power, or lack thereof, to truly affect the lives of those who'd been unfortunate enough to traverse this road alongside him. Instead he tried his best to turn his thoughts elsewhere.

His mind exercised its own will, however, veering him off course, turning his thoughts to how he would not be there to testify at the trial. He would not be there to see Queen's face as he described the scene at the old woman's house. This irked him more than what had currently transpired, yet he knew there was no way it could be helped. He gasped, eyes opening wide.

Taking small breaths in attempts to lessen his pain, he studied the mildewed ceiling above him. He raised a hand, tightly clenching one of the open wounds in his chest. Oddly, his last thought drifted to that of his mother. This took him off guard. He closed his eyes, sucking in short quick bits of air while coming to terms with the fact that, in actuality, she had come to a better end. The best kind one could hope for... an end of her own choosing.

The Tranny

"Lord help us!" Is all I can say as we pull up out front a the courthouse.

Outside the car, there's a whole mess a black people on one side a the lawn shoutin an carryin on, some of em with signs. Across from em a mess a white people are camped out with jus as many signs a their own. Both sides steady rantin an ragin back an forth. There's reporters too, one of em's outta that Atlanta station Lisa watches. Out a habit, I reach my cuffed hands up to straighten my wig then remember it ain't there.

"All for you." The cop up front mutters from behind the wheel where he's starin at me in the rear view through those sunglasses all pigs own.

Clouds move out a the way. The sun shines right in my eyes. I catch site a my reflection in the car winda, dressed up like Jermaine with a dress shirt an slacks. On my feet I got some kinna loafers Lisa dug out a her daddy's boxes in the garage. My face is all black an blue, cheek swelled up.

Some thangs are so horrible they don't deserve to get talked about or cried over. Momma used to say, you talk about evil, you give it power. I won't never tell my lawyer, Lisa or another livin soul how I came to look like I do right now. They seen enough episodes a The Wire to take a good guess. Never did get separated from the general population or get a cell to myself like my lawyer was askin for. Minute I saw the warden, I knew that whatin gonna make it on his priority list.

With tremblin hands, I straignten my pants an thinkin how I'm *disappointed. Tore up inside that I made it this far. Realize deep down, I wished one a them inmates woulda gone on an finished all this. Woulda saved the state a Tennessee a fortune, an Lil' Miss Thang's daddy a whole hell of a lotta time. Plus, it woulda saved Lisa a whole hell of a lot more heartache.*

They got two lines a pigs in between the people an they're tryin to keep some kinna peace. That beats all. Don't nobody give a damn about peace til it gets disturbed. They cain't see it's somethin you got to work on at all times. Ain't jus gonna come when you want it to. Like some dog you got to train or first time you let it off the leash, it's gonna do whatever is has a mind to. No amount a hollerin at after that'll make one bit a difference.

"No time like the present." the pig says as he opens his door.

He makes his way around to my side, another one comes alongside him to help escort me. You'd think they got one a the F.B.I.'s most wanted the way they're carryin on. This is all probly the most action they've had around here in years. Mmm hmmm. I'm thrilled as all get out that I finally give em something to important to do.

As they lead me up the steps, I try not to think about how there's photographers snappin pictures for all they're worth. It's kinna like how nobody's ever around when you dressed to the nines gettin ready to go out an cut up with the girls. But now, you dare venture to the WalMart in your tank top, some pajama pants an your flip flops jus to pick up somethin quick, hell, you'll see ten people you know.

Lookin to my right, I see that I know some a these whites from our restaurant, served em more than a time or two. One woman I know full well eats Lisa's pancakes least once a week an there she is wavin a big ol' sign for all she's worth. All I can make out is a picture of an electric chair on it. God help me! I put my hands up to cover my eyes, but fore I can, I spot Mr. Donaldson. He ain't got a sign or nothin, but he's standin in the crowd, the ones made up a one a those who want to see me fry. Ain't no mistakin it. His eyes meet mine. He turns his head right quick. Didn't take long for him to forget who's responsible for him bein above ground. Shoulda left it to Loretta to help him, mmm hmmm.

A black woman pushes her way through the line a pigs. She reaches out an puts a hand on my shoulder.

"Don't you forget, they cain't kill your spirit! No they can't!" she urges.

I nod, try to smile. She's wearin a Malcom X shirt. Yeah, I get it. I ain't no fool. All this ain't for me. No, I'd say most a these people don't know my name. It's for "them", for all of "us". Damn, cain't they see? Cain't they see when they do that, when they take up for somebody jus cause a their color, it itn't a bit different than the other side goin against us for the very same reason?

One a the pigs pulls the woman back. I look closer, half expectin it to be that devil his self, that wolf that don't even bother with sheep's clothin, but it itn't. It's jus another one I hadn't seen before. Woulda thought that snake wouldn't a missed this for the world since he helped set it all in motion. Thought for sure he'd a been drivin me here, but I hadn't seen hide nor hair a him or his partner. Bet they're inside with a front row seat.

Finally, we're enterin the courtroom. It's all a blur. There's a judge up front an Lil' Miss Thang's daddy waitin with a few others from the state prosecution. Ms. T's daughter is there settin behind em with a few other white people who's probably from their family too. Seein em all here now, it hits me smack in the face, they think I killed their momma. For the first time since this whole mess started, it's sinkin in. This whole room a people believe I'm a murderer!

I take a seat by my lawyer. He pats my shoulder real stiff like. One a them obligated thangs he thinks he should do. I know Lisa says he's makin a name takin up for people like us, but that don't mean he wants to go all out an actually touch one of us. I done made up my mind when I saw a folded blue hanky in his suit pocket an dress socks to match, he's either in the closet an scared to come out, or he's way on back at the part where he don't even know he's in a closet at all. Where he's still fooled his self into thinkin thas jus how everybody lives: all pent up an secret.

My handcuffs get unlocked. Still no sign a that wolf, but the day ain't over. He's got plenty a time to make an appearance. Turnin around, I see the rows behind me are full a strangers. Where's Lisa? I didn't want her to come. Told her that too. Didn't want her to see me this way, but thought for sure she wouldn't be able to help herself. Now that she ain't here, I hate it she took me up on it.

I see a couple reporters were allowed in. The lawyers are jaw jackin back an forth. I turn around again an look out the winda at all the commotion. Lookin down, I focus on one a my bruised hands...Tina. I think a how she must sat in that courtroom when she filed for that divorce from Ike. I think a how it musta been for her to face her abuser, to stand up an say for the first time in front a everybody that she whatin gonna take his shit no more.

That ain't my situation, though. No, she was a victim. I ain't. To every other soul in this room, I'm the bad guy. To them, I'm Ike. This sets my lip to quiverin, fightin off cryin. The thought that all the thangs I've done, all hormones, all the surgeries, all the shit I've taken off people an still held my head high, an here I am in this chair an still all they see is a degenerate nigger.

The room gets quiet. In my hurricane a misery, I look up to see the judge starin at the double doors behind us. All the lawyers turn that direction. Lil' Miss Thang's Daddy drops his jaw like Jesus his self's jus took time outta answerin everybody else's prayers to set foot in here.

Turnin head, I move my seat back far enough to see what it is thas got everybody all in a tizzy, an there she is! Standin there in the middle of the aisle…Lil' Miss Thang! She's shakin like a leaf, tears flowin down her face. Soon as she sees me, we both dry our eyes. I nod at her, smile, then breathe deep. I relax back in my chair. I close my eyes an offer up a silent prayer a gratitude. Straight up to momma, where she's settin, up there on the right side a His throne. Thank you momma. Thank you! Ain't Jesus, but she'll do jus fine.

Lisa comes up along side Lil' Miss Thang an they start down the aisle towards the judge then it hits me. Glad as I am to see em, it hits me why they're here, an I won't let her do it. I won't!

"Judge!" I holler out as I hop up.

My lawyer pulls on my sleeve, but I won't set down. The judge looks over at me from his big ol' perch, lookin like a owl starrin at the mouse he's about to eat, but I stand my ground.

"What is it Mr. Braxton?" he asks all irritated.

I look over at Lil'Miss thang an Lisa who's steady shakin her head.

"Judge, I want to plead guilty." I say loud an clear.

Some gasps go up from the people watchin. Lil' Miss Thang's Daddy an his team are jus starrin. I done made their job a whole hell of a lot easier. My lawyer scurries on around front approachin the judge's bench.

"Your honor, I'm sorry Mr. Braxton doesn't quite understand the proceedings, I ask that you strike…" he's babblin.

I cain't help it. I go off.

"He's wrong judge! He's wrong! I do understand, an I …"

Lil' Miss Thang's standin right in front of me now. She's got red cheeks from all her cryin. She reaches over touchin my arm then leans in.

"I can't live with it." she whispers.

I jus look at her, tryin to figure out what she means.

"*Don't you see? If you do this for me, I can't live with myself.*" she says a little louder.

Her hand squeezes mine, an I do. I see it real clear. I set down.

"*Your honor, I have something you need to know.*" Lil' Miss Thang calls out, turnin to face him.

"*Who's this?*" the judge barks.

Lil' Miss Thang itn't scared one bit. She walks right past her Daddy an up to that bench.

"*Charlotte Grace Danby, sir.*" she announces like she's the queen a England.

He glares first at her then at her Daddy who's done froze all up. Girl sure nough got the floor. Ain't a soul sayin a word or even breathin.

"*Do you know something about this case Miss Danby?*" the judge finally asks.

"*Charlotte Grace!*" her Daddy hisses, takin a few steps towards her.

She turns an gives him the eye. He stays put. Mmmm hmmm. I wouldn't mess with her right now either.

"*I do, sir.*" Lil' Miss Thang proclaims, chest out, proud to be speakin her *truth.*

My lawyer comes back an sits next to me, leans over.

"Do you know this girl?" he asks.

"Sure do." I tell him.

We watch Lil' Miss Thang up there with judge goin on about how I whatin no where around when everythang went down. How it was her who broke in Ms. Terrell's house. How she was only wantin to take some a that jewelry the lady was always gettin in the mail so she could give it to her momma, an she didn't have no idea Ms. Terrell was gonna be home. Tells him she shut that basement door so she could run out fore she got caught. She never thought Ms. Terrell was that close to the top a the stairs when she shut it, an sure nough wouldn't a ever dreamed nobody'd fall an die.

I know part a her story is a lie. I know that chil' wouldn't a broke in there an done all that on her own, but I reckon thas the part she can live with. She can live with lettin that lil' boyfriend a hers off the hook. Another woman takin the heat for a man. She's joinin a long line a females who done that. Mmm hmmm. She's growin up.

As I listen to her finish, I can tell she feels better havin tol' most a the truth. Here I thought all along I'd be doin her a world a good by takin the blame, but I see that I'd a been killin the best parts a her. I sure couldn't a lived with that. That chil' might not realize it right now, someday she will, but she didn't jus come to my rescue today. No, that lil' girl done gone an saved us both. She's done gone an put her name right up there next to Lisa's on my list a Wonder Women.

The Girl

I read once that our memories are irrevocably tied to our senses. That's why I suspect the color of baby blue vibrantly flashes through my mind when I look back on that day. I see my mother there on our porch, her hair beautifully done up in pin curls, a living doll in a baby blue dress, watching as Lisa and I got into the car.

I remembered thinking she looked much like I always imagined she did in her prime, back when she was a contestant in the Peach Princess pageants. As we pulled out of the driveway, she did not move a muscle. She remained fixed in that exact spot even as we rounded the corner out of sight.

She'd been kind enough to call to me that morning, ensuring that I woke up on time. She'd also made pancakes. Compared with her usually self-serving endeavors, these menial tasks were enough to put her right up there with Martin Luther King. Though she did not even once talk about accompanying us, she had in no way tried to throw a wrench in our plans to liberate Queen. I could see it was enough for her, this kind of lackadaisical consent, her underlying condoning of the act – her own brand of activism.

Lisa and I did not talk on the way. The unspoken blame that had been placed on my very friendship with Queen sat firmly buckled between us in the front seat. I didn't have the slightest notion as to what exactly I would say once we arrived or how I would say it. All I knew was that we had to get there.

We had to park several blocks away. Once we neared the courthouse, Lisa aggressively carved a path through the frenzied mob out front. A mob littered with unexpected attendees. There were even a couple of teachers I held in high regard yelling and pushing with the rest of them. Our longtime family physician was present, waving a sign that voiced a hatred of *fags*. For the first time in my life I was embarrassed of my race. Though I'd never seen the people of Murfeesboro react like that before, I did not allow it to distract me.

Numerous black people raged opposite them. For a moment, I felt a sense of hope in that it looked as if they'd come together in support of Queen. My burden felt a bit lighter. As my eyes met theirs, however, I realized I'd never seen most of them. Where had they been hiding? Were they members of that group I heard tell of from the time I could listen? The people from the legendary *other side of town*?

I wondered why, if they'd felt so adament about the rights of one of their own, were they not out and about everyday, making themselves visible in our grocery stores, at our schools, or at community events. It was suddenly evident that they'd just showed up for this. They were not to be confused with freedom fighters. They could be more closely classified as looters, taking advantage while the supposed enemy was weak.

They would have little to no success in providing any real aid to Queen's cause. She was not an individual to them. Her whole plight was but an opportunity for them to be the thorn in the side of their long-time oppressors. My burden resumed. I knew it fell to me and me alone.

I'd like to tell you that I was big, bad and brave as Lisa and I stormed inside that courtroom, but I wasn't. I was anything but. I felt insignificant, small and close to passing out. It was as if the world was ending, as if the floor would open up, revealing burning crevices of hell that had been reserved just for me.

Looking around in bewilderment, I tried to calm myself. The room was a lot like our church sanctuary. Different in that there was a judge instead of a pastor. He sat in his robe behind a large wooden platform, shuffling through papers and sipping coffee.

To his left, instead of a homely, ancient pianist, there was a striking woman dressed to a *T* in a designer outfit seated at a typewriter. Below the judge, a choir of lawyers, my Daddy among them, exchanging information in hushed tones. In place of a congregation, was an audience consisting primarily of law enforcement, a couple of reporters and Ms. Terrell's family. Each of their expressions was every bit as sour as any church member's.

They had not shown up out of tradition or in order to pay homage to a god. No, they'd shown up to worship at the altar of justice. Every last one of them raring to witness Queen receive life in prison or worse, the electric chair.

People gradually became aware of our presence. Person by person, the room fell silent as Lisa and I made our way to the middle of the aisle. Daddy was one of the last to turn and spot us. He made no effort to move away from his flock.

I'll never forget the look on his face. It wasn't a look of anger or shock. It could only be best described as a look of relief. I knew then that I was as much there for him as I was for Queen. That he, like my mother, could not bring himself to do the right thing, but that he would concede to letting it happen.

My throat constricted. I looked back at Lisa. She gently nudged me onward. Where should I start? With Donnie? With the planning of the heists? How the boys had been relentless? How they'd robbed places all over the county and...then I saw her leaned back in her chair to get a better look at what it was that had paused all the madness.

With her men's clothing, without her usual wig to cover her shiny, black scalp, she looked as I thought she must have before she became the Queen I'd known. There she was. No makeup to hide behind - none of the accessories she took such pride in. I felt so close to her in that brief second as we found ourselves in a similar predicament; both of us vulnerable and exposed.

I did not turn away. Though I was fully prepared for her to scowl, or turn her head after what I'd put her through. Instead, she smiled. After everything I'd done, she didn't hate me. I smiled back and immediately knew where I must start, but she shot up in her chair. She started to protest, make sure that the judge knew the fault was hers alone. I quietly walked over and squeezed her hand. What I said to her exactly, with all the chaos of that day, I don't quite remember, but whatever it was, it caused her to squeeze my hand in return then sit down.

I knew I must do what she was about to do. I couldn't pawn it off onto anyone else. Even though I hadn't been the one to shut Ms. Terrell's basement door, I shouldn't have been there, and I should have told someone immediately when it happened. Leaving her there on that floor made me as much to blame. No, I'd never even mention Donnie or the other boys. To do that would have been the Danby way. No, I would begin and end with me.

"Your honor!" I called out to the judge.

He looked out at me, his brow furrowed in frustration. He pushed his glasses further down on his nose so that he could see me clearly.

"Your honor, I have something you need to know!" I found the courage to proclaim.

Now, I would also like to tell you that I saved the day, that I was the hero, and in a way I was, but it wasn't that simple. Owning up, meant that I was no longer Charlotte Grace, the sweet and shy daughter of the D.A. It meant that mother was no longer a former pageant queen turned philanthropic volunteer. It meant that daddy was no longer an admired and prominent lawyer, Murfeesboro's own golden boy.

I had been ready to take full responsibility for all of it, but once I told my part, and the judge pressed a bit, daddy reluctantly owned up to using Queen's spare key to plant the swan. For the first time in his charmed life, he found he was on the other side of things and in need of an attorney, himself. Luckily, his rolodex was chalk full of numbers for some of the state's best. Even more lucky, one of them owed him big time.

Mother religiously attended both of our court proceedings. Her consistent support due in part to a staunch Southern loyalty, yet also due to the fact that she'd had to sell our house. Mine and daddy's trial gave her an escape from the tiny shoebox prison of an apartment she'd been forced to move into.

Daddy was convicted of tampering with evidence, and obstruction of justice. I was convicted of involuntary manslaughter. By the grace of God, Ms. Terrell's children did not push for the maximum penalty in my case. The eldest daughter had children of her own. That no doubt contributed to her pity, not as much for me, but for my mother.

On the day I was sentenced, I watched as she embraced my mother before they left the courtroom. I knew then I'd unintentionally given mother a new role to play. She had not so unwillingly accepted the part of mother to a murderer, and wife of a convict. Once she took on a role, by God she did it up right.

Queen once told me that some things are so horrible they don't deserve to be talked about. She said her momma always told she and her brother Jarvis that to rehearse things, to keep on talking on and on about them only gives them more power over you. For this reason, my years in juvey seldom come up in conversation. I've done my best to leave those years behind me like a blurry nightmare I've woken up from.

They cannot, however help but overflow into my writing. Some of my graduate professors have asked how at my age I've come to possess such a remarkable depth, and understanding. I only shrug and smile as I thank them. There are some questions people cannot handle the answers to. This I know full well. I imagine this day in age, if they're truly driven, they can easily do a little digging on the computer to find out for themselves.

I spare them my speech about how the only way a writer can possibly come by such skills is to suffer. Not your run-of-the-mill death in the family, or broken bone kind of hardships either, but more like the dark-night-of-the-soul grade tormenting kind. The type that only five years in a correctional facility of any kind will leave you with.

When I was first released, mother dutifully offered for me to live with her - a sentence neither of us deserved. I chose instead, to move to Orlando with a girl who was also released around the same time. We were not close, by any means. I suppose we could best be classified as *war buddies, co-veterans*. Both of us having fought the good fight, surviving the unspeakable things that took place during our time inside those slate gray cinder block walls.

She was originally from Florida, and had an aunt there who gave us a good deal on rent. We attended community college during the day, and waitressed by night. Florida was not only convenient, it was apropos in that it was really the place it had all began. Down there in Tallahassee the day Queen's mother gave birth to a second fine baby boy.

Daddy never wrote to me during his incarceration, nor made efforts to make any other sort of contact. I understood his silence, and after that first year, it didn't hurt so much. I was too busy keeping my head down and riding out my own sentence. Oddly, it wasn't until not long after he was released that a letter came. It was genuinely remorseful, though he could not help but offer excuses as to why he'd resorted to such debauchery. More letters followed.

They were all somewhat logical reasons. There was the fact that he loved me and had been watching out for my future, that I had my whole life ahead of me, and of course the obvious fact that my mother and he had instinctually tried to save me from coming to any harm. All in all, I read between the lines. I knew that it had come down to the more truthful fact: he'd done it because he could. More than that, I knew he'd done it because he could live with it. His only crime, in his book, was getting caught.

After it all, my parents chose to live on opposite sides of the country. They always did I think. Daddy returned to his blessed South Carolina, the land from whence he originated. Last year, mother remarried a man from San Diego whom she met through a friend and aside from the fact that mother and Daddy are still living and breathing, that is pretty much all I currently know about them.

When I think back on when we were all three Danbys, I think about that time we visited Augusta for Daddy to attend a Master's tournament. I was eight or nine then. When mother and I became bored with watching the golf, we ventured off to explore the town and find some shopping. We walked along the wide Savannah river that ran through the heart of the city. Jutting over the water and into the sky were several massive, rusted bridges.

That is the image that most adequately represents mother and daddy to me. Existent, and at one time necessary, structures who have eroded into unusable eyesores now only serving, at intervals, to interrupt the landscape of my life. In my parent's quiet moments, if they dare to be honest, I think they too would agree with this depiction.

My last year in juvey, I received news that Queen and Lisa had gone out to Vegas. For reasons I don't think even she was altogether aware of, mother sent me a news clipping. She had printed it out from an online Gay and Lesbian magazine. I had one of the only laughs I had there in my small closet of a room just imagining her even perusing that site. I think this eased mother's guilt, to know that Queen was ok. That was enough for her. It was the only thing she ever sent me about her, and in our sparse phone calls we never once mentioned her.

The article detailed that Queen and Lisa had a friend who'd started a club out there called *Legendary*. There were impersonators of stars such as Michael Jackson, Marilyn Monroe, and of course, none other than Tina Turner. I still have that article framed and displayed prominently on my nightstand.

Queen's pictured at the top of it, in all her glory, dressed as her idol. Tina would be proud, maybe even envious. Queen Mae Braxton makes a better Queen of Rock than Anna Mae Bullock ever did.

It seems like an eternity since I laid eyes on her, and in ways I guess it has been. Ten years is a very long time, but life rolls on. From what I recently read online, she and Lisa franchised the club. There's one in Chicago and one coming to New York. I like thinking of Queen traveling, and picking out flashy décore for these establishments. She always had a glamorous kind of style that was all her own.

I've thought time and again that I might head out to Vegas one of these days. Somehow, I never get further than sitting still in my driver's seat staring out at the hood. I theorize that if she wanted to see me, she already would have. She, like me, has had ample opportunity.

During a recent summer break, I coincidentally attended a writing conference in Nevada. While there, I held a well-publicized reading of my first novel at a local bookstore. I wondered if I might see her then, yet she never showed.

With the ease of technology, I'm sure Queen sees as much about me as I see about her. On occasion, I fall asleep imagining her propped up on a lavish bed wearing that pink robe of her mother's, a hot pink laptop on her lap, catching up on all things Charlotte Grace. I leave her there. I leave well enough alone, not because I think she wouldn't be glad to see me. No, I'm positive she'd envelope me with those long dark arms, and hold me tight. I know she'd say "Lil' Miss Thang! Girl, where've you been?" I know because that's just how she always was, all forgiveness and light.

I've also lived long enough to know that often people stay away, not out of disdain or bitterness, but out of not wanting to relive the events and times that are inextricably attached to you. Like those prisoners of war who are fast friends in a hole where they're kept, but once rescued, quickly lose track of each other, their very faces a reminder of atrocities committed. No matter how hard we try to pretend it's not true, a person cannot be separated from a context.

One night last week, I went against my usual solitary nature and went out for drinks with one of my fellow teacher assistants. Nostalgia got the better of me, and before I knew what was happening, I was recounting for him a few of the memories of my Murfeesboro days. He asked why on earth I write YA adventures. He said I'm missing the mark. He said I should write about my sordid Southern childhood, and all the larger than life caricatures who starred in it.

I chuckled, and told him a half-truth. I explained that there will always be teenagers who need to read fantasy in order to escape. I told him I knew this because I had been one of those withering wallflowers who took refuge in such books. I went on to share that I now feel it my duty to provide similar yet better diversions for the next generation.

What I left out is that I don't want to share her. I want Queen all to myself. I'm a firm believer that what her momma told her, about the rehearsing of things making them powerful, is very true. That's why I listen to Tina Turner every chance I get and on certain nights, in the privacy of my room, I also wear gawdy stilettos. It's also the reason that every Christmas I order a case of lipstick designed by yours truly. I have it sent to me directly from the same company where she got hers in Miami.

All these things represent the only treasure that could be dredged up, salvaged from the stagnant lake of my past. All these things represent the only person I ever met who really knows what love is. The person who was going to give herself over, accept punishment in my place. If shared, I'm fearful all these things would dwindle from the bright flames they are to small struggling embers.

Last spring, I drove to Tallahassee to purchase my first dog from a breeder a student recommended. I wondered how I would choose from all the puppies. As soon as the breeder accompanied me out into the yard, my decision wasn't made any easier. There were so many cute, tiny ones running around, bumping against each other, chewing on toys.

All of a sudden, the only white and brown one of the bunch poked its head out from behind a bush. With a sassy walk, she sauntered right over. She was adorable and she knew it. She sniffed my shoes then pawed one of my feet. I bent down and scooped her up. The moment I held that chihuahua, felt her soft tongue against my hand, I just knew.

As I put her in the car, I patted her head. Instantly, I was transported to that day I patted Lil' Man for the first time. That day he'd ran up to me all those years ago. My pup yipped in my backseat as we drove off. I turned the radio on. This seemed to appease her.

"You know what your name is?" I asked her.

Looking back in the rear view, I saw her cock her head to one side as if to reply, *What?*

"There's was only ever gonna be one name for you." I told her. "You were born to be Lil' Miss Thang."

Acknowledgements: To my husband, Chad, for first listening to the book in its entirety, re –reading it and then offering much needed feedback. To my friends/test readers: *Terry Anastsi, Lucetta Zaytoun, Mariah Zaytoun, Caroline Bond, James Higgins, Barb Shand.* Your invaluable suggestions, corrections and willingness to give of your time, helped to make this book possible.